Penguin Books
Strike Out Where Not Appl

Since his birth in the Gray's Inn Road in the borough of St Pancras, Nicolas Freeling has lived all his days in Europe. Fifteen years as a cook in expensive, and generally nasty, restaurants: thereafter, novelist. His house lies on a historic route from Germany through to France. It has been most things, and now has a future as a light-house. *Love in Amsterdam*, his first novel, was published in 1962, closely followed by *Because of the Cats* and *Gun Before Butter*, which were published in 1963. His other crime novels include *Valparaiso, Double-Barrel, Criminal Conversation, The King of the Rainy Country, The Dresden Green, Strike Out Where Not Applicable, This is the Castle, Tsing-Boum, Over the High Side, A Long Silence, Dressing of Diamond, What are the Bugles Blowing for?, Lake Isle, Gadget, The Night Lords, The Widow, One Damn Thing After Another* and *Wolfnight*. Many of these are published in Penguins, and *Gun Before Butter, Because of the Cats* and *Double Barrel* are also published together in *The Nicolas Freeling Omnibus*.

Nicolas Freeling

Strike Out
Where Not Applicable

Penguin Books

Penguin Books Ltd, Harmondsworth, Middlesex, England
Viking Penguin Inc., 40 West 23rd Street, New York, New York 10010, U.S.A.
Penguin Books Australia Ltd, Ringwood, Victoria, Australia
Penguin Books Canada Ltd, 2801 John Street, Markham, Ontario, Canada L3R 1B4
Penguin Books (N.Z.) Ltd, 182–190 Wairau Road, Auckland 10, New Zealand

First published by Victor Gollancz 1967
Published in Penguin Books 1969
Reprinted 1975, 1985

Printed and bound in Great Britain by
Cox & Wyman Ltd, Reading
Typeset in Monotype Times

Between the two ancient towns of Haarlem and Leiden is a strip of ground that is famous throughout the whole world. Practically every stranger arriving for the first time in the Netherlands looks about him – before he is well over the frontier – and asks, 'Where are the bulb fields?' Tulips will grow anywhere, naturally, but this strip, barely fifty kilometres long and not much over ten deep, is a phenomenon – it was sea till about a hundred years ago. William of Orange, in the seventeenth century, raised the siege of Leiden by sea, and Schiphol Airport stands below sea level in what is still marked on maps as the Haarlem Lake. On the seaward side of the bulb fields, and their only protection, a belt of sand-dunes slopes to the broad North Sea beaches. An engineer famous in Dutch history – his highly appropriate name was Leeghwater, which means The Emptier (I hope that he was born under the sign of Aquarius but that might be too good) – used hundreds of wind-mills to pump the water out, and groups of them can still be seen down in the south of the waterland, near Dordrecht. Farther north, around the bulb fields themselves, one or two have been kept as brightly painted souvenirs. It is the sand from the dunes that has mixed with the polder to make the tulip-soil.

Nothing to look at. Flat, like all of Holland. Drained by ditches running into canals – like all of Holland. A few trees, a few cows, fields looking like any ordinary mixed-farming country. The visitor, gazing eagerly out of the window, from the railway line or the Amsterdam–Hague motorway, draws his head in with a sense of grievance. Is that really all?

Yes, that is all. Even during the few weeks in the spring when the fields are in flower it is a boring sight, and the most attractive manifestation is the chain of daffodil heads the motorist is given to sling on his radiator, and the pretty girls in folk costume handing out bits of cheese on the streets of Haarlem. The fields themselves? Patches of bright crude colour. Instead of being green they are

5

red, yellow, or blue. Gay, certainly. But the violent colours (apposite, in tune with the countryside, in the other famous flower fields of Europe) seem here to swear at the cloudy greys and smoky blues of the pale and chilly lowlands sky. There is something intrusive, almost coarse: inappropriate and jarring.

Would a similar effect be produced by the baring of violent and highly coloured emotions in the people who live here – the pale and placid people of Holland?

One of the best ways to see the countryside is to take the autobus of the North Holland Tramways Company, which is a very Dutch conveyance. A blunt modern singledecker, painted pale grey, with automatic doors and no conductor. You get in at the front, and the driver gives you your ticket and your change in the minuscule neat Dutch coinage from a little desk by his steering wheel, with careful leisure. Inside it is all grey plastic and chrome steel, and you are of course forbidden to smoke. You progress slowly, in silence, with dignity. The quiet orderliness is uncanny: if anybody wishes to make conversation he does so in a hushed whisper, and every now and then in the churchy stillness someone reaches up and presses a button, a little red light goes on, and the driver slows at the next crossroads and bends to the microphone at his left. 'Heemstede.' It comes out in a dry rustle through the loudspeakers. A fattish pale woman gets out and a fattish pale man gets in, his tiny nickel 'dubbeltjes' and 'kwartjes' ready in a pale hand. The doors close with a sigh, immuring one again in the bus smell after the welcome breath of green moisture, and one trundles on again.

'Sassenheim.' One after another of the dreary villages between Haarlem and Leiden. The centre, if there is any centre, of the bulb country is called Lisse. It is just the same as the others but you get out with a sigh of relief to be released at last from that floating coffin, that atomic submarine, and the smell, never really clean but never, never dirty.

Walls white; painted, plastered, roughcast. Metal window-frames painted grey. Huge windows washed and polished every day. Nothing dirty or tumbledown, nothing disorderly, vexatious, or offensive. The world is neat, prim, and unspeakably tidied. A butcher with a great spread of glass and marble: stainless-steel trays with a little piece of beef, a little piece of veal, a little piece of pork; pale fattish sausage and a big heap of mince. The apothecary – a pestle and mortar, flanked by discreet bottles of cough mixture

6

and patent laxative. The druggist – a camera film and a flask of Boldoot eau-de-cologne. Albert Heijn, the chain grocer, with his neat packets of dried beans and margarine to Make You, says his slogan, the Life Cheaper. A kind of greenhouse has a massive title engraved in a slab that says 'Netherlands Reformed School for Lower Instruction'. Next door a pocket-edition power-station that is the Netherlands Reformed Church. Next to a poster saying 'Your Paint Comes From Potter' is another telling you to 'Vote List No. 5 – the Christian Historical Union'.

It is nine o'clock in the morning and all the housewives are chasing dustflecks. The men have gone to factories and offices (no difference can be told, either in the men or the buildings, by looking at them; dark satanic mills are a great rarity in Holland). The bulb industry does not take up much labour: a few husky gardeners in corduroys carrying strawforks, a few pale men in grey suits and white shirts, with diplomas from the Higher Technical School for Horticulture, and some thin little girls wrapping up parcels in moisture-proof paper and typing address labels to Seattle and Yokohama. In the short growing season local women will be enlisted to clip the flower heads and sort the clean, shiny brown-and-white bulbs that look so good to eat but aren't, as the Dutch discovered in the hunger winter of 1944.

Near Lisse there is a country house that once belonged to a Dutch queen. Its park has been turned into a landscaped garden which is a showcase for the bulb industry. There are mossy banks and little streams with golden carp in them, crossed by rustic wooden bridges. There is a tearoom in a windmill, a restaurant, and several glasshouses where you may see precious new breeds of tulip too delicate and experimental to bed out in the neatly raked borders. The trees have been kept; the lawns are mowed. It resembles a golfcourse – a tulip course! It is worth seeing, and attracts very many visitors.

Not far from this park is a building that catches the eye. An old farmhouse with small leaded-pane windows and a thatched roof, the Dutch kind of reed instead of straw. It is painted white, and outside hangs a wrought-iron sign such as one sees in the Tyrol. One can make out a prancing quadruped, and if one spells out (laboriously) the Gothic lettering it says, just as it does by the Wolfgang See, 'Im Weissn Rössl'. It is plainly a restaurant. The Germans, and a great many Germans visit the bulb fields, love it,

7

and the White Horse does an excellent business, which is not un-deserved, because Bernhard, the owner, is good at his job and his food is eatable. In fact, when Michelin brought out a Benelux guide the Cheval Blanc in Lisse was one of the few establishments the inspector felt able to recommend, and this was a great feather in Bernhard's large hat.

Inside the White Horse at nine in the morning it was very quiet. The front door leads straight into the restaurant, which has panelled walls and a floor of large smooth flagstones which are an attraction but take a lot of warming in winter. Wooden benches are built against the walls, and chairs stand on tables because Gretel is scrubbing: Gretel is one of the two 'girls'. Towards the back is a bar, with a fat copper pot of flowers standing on it, and an espresso machine. At the side of this bar is a lower table which makes a cash desk, and beside this table is a door through to cloak-room and lavatory. Behind the bar is a hatch through to the kitchen. The walls are decorated with old prints and bric-à-brac of the sort hunted up in fleamarkets to give a now-as-ever-shall-be look to restaurants – brass lanterns, hunting horns and antique pistols.

Opposite the cash desk, on the far side of the cloakroom door, is a table under a huge tank of tropical fish. This is Bernhard's special corner table, where favoured customers come to have drinks, where the butcher comes to haggle about beef, and where he himself sits all day – or would, if his wife did not drive him out for exercise.

Besides Gretel doing the floor there were two other women there. Marguerite, Bernhard's wife, was sitting behind the cash desk finishing the accounts of the day before. Saskia, standing with a cigarette in her mouth and a soft yellowish duster in her hand, was rubbing up the polish on the copper flower-vase, which was full of flowering sprays, because it was April. She went out every after-noon for a walk and came back with fresh branches. Flowers for the tables she got from the growers, extremely cheap. Plastic flowers are not among Dutch vices.

'Gone nine yet?' asked Marguerite. She was wearing a gold wrist-watch, an Omega at that, which certainly kept good time. Was it winding it, or just looking at it, that she found too much trouble?

8

'Five past I make it. Say seven.' Saskia's watch was an old-fashioned silver one worn on an expanding bracelet. She pushed it up her arm, as she often did, and rubbed the line of pink indentations. Her arm was thin, brown, wiry, with little flecks of a deeper brown and a shimmer of fine hairs blonder than her faded, beginning-to-grey head.

'I'll just slip over to the bank. Time Benno got up – I'll call him.'

The safe with yesterday's takings was in her bedroom. She pushed the bills together, snapped an elastic around them, slid them in an envelope and wrote yesterday's date and day of the week. Tuesday, April 13th, it went in her flowery decorative handwriting. Lunch covers sixty-five, dinner covers twenty-one. Weather cloudy all day but no rain. Thermometer at midday eleven degrees.

'Iron my blouse, will you, Sas? Not the one with the little flowers – the fern pattern. I'm going into Haarlem – no point in your coming; I'm not doing any real shopping. Those glasses we ordered – the round wine glasses, remember? – they haven't come yet?'

'They'll come by Van Gend and Loos. You never see his lorry before eleven.'

'Well, if they don't come today remind me to ring up and complain. Have you got a fresh jacket for Benno? – he spilt coffee down his last night, the beast. Well, I'm off.'

She picked up her handbag, a large shiny affair with a gold clasp, hitched automatically at her girdle, pulled the jacket of her suit down a bit, and examined herself in the large glass that stood behind the bar. This glass was to keep an eye on customers when one's back was turned to them; it was handy in many ways. It showed her a healthy sturdy reflection, with ash-blonde hair cut fairly short and set every week in Leiden, big white teeth, and the high rosy complexion that is so Dutch. At forty-five Marguerite had a large firm mouth, small shrewd electric-blue eyes, and the beginnings of a double chin. Her figure was solid, with a splendid bosom, a tummy well disciplined, and a powerful behind. Her legs were a trifle heavy but long and well shaped, and she was vain of her hands and feet, which were thick, and the fingers obstinately pink, but small and very taken care of. She wore black patent-leather shoes that matched her bag, with very high heels. She did not bother with gloves to go to the bank, nor a coat – it was five minutes by car to the village and the sun was shining this morning, watery but optimistic.

Saskia's eyes followed her out, then took a good sharp look to be sure that Gretel, in an apron over her overall, was doing the floor properly. She breathed on the copper, rubbed it dry, put it down satisfied, slipped the duster in the drawer with 'reserved' cards and a spare corkscrew, and pulled off her rubber gloves, which she dropped in the little sink behind the bar where glasses were washed. She gave her hair a pat, her green jersey a pat, her darker green skirt a pat – though none of these things was the least out of place – and sauntered towards the door. Marguerite, in her shiny cream Fiat thirteen hundred, was just driving off; she glanced back and waved and Saskia waved back. Brr, there was a chilly wind; she shut the window that had been opened to air the restaurant. Antje, the other girl, could be heard clattering on the stairs. Saskia stepped into the doorway leading to the back and glanced up. Bernhard, puffing, was coming down the stairs; he patted Antje on the behind as he passed her and her dustpan and Saskia stepped back quickly. Antje, whose turn it was upstairs this morning, picked up the Vim tin and headed for the bathroom.

'When you come to the tables, Gretel, be sure not to put too much polish on. It not only wastes polish; it never shines properly.'

'Morning everybody.' Bernhard's morning voice, a bit woolly and coated. 'Breakfast ready?'

'I didn't know you'd be so quick,' said Saskia.

'I take the same time every morning,' irritably. He opened the hatchway with a pointed slam. 'Ted? Be a good lad and make my breakfast, will you? Never can rely on the women in this house.'

The cook was eating his own breakfast and got up with poor grace. Saskia, looking out of the window, paid no attention. Bernhard lumbered half way down the restaurant, glanced out of the window himself – without much interest, merely checking – and picked up the post and the morning paper that lay on the table by the door. He lumbered back and sat heavily in the corner. A smell of bacon and eggs, with a pleasant frying sound, drifted through the open hatch. Bernhard – a great handsome hill of a man around fifty, with silvery hair and pale massive features – threw a big grey bloodshot eye at Saskia and unfolded the paper with a malevolent crackle.

'Get me my coffee, Gretel.'

'Gretel's busy. I'll get it.'

Ted slapped the dish with bacon and eggs on his counter by the hatch. Saskia took a plate from the hot cupboard, a knife and fork, and the dish, together skilfully like a waitress, and bumped it all on Bernhard's table. He pretended to be deep in his paper. She walked slowly back for the coffee, taking her time. The door opened and Marguerite came in breezily.

'Chilly wind. Morning again, darling.' She kissed his cheek in passing, in a wifely, impersonal fashion.

'I'll go and do your blouse,' said Saskia.

It was absurd to think that Commissaire van der Valk was not yet used to his new surroundings and his new life. He had been here six months, and if he wasn't used to things yet . . . Perhaps he had changed, he thought sometimes. Perhaps he was in some ways a different person? Six months on crutches had given him plenty to think about, and time to think in. And possibly, at the age of forty-four, one did not adapt, old tortoise that one was, to a new carapace as quickly as one would wish.

A good life, this, for all the grumbles. He had jeered at his luck, at first. What, it took a bullet to get promotion, the same rank any man of his age and talents had reached four years ago? A permanent disability; was that what it took to make him respectable? But he was contented, and knew it. His job was – compared to what had gone before – something of a sinecure. Still, he was not on the shelf yet; he was commissaire in charge of the criminal brigade, responsible for a town of some fifty thousand people and the countryside within a radius of twenty-five kilometres. And the town was agreeable, much of it sixteenth- and seventeenth-century buildings, with too much dignity to fall into the merely picturesque. This historic centre whose driving force was (as it had been for four hundred years) the university was blessedly freed of cars by the canals and humpbacked bridges, and the industry – a light, clean industry not over given to stinks or loud clangs – was grouped at a respectful distance. Paint, printing, shirts-and-blouses – a well-behaved industry!

Three months in hospital, as good as paralysed from the waist down. Three months remedial exercises. Six months convalescent leave – they had treated him very generously. But after a year Amsterdam had moved past him. He no longer had his ears and fingertips tuned to the pulse of things – he no longer spoke the new argot or recognized the new catchwords. It seemed a small thing, but to him it was more radical, more definite, than the notes after his last medical stating that he did not, and now never would, meet the physical standards exacted of the Amsterdam police. A lot he had ever cared about things written on his dossier!

But the authorities for provincial Holland were more accommodating, and the notes on the dossier of a moral kind – that was wrongly put, he told himself; let us say less physiological – had been glossed over, as it were, out of sympathy for the stick he would now always need to walk with. He had been given promotion to the grade of commissaire, the command of a brigade, the perks that went with it – and that was not negligible!

In Amsterdam no mere police officer got a house – a whole house – in the centre of the town. And it was a nice house, in the old style, tall, narrow, gabled, with a tiny back garden. Arlette was delighted with it. And with this went the 'standing' – as 'The Commissaris' he was something in the upper crust of the bourgeoisie, equal to, say, a full professor at the university. He would get his name in the local paper for subscribing twenty-five florins to a charitable cause – grieving heaven, there were an awful lot of charitable causes, and woe betide him if he did not contribute to all of them.

His eccentricities, moreover, were here put down to wounds received in the course of duty, and to being an Amsterdammer. When he entertained municipal importances, they made, perhaps, faces at the food they got and the pictures on the walls, but they also made allowances. He was fortified by his status, and the notion that at forty-five he could be considered to have mellowed a bit, and he survived . . .

He no longer ran about – he sat behind a desk like a minister. Come to that, he no longer made jokes about town councillors, he was no longer rude to lawyers and doctors, he no longer sang songs. The slow, dramatic limp on the rubber-tipped, silver-mounted, impressively polished walking-stick helped him very much, and he found this a good joke. . . . Nobody forgot he had been wounded – it was a most useful stage property and he refused to be separated from it an instant, though he could walk quite well, when not too fatigued, without. Better than being compulsory-retirement material, for a man with a boy in the first year at the university and another in the last year at the lyceum!

The new standing showed itself in subtle ways. It was a shortish walk to his office – five minutes even for him. He accomplished this four times a day, not dressed in the tweed jackets and shapeless trousers of Amsterdam, but in a well cut, countrified – almost horsy – suit of West of England wool, very small black-and-white dogtooth. With the stick, and a hat (Arlette, giggling, insisted on his always – always – wearing the hat), he looked like a colonel in the cavalry, convalescing, perhaps, from a fall at polo. And if he detested horses she more than made up for it – she loved horses, always had. She was forty now, needing exercise if she was going to keep her figure, and twice or even three times a week she put on breeches and boots, and – carrying her little whip – went to have riding lessons at a snobbish manège out in the country near Lisse, in her little 2 CV Citroen, the ugly duckling as it is called in Holland. She had turned into quite a good horsewoman, with a firm seat, and strong hands; a bit clumsy, but a creditable jumper. And Francis, the peppery owner of the riding-school, who played the part of cavalry colonel so much better than Van der Valk ever could, approved of her too, and hardly ever shouted 'Keep your belly in, cow that you are'.

Francis looked like General Weygand, knew it, enjoyed it, played up to it. His boots had to be perfect and his breeches shabby; he combined disreputable Harris jackets with Lanvin scarves and pullovers: his monocle and his gold cigarette-case, his clipped sharp voice and his tremendous oaths were essential parts of his 'Saumur' art, which was most successful and known throughout horsy Europe. 'That bottom of yours, dear Countess, would give even a carthorse a sore back,' he shouted in public at his wealthiest, most snobbish client, and she loved it . . .

Francis would light another Egyptian cigarette with an irritable snap of his lumpy old aluminium storm-lighter, hit his boots frenziedly with his switch, and say 'Bitch, bitch, bitch' on a rising scale of assumed indignation that was a joy to listen to. He had certain surefire jokes that were repeated all over Holland, such as the remark (in the hearing of at least ten wealthy bourgeois women) at the sight of the elegant Military Attaché of an Arab country: 'Don't give that damned Wog any mares – the moment he's out of my sight they'll start making love.' Such remarks, shattering, surest death to any reputation in ordinary Dutch circles, were tolerated and secretly enjoyed among the horses. Francis' reputation as licensed iconoclast came perhaps from a peculiar bourgeois notion that there was something fast and raffish about a manège, and that all sorts of things were permissible there that would have caused lifted eyebrows and glacial coughing in any other Dutch circles . . .

As for Arlette, she enjoyed Francis, enjoyed the horse, enjoyed even the interminable horsy talk, as well as the fresh air and the violent exercise that were so good for her waistline.

Van der Valk, laying the stick with its chased silver band across his polished desk, tried to make the act as good as Francis but he failed. He had, though, cultivated a slow, quiet voice and an air of weary wisdom that was not without effect on subordinates and on the commissaire, his colleague, head of the municipal police, a baldish personage given to self-important dyspepsia about his administration. Had Van der Valk known it, he had brought with him a glamorous reputation; he did guess, though, that the unaccustomed respect in which he warmed himself was that accorded to Major Held, coming home on crutches from Stalingrad with the Knight's Cross pinned to his bosom and making the girls go weak at the knees, and he enjoyed this.

The new job was, too, very pleasant. Regular hours; no goddam weekend duty. He could pack up and go home – and did – upright and distinguished with his stick, raising his hat to people, rather ahead of closing time. No beastly evening chores, no reports to be typed, free from Friday evening till Monday morning. . . . There was, to be sure, responsibility. If he got a crime wave – ha, then he would have to sit up all night and like it. So far no such thing had happened. Except for an attempted voluntary homicide (two loutish youths who had been supplanted with girlfriends and had tipped the supplanters' Volkswagen into the canal coming home from a dance at one in the morning, materially aided by a big fourth-hand Chevrolet) he had had little work. Puff-puff – petty puff-puff – of a provincial town: burglaries, embezzlements and frauds; juveniles robbing the till in sweet-shops, terrorizing old women with air pistols, putting obstacles on railway lines (vandalism in public parks and breaking up the furniture at pop concerts was the affair of the municipal police) – there was always plenty to do, but it wasn't the kind of thing one sat up at night for.

When, therefore, he heard that Bernhard Fischer, owner of the

White Horse Inn out in Warmond, had died suddenly in confused circumstances, he was at first pleased, then irritated. Something had happened at last to give him a headache over the weekend, not to speak of losing golf, a ridiculous game he had taken to for exercise and which he was getting to enjoy.

A Saturday. Day for a ritual he enjoyed and looked forward to: English afternoon tea. Since this mania for fresh air and bumping on a horse had possessed Arlette, she seemed to eat more than ever and still stay thin, which he grudged. He was not on a diet, but he had to be frugal, watch his drinking carefully, and not smoke before five in the afternoon, and then only cigars. Weekends, apart from suburban joys like golf or gardening, brought the pleasure of naughty, illegitimate cigarettes. There was a suburban ritual too, and passwords given while he washed the soil off his hands. 'Why is it that the servants always eat the cucumber sandwiches?'

Buttered toast, and cherry cake, as well as Marmite. Goody, goody gumdrops. Arlette poured out tea, the Copenhagen porcelain that had been her promotion present. Darjeeling tea, no lemon at teatime, very austere (China tea with lemon, in a tall German beerglass, was made for him by the typist at ten-thirty on office mornings, while everybody else was gorging milky coffee).

'Have a good bump?'

'Jumped over hurdles with Janine. I made fastest time. That horse of hers cost a fortune but she's not really up to it.' He had heard quite a bit about Janine in the last months – Arlette had got quite friendly with her. She sounded an absurd woman. Her real name was Jannie, pronounced Yanny. She came from the South and had the local accent, which she had replaced by French spoken with a strong Belgian accent of which she was absurdly proud, and the name Janine went with this. You could not really blame her. Her husband, Rob, was the best bicycle champion Holland had produced in more than twenty years. World road champion, an excellent six-day rider in winter, a devil in one-day classics, he had become a rich man. Now, just retired at thirty-six, he had bought a seaside hotel and was making a good thing out of that. Janine had not only an expensive horse and two mink coats, related Arlette, but a very classy BMW two thousand coupé. She was a vulgar, noisy girl, greatly snubbed by the haute bourgeoisie of the riding-school for having made her money out of bicycle racing. Van der Valk agreed that this was pathetic as well as amusing. The girl herself, it seemed, was funny and Arlette liked her, laughing unmaliciously at her horrible French.

'Any news?' not very interested in Janine or her horse.

'Well, yes – that is to say perhaps. Might not be news to you, but that's not my business.' Peculiar remark.

'Out with it.'

'You've heard of big Bernhard – Im Weissn Rössl?'

'Yes.'

'Dead.'

'So? No, I hadn't heard.'

'He was too fat, and it seems the doctor told him half jokingly to ride a horse. Everybody laughed, but less when he took it seriously. Francis had twenty fits – "I don't keep oxen for overweight Germans" – you know, no need to repeat it. The wife, Marguerite, was angry because she felt humiliated and that he'd made a fool of her.'

'Yes but what happened?'

'Nobody quite knows. He was in a field and got off to look at something and upset the horse in some way and apparently it kicked him, and he got it in the temple – he must have been bending down, they thought.'

'I suppose that can't be unheard of, or even uncommon, in a beginner who loses his head.'

'I don't know. Everyone seems to have been satisfied with that interpretation, but I heard some whispering out there that the doctor wasn't satisfied – I know, I'm repeating gossip, but there, you did ask.' He was so busy listening to this tale that he failed to notice that Arlette had eaten all the toast. With a slight sense of shame he realized that perhaps he did wish that someone was 'not satisfied' about a sudden death. He hitched himself along the sofa till he could reach the telephone, and dialled the central 'police' number.

'Commissaris Van der Valk. Who's that on the switchboard? Ah, you, De Nijs. Heard anything of a death out at Warmond – man kicked by a horse? You haven't? – good, get on to the gendarmerie barracks out there and put them through. Yes, I'll hold on here. . . . More tea, please. . . . Warmond? Commissaris, criminal brigade. What's this about Bernhard Fischer?... Nothing much, nothing much, read your standing orders. . . . I don't care if it is Saturday, get your thumb out of your behind. . . . I quite see that. . . . Now ring this doctor and tell him – ask him to be so kind – as to ring me at this number. Right.'

'Stupes?'

'No more than usual. Doctor thought the thing peculiar: he mentioned it to them but he wouldn't commit himself before he'd made a full examination, so they did nothing. They've done the usual things, measurements and photographs and so on, but there's been no action – say they were afraid of my blowing them up for wasting my time before they got a medical report. Usual shilly-shally.' The phone burred again discreetly.

'Van der Valk. . . . Yes. . . . Quite. . . . Quite. . . . Yes. . . . Very well. . . . Yes, I would. . . . Many thanks. . . . I'll have a talk with you then if I may.' He banged the hook and dialled the police number again. 'De Nijs, I want a car and a driver, here in front of my house, in ten minutes, right? Good lad.'

'You're going out there? Straight away?' asked Arlette, alarmed at having conjured up this bustle.

'Can't expect weekend peace to last for ever.'

'You don't really have ideas that something is not above board? Aren't you just agitated because you feel guilty at being lazy and having a comfortable life?'

'Rather like that,' he agreed, grinning at himself and the clever-ness of women. 'Fusspot is short of activity. Feels the need to be officious, punctilious, generally get good marks for being switched on. If I should be held up, keep supper for me.'

'Quite like old times,' resignedly.

He sat in a Volkswagen and examined the countryside, switching himself on, noting the degree to which new leaves had unfolded, how far the budding stalks of tulips had pushed, mapping the cloud formations. Many many times he had sat in Volkswagens from the police car-pool and driven out towards some little problem along narrow countrified roads with straggly trees bordering them, and deep drainage ditches, crossed every now and then by rickety planks to messy little farmhouses beyond. He never thought about what he would find when he arrived; he had his mind on the road – you had to, for the drainage ditch waits. . . . It's not so much that the Dutch driver is careless and undisciplined, more that the driver's seat of the car is the one place where the

Dutchman throws off his terror of government and becomes a devil of a chap, all aggressive to show what a brave tough fellow he is underneath.

What an extraordinary self-confidence I possessed, thought Van der Valk, easing his stiff hip, pushing the stick parallel to the leg he had stretched as far as he could (never far enough in small cars, but no matter). The amateur psychiatrist. The silent understander of the human heart. Dear Lord what a clown. But what a lot he had learned, this last year.

He had learned that he was a far less good policeman than he had thought, which was very good for his vanity. He had thought himself clever when he had just been eccentric. What made him look clever was simply the spur of frustration awaiting anything of originality in our century, our generation of polite mediocrity, where everything is organized – Holland! – and nobody can improvise because it is not allowed. Most people's standards of thought and conduct he had found ignoble, and the revolt against the pressure-to-conform had produced a flint-and-steel analogy. Sparks of intuition that he had mistaken for big talent. He hadn't any big talent: he had a small talent. And it wasn't enough.

He found himself thinking of the last case he had had in Amsterdam. A woman, married peaceably for twenty-three years to a steady plodding fellow, a marriage seeming a model of stability. Their life was comfortable if not spectacular, they had two nice average children with no problems. A good husband, who went out once a week to play cards, once a week to his 'club', once a week with her to the pictures. What could have gone wrong? The husband had decided, sensibly, not impulsively, that he was getting nowhere with the firm where he had been for seventeen years, and decided to move to Germany, where he had found a house, a better job, and twice the salary. That was not enough, was it, for her to go out, buy quite a large sharp kitchen knife (bad that, in law, where it is called premeditation) and stick him with it, dead dead, before going, calmly and reasonably, to the police to tell them?

A homicide; the station called Van der Valk. He had found her sitting quiet, undishevelled, unhysterical, in a police waiting-room (metal furniture, upholstered in sponge rubber, covered with grey plastic, circular perspex table with ashtray thoughtfully provided, four climbing plants on the wall and a geranium on the table in a white pot); she was drinking tea. He sat down to read the report of her quite coherent tale.

'What made you do that?' he asked quietly.

'I don't know,' she answered, putting down her teacup.

They never got any further. Not that there was no answer; there were too many. As a distinguished sociologist had recently remarked, 'Anything, on any page, of the *New York Times* is sociology.' Ha. The world was so full of phony 'behavioural sciences' that everything was important, and nothing mattered any more. Officers of Justice, who in Holland combine the functions of examining magistrate and courtroom prosecutor, send for three or four head-shrinkers nowadays at the first drop of the pencil, but they got no further than Van der Valk had. What, a harmless, unagitated, untense woman had knifed her husband? And she had brooded, to the stage of going out for something more lethal than the little knife she peeled potatoes with?

They had produced page upon page of clotted nonsense disguised in jargon. Van der Valk had seen it, and seen it to be nonsense. Dutch assize courts were generally good; six months later when the case came up the president had tried hard. He had been quiet and kind. But by then there was too much paper, and the poor woman had been dulled into total apathy. They couldn't swallow the premeditation, and she got three years' 're-education' and what the good of it all was nobody would ever know, and from that moment Van der Valk had told himself that he was a clown. He should resign from the police and hang out a charlatan's plate. 'Neuro-sociologist' in polished brass.

The Volkswagen stopped with a jolt in the little village and Van der Valk got out stiffly with his stick. The neuro-sociologist would now begin diagnosis. His driver went off thankfully to drink coffee with the local boys-in-blue, and he went in search of his doctor.

Doctor Maartens was, he was glad to see, a man who seemed both sensible and competent. So many doctors are neither that this was a welcome rock to stand on. Youngish, a round face, grey flannel trousers, a navy-blue blazer. The white chalky hands of all doctors – it comes from washing too often in hard water. He smoked cheap Dutch 'brown' cigarettes with a healthy air, not at all worried about his lungs, and had a hard no-nonsense handshake.

'Come on into the torture chamber. I hope you're not furious – I dropped a monstrous clanger, letting anybody see I wasn't happy, but' – obstinate look – 'I'm still not happy. I saw nothing disquieting up there – they called me, and I came of course, had a waiting-room full of sniffles and miseries, all most indignant though it's not good form to show it. All I could do there was agree officially that the chap was dead – I had him brought down here.' Doctor Maartens was talking too much, and plainly had guilty wishes to explain, to justify: Van der Valk went on saying nothing.

'I felt a bit disturbed, uh, because the head injury wasn't quite what I'd been led to expect. I don't want to be technical, but it didn't seem the right shape. Well – I didn't want to make a fool of myself – I rang our local vet, who handles these horses when they cough or whatnot. Asked him about characteristics of kicks and so on. He agreed with me, and it was then I told the local police I wasn't ready to sign the certificate without more thought, or evidence, or both, and that they'd better take him – means town, I suppose, since naturally we've no mortuary here. I don't know whether that will automatically mean an official autopsy – doesn't lie within my experience – be glad to have your thoughts on the subject and that's why I'm pleased you saw fit to come.'

'I can arrange all that's necessary, but will you give me a brief untechnical outline of your not-quite-happiness?'

'Certainly. It's the kick. Nothing fundamentally improbable about the kick. The first thought was a momentary vertigo, a dizzy spell – Bernhard was overweight, blood pressure and so on. It's possible, though I doubt it, for reasons I'll give you. But he could easily have been standing stooped or bent behind the horse, I suppose, and made it nervous or irritable in some way. I would accept that, I imagine, if I was told that had happened. But a horse kicks upwards, hm, or horizontally as it were, at knee level – Patty, the vet, my esteemed colleague, I should be saying,' – he had an engaging grin – 'can explain much better than I can. Now this bump on Bernhard's head has characteristic of a downward slant, hm? I was stupid – you'll find me indiscreet – but I went to the smith, and he found me a shoe, and I messed about for quite some time hitting a plank of soft wood from every angle . . . look, I'll show you – in my garage, we can go out this way – if you don't mind.'

'I don't mind a bit.'

20

'What's wrong with your leg?'

'Rifle bullet. Went in here and came out here.'

'Ow. War?'

'No – woman. Possibly round the bend, but nobody was called on to decide – she shot herself – probably thought she'd killed me.'

'Most interesting. Like to look at that. Made a good job of getting you mobile again, what?'

'Took a long time.'

'One doesn't see things like that in this kind of practice,' with regretful enjoyment.

'Happy to oblige you any time.' They both laughed. 'Still, you do get horses' hoofs.'

'Here, this is what I mean.'

'Aha.'

'You don't find me overmuch the enthusiastic undergraduate?'

'I only wish we had more of them.'

'Put it in the vice this way, vertically, and here is where we get an approximate result – I'm bound to say roughly approximate, but Patty bears me out – to what you'd expect from a horse, if you were stooping, crouching, even kneeling – here close by, there further off, at the limit, call it, of a horse's kicking range.' Van der Valk did not state his respect for the thoughtful way it had been done.

'Now this drawing is what the actual injury looked like. You see, he'd need to have been sideways, even a bit upside down. The hoof, Patty says, moves in a plane like this. . . . I started making various suppositions; perhaps he fell but remained entangled, got dragged perhaps – or if there were a second horse – but Francis pooh-poohed all that. He's the expert after all, been a cavalry officer and so on. Naturally, he's concerned about it happening on his premises.'

'You talked to him, did you?'

Maartens looked uncomfortable.

'He questioned me closely – I took it that he was thinking of a possible suit for negligence or something of the sort. Since his responsibility could be brought in question, I did think he had a right to know that I was not quite . . . ' Not very surprisingly, Van der Valk felt curiosity about Francis.

'The news spread quickly, you know. But was it only to the vet that you hinted what you had in mind? The smith . . . Francis . . . '

'They would not, perhaps, have found it difficult to conclude – from my attitude . . . '

'He's a chatterbox, this Francis?'

Maartens looked at him as though astonished to hear a policeman ask so naïve a question. 'He's not just a gossip – as the smith would be. But he's the type of person who tells people about things that are bothering him, to make him feel better. But discretion in a village is virtually nonexistent. I made a bad mistake, I realize.'

'It forces me, virtually, to take some action towards deeper enquiry. You've set, without perhaps meaning to, a police apparatus in motion. Do you regret that? Do you want to qualify your certainty that you feel dissatisfied?'

'I'm sorry,' sturdily, 'but I am not satisfied.'

'That's all right. I'm not blaming you. My reaction was sudden, perhaps, simply because my wife heard fragments of this gossip. I rang you, you invited me to come and see, and I am sufficiently impressed by what you show me. We'll arrange a medico-legal examination.'

'And if it turns out to be a perfectly natural death I'll lose my practice.'

'Does that prospect worry you very much?'

'No.' Firmly.

'It's always an occupational hazard. For me too. Now where is this manège exactly? My wife goes there, but I've never been with her.'

'Just up the road. Ten minutes' walk.'

'And the restaurant?'

'Ah, for that you need the car. Five minutes along the road going back towards Lisse.'

He decided to walk; good exercise. He dropped in on the tiny local gendarmerie bureau, looked at the measurements and photographs, gave nobody any blowing-up, and left the driver where he was, which was comfortable. He started to walk quietly up the road, using his stick.

The manège was a large farmhouse with a slated roof, a rarity which gave it a formal wealthy look; it might have been built as a country house, early in the nineteenth century. It was surrounded by trees which left a semicircular space in front where cars were parked, and showed a cheerful country-house façade: the serious part – stables, 'pistes', exercise courts and yards – lay behind and masked by trees. Beyond these trees were fields, in which could be glimpsed, scattered about, obstacles, brightly painted wooden hazards for horses to jump.

The front door stood open; he passed a second glassed door and found himself in a large hall, decorated with pennants and rosettes behind glass, medals, cups, and trophies in rather tarnished silver, and a great many large flourishing photographs of the clean shiny bellies of horses (photographed intentionally from very low) stretched to clear dramatically high barricades. In this large room five or six people were drinking coffee and chatting. When he appeared the chat stopped to take him in, but only for one well-bred moment. Curiosity as vulgar as any other, but covert. Arlette had told him that it was good form here, following Francis, to be rather shabby. It struck him that it was a bit overdone; several boots could have done with a good rub and he observed (he was inclined to be a bit of an old maid where clothes-brushes were concerned) the shoulders of one or two jackets with distaste.

He advanced across a floor laid out in parquet, or rather a pattern of hardwood blocks about forty centimetres square. (Yes, that showed country-house rather than farmhouse origins.) It had been recently cleaned but was smeared with mud and scarred by dashing cavaliers who would not dream of going to bed at home with their spurs on, but were quite ready to do so here, where they hadn't paid for the sheets. At the end of the hall was a kind of little bar strewn with dirty coffee-cups, and a girl behind it of about eighteen, in breeches and a sweater, was looking at him in an enquiring way. An apprentice in the business, he guessed, learning to be a 'piqueur' – he had picked up scraps of the jargon from Arlette, who was amused at the rather mangled cavalry-school French that floated about.

'Good afternoon. I should like to know where I might get hold of Mr La Touche.'

'About riding lessons, was it? We can probably fix you up – you've ridden before, have you?'

He smiled. The days were past when he presented little dogeared cards. Eighteen months ago he would probably have said, 'Oh yes, I ride anything.' Now he put his stick under his arm.

'Van der Valk is my name. Be so good as to tell him.'

'I'm afraid he's rather busy,' began the girl in a cheeky way, but one of the women, a thin brown thing with very splashed boots and three diamond rings, lounging sprawled over a coffee-cup, intervened.

'Don't be dim, Elsie – it's the Commissaire of Police, from the town.'

'Well, nobody told me,' going out of a French window at the back of the bar with something of a flounce – oh yes, one can flounce in riding breeches – and crossing two little girls in blue jeans, their brown hair held at the back with elastic bands.

'There you are, darlings,' said the thin woman. 'Good day?'

'Ooh yes – Willy let me have Merman – he pulls like anything but he's terrific. Bambi's coughing so I couldn't have her today. Jane had a fall for no reason at all,' looking at her younger sister with contempt. Van der Valk put his stick under the other arm in a lieutenant-colonel's gesture and smiled austerely.

'I knew you,' said the woman with a social brightness that had a touch of sly vulgarity.

'Oh I'm not in disguise,' politely, 'and there's nothing official about my visit.'

'Your wife rides here, doesn't she? – I know her by sight. Isn't she French?' The tone seemed to imply that a respectable police-officer's wife should not really be French.

'She is, yes, but the horse knows no frontier,' with ponderous gallantry. One had to be polite to so many people . . .

'Her old general's being a bit tiresome, isn't he?' This was coat-trailing, and he was inclining towards a snub when luckily Francis chose the moment to enter, in a draught, giving the door a kick and leaving it open. He came round the bar, passed the brown woman, and gave her slouching bottom a flick with his switch, saying, 'Hitch it up, girl, hitch it up.' He surveyed the company present with a rapid semicircular turn of the radar screen, and gave Van der Valk something between a bow and a salute in the gesture with which he drew off his glove.

'Delighted at the pleasure of making your acquaintance. Good wind blows you our way, hey. Come on upstairs, my dear fellow. This place is very untidy, Els, get these coffee-cups away.' He put his boot on a chair and with a skilful shove sent it sliding theatric-ally. His eye rested on the two little girls, drinking Coca-Cola between giggles.

24

'Drink that stuff and then go and burp in the car, not in my house.' Indulgent smile from mama and an ostentatious clatter of coffee-cups. All the mares had come to attention at his entrance, noticed Van der Valk with amusement, and were hoping for a lump of sugar from boss-man, but were frustrated by his throwing open a side door and starting up a flight of stairs, bawling, 'Marion? Marion!'

'Permit me to show you the way,' he said to Van der Valk; formal courtesy towards men, and women too no doubt, if the occasion warranted.

'Damn this bloody prayer carpet,' kicking a rug that lay crooked on the landing. He threw open the door and flicked his hand in an invitation to precede. 'A friend here, Marion – how about some whisky?'

'Not for me, alas – I'm the British in colonies – only lime juice before sundown.'

'Ha – good, that. Pity. I'm not allowed them either but it would have been a good excuse for cheating. Where is that damn woman? Sit down, do.' Handsome sofa, covered in attractive lees-of-wine colour. It was a big sitting-room, L-shaped, with a huge open fireplace piled with logs. Two large portraits: Francis, and the wife, presumably. Well-painted oils, skilful, with a certain technical flourish, and some individuality and dash about them. Over the chimney-piece was a large oil of three splendid horses standing grouped in a field, handsome and spirited as Valkyries in front of an operatic cloudspace. This attracted Van der Valk, not that he was any judge. La Touche saw him looking and nodded approval.

'Admirable. Good horse painters very rare, you know. Dickie does those – the portraits too – amused Marion,' indulgently. 'Ah, here she is at last.'

A thin, tallish woman, much too thin and consequently too tall, had come in at the door on the far side. She had a suntanned, painted face – about half real tan, judging by a quick look – emerald eye shadow over bright brown eyes, brown hair with blonde lights, and fuchsia lipstick to match her suit. The suit was well chosen for the thin body – shaggy mohair in a large complicated overcheck of fuchsia, havana and off-white. She had diamond earrings, a pearl rope round a throat beginning to show lines, and a brilliant smile.

'Mr Van der Valk, my dear, our police Sherlock.'

He got the impression that this was no news to her, bowed, and kissed the outstretched hand, and was glad he had done so; a grave warm smile told him it was the right move. Francis galloped on like someone bringing the good news from Ghent to Aix.

'And of course our Arlette's husband – charmin' woman your wife, charmin'. Get us a drink, my dear, a tonic or something; I've got to take my pill – what about you, you're not drinking but a tomato juice or something – lime juice, that was it, Kenya or Singapore or wherever the damn place is – a little polo, m'dear chap, no proper horses out here, unless you count th' racecourse.' His hand twirled an imaginary mallet skilfully. Marion was still looking at Van der Valk carefully.

'Delighted.' Voice like the smile, like Jersey cream, gentle to marry with the jerky military gunfire from the other side of the fireplace. 'Do make yourself comfortable.' She moved towards an ornate presentation-silver drinks tray – all the accessories in the room had that hussar-regiment anteroom look. The furniture was feminine – there was a Louis XV secretaire between the two windows – but the huge silver ashtrays, the silver cigarette-box, and the silvermounted leather boxing-glove from Hermès that turned out to be a table lighter, balanced the sexes.

Francis, now that he had his wife handy, attacked briskly.

'So don't tell me you're worried about this death? Not a social call, I take it? Couldn't say anythin' downstairs – gossips!'

A heavy tall cutglass tumbler was put in Van der Valk's hand, with the attractive oily look that means Rose's lime juice, and the million tiny bubbles of Perrier water. Francis got a large ornate champagne glass with a hollow stem and a lemon sliver, and jerked a bottle of pink cachets out of his breeches pocket. The drink was cold, delicious, just rightly dosed – no doubt of it, Marion was an excellent hostess.

'I've heard nothing to invite worry. I heard gossip. The doctor was in a bit of a flap – young of course; inexperienced in that kind of situation. I'm bound to pay a call – imposed on me by protocol – thought I'd like to hear the story first hand from you – I've no use at any time for shreds of garbled blither.'

'Quite right,' large emphatic approving nods. 'Delighted. Settle the natter of silly women – bitch downstairs – more money than sense – grocers! Canned sardines that aren't sardines, sand in the sugar, what!' Like many men who shout how much they detest gossip, realized Van der Valk with pleasure, Francis was himself an accomplished backbiter.

'Bernhard? – you knew him at all? No? Great mountain of a chap, typical Bavarian, overate, overdrank, no exercise, high blood pressure, physique in a shockin' state, shockin',' palming and swallowing his pink pill with relish and a gulp of tonic. 'Cigarette?' An oval baroque case, gold for a change, with oval baroque cigarettes. Van der Valk, who indulged in Gitanes at home as in a secret vice, shook his head to avoid breaking the flow.

'Damned idiot decides he wants a horse. Marguerite – that's his wife; charmin' woman – won't have him near hers of course, and what does he do but insist on my buyin' him one, great Belgian lump of a Hanover that will carry his weight. He comes here and bumps around solemnly a few times – shameful exhibition but I ask you, what can I do to stop it? That restaurant is very handy for us, several of our people have lunch there, we rendezvous there often, have the horses rubbed down and fed in their stableyard, Marguerite's a fine woman – damn it, I simply can't refuse. But I keep the great lump out of everybody's sight. I had nobody to waste their time on him anyway, and after he'd been taught some rudiments, how to saddle up and so on, he'd go ambling about, State Coach opening Parliament – that sort of pace and action – that sort of horse! And there, I might have known it' – irritable flap of a hand on the coffee-table – 'fellow goes messing about with the horse instead of looking for someone who knew what he'd be doing – heavy breathing, clumsy movements, scared probably, make the horse nervous for sure. Lash out, catch him on the temple and the fellow goes over like a sack of grain, which was just what he was, god-forgive-me-for-speaking-ill.'

'Who found him?'

'Horse went back to the stable, reins hanging, and the boy thought of going to look see. Told me at once, naturally. Wasted half my morning. Just a stupid banal accident – I knew perfectly well what had to be done and that there was no point in any of it. Phoned young whatsisname – he's an efficient young chap, quite bright, perfectly polite – and he lost his head hawing about, so I said we'd get the gendarmerie to look at things, just to get the record straight, what? I took a dim view at first, but Marion pointed out sensibly that he was worried about taking responsibility all alone. They came, but they saw no point in it either. Photographed footprints and so on, said it seemed likely what happened was what had been obvious from the word go, and buggered off again.'

'Was there anything wrong with the horse?'

'Not a thing. But a horse can stumble, or limp momentarily, without there being anything to show – they are very sensitive. That could deceive a beginner. Horse was right as rain.'

'And the saddle – it hadn't slipped or anything?'

'No no – harness was all properly fitted – he'd been taught that, at least. He'd got off, not fallen. Young Maartens suggested he'd been dragged, but that's impossible with modern saddlery.'

Van der Valk was amused. The whole thing had plainly happened with no more reason than to waste Francis La Touche's morning!

'I'm very so-rry, naturally. We close the manège for the day, and go to the funeral and all, and of course I'm sorry for Marguerite, but she certainly doesn't miss much! Fellow lived on his reputation; he did nothing she can't either do or get done as well or better. Admirable business woman – like my dear wife here, ha.'

The dear wife had not said a word nor taken a drink, but sat effaced, discreetly immobile, smoking a cigarette – American filtertip, king size, noticed Van der Valk automatically. Francis, carried away by his grievance, had forgotten to 'zézayer' – the elegant cavalry dropping of the terminal 'g'.

'She won't miss him?'

Francis realized that he had been indiscreet and embarked on a rather hurried justification.

'Well, he was very popular, you know, pals with everybody, that wasn't what I meant – I meant only that my wife, now, is also an excellent business woman, I'm delighted to say, but in the event of my being kicked by a horse – that'll be the day, ha – she'd have no resource but to sell the stock and an excellent property which is worth a great deal, I'm glad to say. Very technical business, this. But a restaurant – that's a simpler affair, and Marguerite knows it inside out. The butcher and the pals in the village, who sat there by the hour drinkin' and gossipin' – that's who'll miss Bernhard most.'

'There's nothing to worry about,' said Van der Valk soothingly. 'Delightful place you have here – I've heard a lot about it from my wife of course. Curiosity, really, that made me snatch at an excuse to come and see for myself.'

'Come again. Delighted to see you any time. Charmin' woman, your wife. Ride at all?'

'No, alas,' tapping his stick.

'That? That's no obstacle – I knew a French colonel – left leg tin from knee down and one of the best jumpers in the country. Had it here in the thighs, that's where it counts.'

I don't have it here in the thighs, thought Van der Valk, strolling back towards a police station, a police driver, a police Volkswagen. Was it *Twelfth Night*? Higher, sir, higher. Taurus, that is heart – no, sir, it is legs and thighs. Something like that. He was a Bull, but he disagreed. Power, in his book, sprang from the nape of the neck.

He had another look at photographs. The ground was soft from rain, but there were dozens of foot and hoof prints. Nothing for Philo Vance to get hold of.

He went home to supper, which was pizza ('The trouble with Dutch tomatoes,' said Arlette reflectively, 'is that they look beautiful but they've got no taste'), watercress salad, and Camembert with an apple, and feeling comfortable with a cigar he picked up the phone to ring the hospital.

'Switchboard? Give me whoever's on night duty at the desk. Hallo. Commissaris here, criminal brigade. I asked for an autopsy this afternoon; has it been done? No no no, the report can wait – I want to know who did it? Haversma? Will he be at home at this time? Put me through? – that's kind of you but there's no need, thanks.' He knew those switchboard operators. He knew Doctor Haversma, too, and quite well. He and the Head of Pathology at the University Hospital played golf together – though they were the only ones that called it golf.

'Hallo, old son? The subject you worked on for me today – of course I couldn't care less about the report, keep the rubbish for the file – but I'd like a little shop chat, and not on any phones. How about golf tomorrow? Tell me one thing now – is that young chap in Warmond talking through his hat?'

No, the young fellow was not talking through his hat. If it had been a circus pony and a contortionist – but not the staid and venerable Hanoverian bought by Francis La Touche to carry two hundred pounds of restaurant owner. Van der Valk went to bed and slept peacefully.

Francis La Touche was having breakfast in bed. The bed was a large and lavish affair, with a buttoned padded satin headboard and embroidered percale sheets. Francis was being fussed over, and he enjoyed being fussed over. The morning was a time for luxury, and on Sundays particularly so, because of the immense trouble and expense of getting English Sunday papers that early. He lay now in a wonderful litter. By his feet was a huge tray with the ravaged remnants of an Edwardian meal – he liked things like devilled kidneys, kedgeree, soft herring roes, and he would have had lamb cutlets were these not so difficult to get in Holland. Strong Indian tea in large Worcester cups with little roses on them, and the smell of kippers and airmail newsprint. Added to his Egyptian cigarettes the Ardeny scent of expensive perfumery that Marion had left in the room an hour earlier was almost gone, and to emphasize this air of masculine conquest Francis was now shaving with a busy sound that was also defensive, for Marion had said nothing yet, either last night or this morning. She was sitting on the bed reading theatre notices; Francis did not only read about The Horse, but went in for intellectual food, this kind of Sunday paper being quite a pleasant sugar-coated substitute for thinking. He had to turn the razor off at last.

'I don't feel at all well.'

'There doesn't seem much wrong with your appetite.'

'Find me my pills.'

Obediently Marion walked across the carpet to where his breeches, jacket and pullover were flung in a heap; he never omitted this ritual of on-the-floor, just as he never forgot to put his shirt and underclothes into the bathroom basket.

'Not at all well.'

'I'd better phone Maartens then, had I?'

'No. I'm not at all certain I haven't lost confidence in Maartens – he let us down badly there yesterday.'

'It wasn't Maartens who was indiscreet. It was you.'

Francis unscrewed his pill-bottle and kicked fretfully at the breakfast tray.

'Take this damn thing away, Marion, I can't move without that blasted clinking noise.'

'I know; you mean I'm making the blasted clinking noise. I'm not going on and on – you were indiscreet and there's an end of it. Just remember that if Mr Van der Valk starts becoming an habitué around here you've nobody – nobody to blame but yourself, so please think it over and make the best of it. He's not a stupid man.'

'Marion, if you don't mind, I'm feeling very tired and I haven't slept at all well.'

'Here, have some sugar.' She threw the literary section of the Sunday whatever-it-was back to him, picked up the tray expertly, and swished off, her taffeta morning-coat making a more attractive sound than the blockhouse of newsprint Francis was busy building.

Sunday is the day of the dark suit and the white shirt, of early Mass and the sermon to which Commissaire Van der Valk does not listen, of the lavish breakfast – a Boiled Egg and Toast, instead of just coffee and bread. Holland has a peculiar tabu that runs No-Fresh-Bread-May-Be-Sold-Before-Ten which Arlette combats, now that she is Bourgeoise, by making her own, but not on Sundays.

After breakfast there is a great panic to get out to the golf course, for several reasons. The morning sun is often replaced by afternoon rain, and anyway the place is emptier, for most golf-playing dignitaries go to ten o'clock church services more ponderous and worthy, the sermons longer and even more crushing. Also it gives one an appetite for Arlette's roast beef. Even at ten o'clock on a Sunday morning it is often icy cold and a blustering north-wester is driving sheets of rain at one, but today everything works and at twenty past the Commissaire, a perfect figure of fun, is driving Arlette's milky deux-chevaux out to the sand dunes. The figure wears a black tracksuit now gone greenish, with khaki rainproof trousers and an English suède windcheater. On his head he has a green beret: the whole get-up makes him look, says Arlette, like a very old and ratty white mercenary from the Congo. But Doctor Haversma as well has violent reactions from the primnesses of his week and has a tweed deerstalker with the brim turned down all round, and German plus-fours in the Campbell tartan, as though hoping to be mistaken for the Duke of Argyll bawling the factor out about salmon poaching.

They share seven golf clubs with a warped look, and at least seven balls, for Van der Valk, being a detective, is quite good at finding other people's in trackless jungle. They do not know whose ball is whose, but this matters little, for they know none of the Strict Rules either. They take no helpers; it would not do for anyone in Holland to hear the language used by two high civic functionaries, which is elementary-school with a faint smack of Chatterley charm. There is, too, a tradition of elementary-school humour in fake foreign languages ('Pivot, divot' and 'I haf kein schwung in my schwing'). Today, though, Van der Valk had eaten breakfast absentmindedly, and had as little idea how-many-after-Pentecost it was – it was the Third Sunday after Easter – as any mother-in-law in a Mauriac novel.

'What about this blood pressure and the other things I've been hearing about? Couldn't he have had vertigo or something and been kicked while lying on the ground, or perhaps sitting?'

'He could, and again he could have been struck by a mini-meteorite while in orbit.'

'Any sudden crisis would show up in the bloodvessels or wherever, wouldn't it? He wouldn't have had a cardiac or cerebral attack?'

'Correct. Does this young chap say he was subject to vertigo?'

'No. He said he didn't believe in it, for reasons he'd tell me but he didn't.'

'I can. Constitution is remarkable, going by these lurid tales of overeating and drinking you tell me.'

'Hearsay.'

'Because you can take it from me he died from being hit on the head by an object forming a depressed fracture; cranial trauma and nothing else. Damn, I'm in that piddle of a pond again.'

'He might have been hit by a golfball. Picking it up afterwards for me to find in his pocket.'

'Was there anything interesting in his pockets?'

'A box of cigars, three dirty handkerchiefs, a large assortment of keys and a bottle of laxative pills.'

'You're not satisfied, then?'

'Not the least bit. I say – a brand new Dunlop.'

After the roast beef was the equally classic apple tart with cream.

'Sit down. I want to talk.'

Arlette, who had overeaten slightly – also rather classic – poured herself a small glass of kummel.

'Tell me about these people. You've often made remarks about one or the other. Could you make a potted biography? Like Stendhal.'

'Bigillion, a good heart, an economical and honest man, chief greffier to the Tribunal of the First Instance, killed himself around 1827, fed up I believe with being cocufied, but with no real bad feeling towards his wife' – it was one of his favourite passages from a favourite bedtime book, *The Life of Henry Brulard*.

Arlette lit a cigarette slowly, remembering an occasion in the north of Holland when she had been told to study the habits of a suburban street. She had been horrified – younger then. She was no longer alarmed that people she habitually met and talked to were criminals.

'I began by being disgusted with the atmosphere. Later I found it amusing, but I was sorry for Janine, who is more sensitive to snubs, and I remember what that was like – you know the way they have here of being anti-French and how it hurt my feelings once upon a time. Recall that cretinous woman who said she couldn't understand anyone ever going to France – what was there in France? – nothing! These sisters have something the same act, and one reminded me the other day – she said, "Paris is finished of course – you can't get anything there!" They go into ecstasies about Mary Quant! They talk pidgin English and tell each other about London; they buy copies of the *Observer* and leave them lying about. Lot of namedropping – they gas on about Harrods. I'm isolated, which doesn't bother me, but is rougher on Janine, who sticks to me for support and talks French – she's Dutch of course, but out of a bread-and-cheese family, and talks French to hide her accent, which is like them, but rather sweet. She's shy, really. Do I go on?'

'Marion.'

'Can't make my mind up. Times I think she's a bitch, others I like her. She has a good act of letting Francis rule the roost, but on the quiet I think she makes the decisions. That might be why he blusters – that act of shouting at stable-girls. She surprises one sometimes – nobody's nasty all the time, are they?'

'Make a pretty convincing effort sometimes. Go on.'

'Francis forces things sometimes by simply shouting her down – even making scenes in public – but she knows how to give in graciously. Where money is concerned I'm sure she has the last word – they achieve quite a good balance.'

'Marguerite?'

'She's the kind of person everyone likes. Immense charm. Lots of vitality. Dresses oddly – she's stocky, solid, with a lot of bum and those great massive breasts that strike you down – but she has a lot of good looks. Healthy-looking, like an eat-more-fruit advertisement, marvellous eyes and teeth, looks fine in breeches and on a horse, always very tanned. And people like her – not only the men but the women too.'

'Remarkable,' without irony.

'Very. She's shrewd too – has I'd say a cold calculating eye for things on occasion. She has an extravagant generosity though – gives big tips, gave Marion an antique porcelain tea service for her birthday that must have cost a fortune. They are friendly – she's one of the inner ring there at the manège, along with people like Stefan – he does international show-jumping – and the big oils, like Kampen's coffee and Miersma the dry-cleaners – shops you see in every village in Holland. That crowd have yachts and private planes. I'm the lowest of the low, I can tell you, and Janine, who thought her fur coat pretty grand when she started, soon discovered she was small fry. They go over to England every week, some of that lot – the husbands have conferences with Shell or Unilever, and the wives go shopping and hairdressing, and the theatre in the evenings, and whichever nightclub is in the wind.'

She was no longer intimidated by his making notes. She knew that he was not writing her down word for word. On the contrary, he was looking for the gaps in her sketches. People with dry-cleaning empires had cracks, pasted over but deep, in their glittering image, and she was not expected to know about them.

'And Bernhard?'

'I haven't seen him that often. He's only been a regular at the manège in the last couple of weeks, but I've seen him a few times at the restaurant when the horses rendezvous'd there. Like a bear, wore a cook's jacket but no hat or apron to show he was the boss. Used to get up and act mine host and then go back to natter with pals. I thought him rather nasty – simply because he was servile to people he knew had money, and inclined to look over the top of your head if he thought you hadn't.'

'How was Marguerite with him?'

'I wouldn't know, really – a bit offhanded: affectionate phrases but sounding a bit crisp – you know. They seemed to know well enough how to get on with each other.'

34

'Have you seen those paintings they have there in the living-room?' irrelevantly.

'Francis, you mean? I've only been in the living-room once, when it was her birthday. I brought her a bunch of flowers and she thanked me as though they were diamonds – you couldn't get in the door for flowers! We were invited upstairs for drinks – sweet vermouth, ugh – and I remember seeing them. Rather good, I thought. I've seen the painter – he's often pottering about; seems to specialize in horses. Maybe they think a lot of him on account of that – rather a tatty chappy by their standards. Supposed to be French – doesn't look it. I've no idea – never as much as exchanged the bonjour.'

'Isn't that odd? He must know you're French.'

'Oh I dare say he's not even aware I exist. More coffee?'

'What does he look like?'

'Oh young, thin, quite goodlooking in a sallow way. Wears those terylene suits that go shiny and look so cheap, so he has a kind of slummy smartness. Doesn't look like an artist.'

'What do artists look like?' laughing.

'Oh, I only mean he's conventional-looking – hair cut short, wears a collar and tie. I say, there's a concert in the big amphi at the university tomorrow night, an American soprano doing a Schumann group; we might go, don't you think?' He hadn't quite finished fishing.

'You know a thin woman with brown hair and skin, lot of diamond rings, got two little girls with ponytail hair?'

'Maggie Sebregt,' promptly. 'They turn their names into something sounding English. She's the daughter of some big oil in Utrecht that makes gearwheels or cogwheels or something, and she's married to Robert who is tall, thin and sententious, something quite haughty in the civil service. I can't stand her – she's one of those women with an infallible nose for the misfortunes of others, who take the keenest pleasure in discussing them.'

'Lovely. Does me a lot of good, all this. I feel filled with useful activities.'

'Yes, well, don't forget there's the washing-up still to do.'

Although the riding-school seems lost in a sleepy village atmosphere, Holland – and especially metropolitan Holland – is very small. Lisse is roughly half way between Amsterdam and The Hague, and no more than an hour in the car from either. From Lisse to the seacoast is only a few kilometres, and the strip of bulb fields lies between. The sand dunes, which have been made into a sort of nature-reserve, form a barrier through which one cannot cut direct, but it is not far from Lisse to the seaside town of Noordwijk, especially for the fast sports coupé that Janine got for her last birthday.

Janine and Rob were spending Sunday afternoon in the flat on the top floor of the hotel-café-restaurant Rob owned on the sea boulevard. It was a messy, ugly building of discoloured concrete that had several times had bits added by various owners in expansionist moments, and had climbed beyond modest seaside-café beginnings. It was on three levels – the café, with a big glassed terrace several steps above the sandy bricks of the boulevard; the restaurant, at the back and several steps lower, reached from the carpark on the landward side; and the hotel, an irregular cube perched above both, with balconies looking out to sea, an expensive but small hotel of twenty-four rooms or so.

Well run, all this would be a moneyspinner, and Rob did run it well. He was not, of course, on the level of the gang that goes to London every week – besides being socially inferior, a hotel is too easy-come-and-easy-go: one is overdependent on Holland's capricious summer weather, and the staff problem is always acute. But he was a lot richer than he seemed. Even staff was not too great a worry – he had friends in Italy, who kept him supplied with chambermaids from Calabria, and he even had a smattering of their dialect – he had always been popular in Italy. He taught them enough Dutch and German to understand the customers, and both restaurant and hotel ran smoothly.

Rob had bought it a year ago, when it was, on the outside at least, much as now, though far more run down and slipshod. There is now little debt, though this is due more to Rob's work than to Rob's money. He has worked like a tiger and has got the place nearly up to the standard he knows he wants, and it has just begun to make real money again. It has lost the evil reputation for bad food, sloppy service and exaggerated prices for cut drinks, and next year, the German couples from the Rhineland tell Rob, they will be back for a second season. Throughout the summer he will have to go on working like fury, but in October this year, he hopes, he will be at last free for a long lazy trip round Southern Europe, and take Janine with him, which she so longs for.

Sunday afternoon was the only time of the week when he allowed himself to sit back for an hour, but though he was pretending to read *Match* he was busy thinking about all this. Janine had had a hard time all this year – all these years. And this last six months he had been too busy to pay much heed to her. Well, he would try and make that up to her. He thought this riding business kept her fairly content, but she deserved more. . . . He hadn't said anything; he was intending to keep it a surprise. Say to her, casual, in the first week of September, 'Next week, treasure, we're going to make a cruise on a liner – go and buy yourself some clothes.' It was something he'd always wanted.

The room was a large oblong sitting-room with glass all along one side, looking out to sea. Even at this height, this far back from the beach, the window was constantly obscured by salt, which made the glass smeary and expensive to keep clean, besides corroding the metal window frames. When the wind blew, which it did seven days in ten throughout the year, one could not open these windows without vases of flowers getting knocked over.

The room had big armchairs and sofas upholstered in black leather, and white polar-bear rugs. The coffee-table was square, very large and massive: black Japanese lacquer with red and gold, covered in glass and the usual patterns of water-lilies and flamingos and spiky curved-roof pavilions. On the walls were several modern paintings, the kind one bought in St Paul de Vence. But most of the long wall, opposite the window, had been excavated into shallow curved alcoves with concealed lighting that could be adjusted with a rheostat. Here on shelves was presentation silver (or pewter, or electroplate) in every conceivable pattern from curliest rococo to bleakest Swedish – but mostly silver, for Rob was the best bicycle champion Holland had had in thirty years, since Long-legged Jan Mossup, or since ever, said some, for he was not only a sprinter.

He wasn't so vain as to allow pictures of himself in here, though Jannie (he wasn't allowed to call her Jannie, but he still thought of her as Jannie) had four silver-mounted cabinet photographs in the guest bedroom. But the café, downstairs, had the walls totally filled with photo-montages of Rob Zwemmer, world champion on the road, in the barred leather headdress of a track racer, in the

37

peaked linen cap of a road runner, bareheaded, his hair swept boyishly back by the speed of his passage . . .

No no, he wasn't vain. He had been cute enough never to make a serious challenge to the French in the long-distance races in stages. Only once had he tried the Tour de France, and he had reached the Pyrenees in a heatwave, and dropped out on the terrible Col du Tourmalet. So had forty others, but his had been the most remarked casualty. It wasn't a disgrace – the same thing had happened to Louison Bobet, who won three Tours – the same thing happened to Anquetil, who won five . . .

Nor could he challenge the emperor of Belgium, Ricky van Looy, who had two world championships, and a record in one-day classics over the wicked cobblestoned Flanders streets that nobody would beat. Nor could he match the fantastic total of winter wins in six-day events, on the covered city tracks, of the other Rik, the wonderful old Van Steenbergen (Rik One and Rik Two they were called, in the bicycle world).

But he was a complete runner. Who else with his record on indoor tracks (the brass band blaring in the smell of beer, the technique of sleeping in an unsoundproofed cabin while his partner took his stint of round and round, up and down, whizzing to the top of the banked steep track and accelerating down in a wicked diagonal sweep, and as suddenly idling down to cruise tempo, with the Oy-Oy-Oy of the music in the strapped padded ears – the smell was meat and the noise drink; never would he get them out of his grain and fibre), who else with that record had won a Tour of Flanders, a Liège–Bastogne–Liège, a Walen Arrow, and, greatest of all, a Paris–Roubaix in the teeth of them all, thanks to his punch. For he was a good track racer and a good road runner, an excellent sprinter and for a Northerner a remarkable climber, but above all he was a puncher, able to excel himself at a given moment. It was his punch that had won him a Midi Libre over the thirst-dried causses of Languedoc: it was his punch that had won him victory over the terrible Spanish climbers among the saw-edged rocks of the 'Dauphiné Libéré'. The punch – he could do it once, at most twice, over a week's racing: his famous 'coup de reins'. He would have agreed with Van der Valk that power, after you have learned to conquer heat, thirst, pain, fear, springs from the nape of the neck. To be a bicycle racer you have to learn to do a stage of two hundred and forty kilometres at an average over forty to the hour, to climb a col of two thousand five hundred metres through roads with bends of a hundred and eighty degrees, under the merciless sun and the no less merciless rain, to go downhill at a hundred and twenty an hour. If you can do all that you are worth the money you earn.

He was thin, and looked fragile in his expensive suit – English material, Prince of Wales check, but cut more extravagantly than the clients of the manège would have considered permissible. They would, indeed, have curled the lip and given little deprecating laughs: what else could one expect from a boy who had made huge sums of money just riding a bicycle? No difference between that and a pop singer, that anyone-who-was-someone could see. Making money, to them, was something one did without the eyes of a crowd – the crowd might see how the trick was performed and that would never do.

Thin, with a narrow head, blond hair cut short, candid blue eyes. Anquetil, not surprisingly, was his great hero; Rob was another one who used his head. Rob had studied the terrible Norman for ten years with extreme care, and profited from something the same temperament. He was Dutch! – not for him the flamboyant fury of a Fausto Coppi, capable of winning on his own half an hour before the next – he had learned how to dose his effort, how to make 'psychological wins'.

He was thirty-six, a calm, controlled man, very much in charge of the enterprise to which he had set his hand.

Every winter he had done two hundred kilometres a day, rough country roads with spare inner tubes slung round the neck, the rain slashing his face, wind in the eye. Six-day events were for money, and also to learn racing in a crowd, to keep balance in the desperate wobble of a sprint, to learn the hard lessons from riders who elbowed you, pinched you against the barrier, held you by the jersey. He wasn't a salon runner, as the French called it contemptuously. He was hardened. And he had been a lone wolf all his life. He had been sacked by Pellenaers from the Dutch team for disobeying group discipline. All Brabant had pelted him with eggs for that, and a national glory had turned into a national disgrace like so many more. He hadn't budged, and now he was 'Our Robbie', the glory of South Holland. He hated the coldblooded metropolitan west, where there was no sport but football (which Rob thought a show-off game for oafish exhibitionists) and where oafs giggled at his soft, peasant Brabants accent.

He would have liked to stay in France, where no rider, save perhaps the grave and courteous Raymond Poulidor, was more popular with the French crowd. In France he had been happy. He had learned to stop being uncouth, a tonguetied sweating clod – he remembered so well; Stablinski had beaten him by cunning in the Four Days of Dunkerque, and they had been interviewed together in front of the television. Jean deserved to beat me, he had thought, destroyed with shame and envy, listening to the Frenchman say calmly, 'You have to exteriorize yourself' – what on earth did it mean?

He could talk French now well enough for anybody, a queer mixture, with Northern and Catalan expressions but perfectly understandable. In France a rider was respected and an individual was prized, and he had plenty of money. He would have stayed, but at the last moment he lost courage – for the first time in his life. When it came to buying property he was frightened of the flowery phrases of French bureaucracy, of the chalky old notaries and their exquisite Tourangèle accents, of the odious smooth young men in préfectures, showing all comers that they were Parisian, serving a short apprenticeship in this dusty provincial corner. . . . When it came to tax and capital, to economic outlay and return, to planning permission and the Préfet's Decision, he turned away instinctively, to his own people, to work his own way stubbornly through paper. And he had liked France . . .

Little thanks he had had – Janine had not really forgiven him, even now – but that was neither here nor there.

There she was, sulking again this morning, sprawling childishly on the big sofa instead of sitting straight. She was graceful and a gawk at the same time . . . but Robbie found this idea a bit 'twiddly', a bit too like a notary embroidering sonorously upon the statute of eighteen eighty-one, as amended by the law of July ninth, nineteen sixty-one, relative to Immeubles. . . . He did not like twiddly ideas; he liked things simple.

Janine was thirty-two, four years younger than Rob. They had married when he was twenty-two and she eighteen, and had eaten together the bread of poverty and frustration. She had had three miscarriages, had lost two children prematurely, and now had her tubes tied; the doctor had said that there must not be another time . . .

She was a silver blonde, not white, not ash, and certainly not out of any bottle, but a silky silver, cuddly and delicate, and she wore it long, in ringlets that fell in a tumble to her shoulders. In her childhood she had dreamed of the cinema, and it had been Rob who had told her bluntly that she was not the new Bardot, but that he liked her the way she was. He had given her the roses from one of his first amateur wins, a ridiculous thing called the Tour of Overijssel, and she had gone, not long after, to Antwerp for the day and reappeared with a blue rose and the words 'Rob, I am yours for ever' tattooed on her right hip. Rob had been profoundly shocked, and had seen to it that there were no further fantasies dating from her Bardot period. She had skin to match her hair, soft and tender with a pale bloom on it, and the French journalists – had they had a memory of a White Lady of some years before? – called her 'Pêche Blanche'.

And how she had worked, after they married without a penny, and her father, a skilful collector of unemployment benefit, threw her out in a rage. A stupid bicycle maniac, and from Brabant at that! He had quite believed in the second Bardot, and had indeed counted on being kept in comfort by his grateful daughter, the moment she 'arrived'.

She had worked as a chambermaid, as a waitress, her hair pinned up, as a hairdressers' assistant, as salesgirl in a dress shop, as everything . . . everything honest, Janine would add, hotly. She wasn't going to end as any stinking prostitute in the docks, thank you. She would never admit even to herself that she might have done . . . something – to keep Rob going after his first world championship – he was twenty-fourth, and starting offers were very thin on the ground.

Her loyalty to him was total – it struck him now that he had forgotten that, lately. He put down his magazine and went to sit on the sofa awkwardly, squashing a corner of *Elle*. Poor Janine, who so hated her growing-up years that now she would only talk French, only read French – the language of her success. He wanted to show affection for her; awkwardly he started to play with the silky nape of her neck – her power. . . . She shook her hair irritably but did not stop him. Affection – as it does – turned into desire; he unzipped her frock. Her spine was slightly bony, but that peach-like back, cut horizontally by the black brassière. . . . He fumbled a long while with the cunning hook-and-eye system and for a wonder she still did not stop him. In the end, she just had to do it for him . . .

Monday morning, and Van der Valk in his cavalry get-up – flannel shirt, with little red lines forming squares, a tie of different shades of green woven into each other. He paraded towards the office, manoeuvring the stick and contemplating horse-chestnut shoes under the twenty-and-a-half centimetre wide trousers. This morning he wore his short overcoat, a nice fawn thing with a furry lining and elaborate pockets that gave him much pleasure: April is a damned cold month in Holland. He had a rich sombre scarf too; midnight-blue silk . . . bought by Arlette in Paris the first day he walked without crutches.

In the office he ran through his reports, which included this morning one from the hospital Pathology Department, signed by Doctor Haversma. He brooded some time: life was fairly easy at the moment. . . . He had three criminal-brigade inspectors, or Adjunct Officers of Police as they are called nowadays, as well as a specialized technical squad. He went round to the Palace of Justice, where he had a tactful wary chat with the Officer, and came back thoughtfully, rubbing his nose. Back in the office he stroked his carefully shaved jaw – he was getting pompous nowadays, and had had a very super German razor from the two boys for Christmas.

He felt contented with his staff: good boys. That oriental-carpet warehouse that had been broken open last week – they had cleared that up in a clean, decisive manner with no loose fringes left for him to trip over, and he had an agreeable free-handed sensation. He left his duty inspector to hold whatever forts needed holding, went and borrowed Arlette's deux-chevaux, and drove out towards Lisse.

The restaurant of the White Horse seemed to be doing business as usual – a girl was laying tables which had been freshly polished that morning, there was a good smell of veal stew with mushrooms, and a slim woman of indeterminate age in an almond-green skirt and jumper was writing out menus behind the bar counter.

'Good morning. A table for lunch? Or was it just coffee?' briskly.

'Have you such a thing as a glass of cold white wine?'

'Certainly – Rhine, Moselle or Alsace?' pronouncing it Elzass in the German fashion.

'The dryest, if you please. Is Mevrouw Fischer here this morning?'

'I'm afraid not. Have you some business with her?' dubiously – he did not look like a traveller in ice-cream wafers somehow.

'Van der Valk is my name – I am the district commissaire of police.'

'Has Mr Mije been transferred?' suspiciously; he smiled.

'No, he's here and healthy, I'm glad to say. I am his colleague of the criminal brigade.'

'And what does the criminal brigade need of Mevrouw Fischer?'

It didn't sound aggressive, nor even vulgar curiosity: it was politely spoken and with assurance, as though it were her business to know. As though she had a right to know, he thought.

'Are you perhaps the manageress?'

'I am, yes – Miss Groenveld, at your service – I am in fact part-owner; Heer Fischer and I were associated many years, so you need not hesitate to tell me your business.'

'No business – a conversation.'

'You can speak in confidence if that is what you wish.'

'I see. Well, there is no need for any stiff formality. You may not know, perhaps, that when anyone dies suddenly in an accident my department is automatically notified. You doubtless do know that in Heer Fischer's case the local doctor thought fit to ask for a post-mortem, because of his overstrained health.' She didn't look as if she was swallowing this – she was watching him narrowly.

'I'll get your wine myself – the girls are busy.'

When she came back with it – rather a mean glass, one of those deceptive green German things, but a respectable wine, with condensation forming on the outside – she had thought out her approach.

'We were waiting for word about the funeral. I may tell you that is where Mevrouw Fischer has gone – to arrange for cards to be sent and the cemetery authorities and – uh – so forth.'

'Yes, that is my purpose here. The funeral preparations can go forward whenever you wish – there's nothing to prevent it.'

'Why should there have been anything to prevent it?'

'A bureaucratic regulation – after a post-mortem the Officer of Justice signs an official release authorizing the funeral.'

'I don't understand the word authorize – do you come round to tell us that in person?' Hm, she had detected his little subterfuge.

'Just courtesy. And shall I confess a certain curiosity?'

'Curiosity? – because that fool of a doctor wouldn't take the simple responsibility of signing a death certificate? I can satisfy your curiosity, Commissaris. He said that there was nothing wrong with Bernhard's health, and even encouraged him to go riding that horse. Then when poor Bernhard did have a cardiac failure he couldn't admit it, because it would have meant admitting that he hadn't made a right diagnosis – I can tell you that this post-mortem shilly-shally won't do his reputation hereabouts any great good.'

Now did she genuinely believe that? Surely she must realize that his visit was a result of the post-mortem findings.

'Shilly-shally,' he repeated as though he liked the phrase. 'Doctor Maartens' decision was perfectly proper, and it would be most regrettable if through careless words he were exposed to criticism.' The snub was sharp enough to sting her.

'Why is that?'

'His interpretation was confirmed by the post-mortem. The findings have been communicated to me, and Doctor Maartens has no part in the decisions arrived at, which depend, as I have said, upon the Officer of Justice.'

She was watching him as though he held the last number for her bingo card. Greedily.

'I will ask you to come into another room.' He had spoken in too low a tone to be overheard but he saw what she meant. He followed her up a flight of stairs into a sitting-room furnished in expensive but tasteless comfort. Limoges enamel and Venetian glass – many expensive semi-antique objects pretty enough in themselves but without coherence.

'Sit down – you do understand that if the restaurant is open it doesn't mean that we aren't upset. We didn't know when we could arrange the funeral, everybody gave different answers, there have been rumours floating about. . . . We agreed completely that it was sensible to behave as normally as possible.'

'Very sensible. I advise you to go on like that. Above all, pay no attention to rumours.'

She looked encouraged.

'Since it might have taken several days as far as we could ascertain' – rather a grandiose word, that – 'we just said we would close the day of the funeral, not before.' It sounded almost appealing, as though she wanted to be approved of.

'Perfectly proper.'

'So we will put a notice in the local paper to that effect.'

'Ah, the local paper – have the papers been round here?'

'No – just a man to get a sort of obituary thing – Bernhard was very well known – and of course the *Caterers' Journal*.' One good thing – the national press seemed not to have caught on. Wouldn't either if he could help it.

She hesitated a moment, then plumped out with it.

'You talked downstairs almost – almost as though there were something in the rumours.'

'I haven't heard these rumours.' He was being rather mean.

'Village gossip,' angrily. 'But if one pays attention to it people become convinced there's something in it. They were saying that Doctor Maartens . . . '

'That Doctor Maartens?'

'Was not satisfied it was a natural death,' in a rush – she was rid of it!

'That is perfectly true. And very properly he did not wish to commit himself to so grave an allegation, and that was why he requested an autopsy. And that leads me to ask myself questions.'

'What questions?'

'I haven't said I wanted to question you, Miss Groenveld.'

She was saved from embarrassment by the squeak of a hand-brake being put on and the mutter of a car engine dying at the same moment.

'Oh, there's Mevrouw Fischer now – I'll just go and tell her you're here.'

'The girl will tell her, I've no doubt,' peacefully. She looked at him quite angrily, being used to getting her own way, but composed herself by straightening ornaments that didn't need setting straight. The door opened and a woman came in in a bustle. She would always be in a bustle.

She was as Arlette had sketched her, solidly built with a square and almost heavy face that was goodlooking because full of warmth and animation. She was neatly dressed in a black suit, a frilly batiste blouse, high-heeled shoes and black suède gloves. Seeing him she assumed an alert wide-awake expression as though he were a bank manager who would certainly regard her as a good prospect for a mortgage.

'That's arranged, darling – but introduce me. I am Marguerite Fischer.'

'This is Commissaris – Van der Valk you said, didn't you? – from the town – in charge of the criminal brigade, darling,' with faint emphasis on the words, but no more.

'Delighted to meet you,' with a firm handshake almost like a man's. 'Do you know anything about what's holding up the funeral?' She sat with something of a thud and her knees apart, as though accustomed to wearing trousers, saw him glance, and crossed her knees at once, pointing her ankle to make her legs slimmer, arranging the tight skirt with little tugs.

'Now that you're here, Mevrouw, I will say what I came to say. I had got as far as telling Miss Groenveld that there are no further legal formalities and that you are at liberty to go ahead with the funeral as soon as you like.'

'Oh that's good – I was beginning to think it might take simply days.'

'More to it than that I'm afraid, darling,' softly.

'I prefer to explain myself, Miss Groenveld. We had not got so far in our conversation together. I speak bluntly, Mevrouw, since I see that you are a well-balanced and intelligent person. Doctor Maartens was not happy about the sudden death of your husband – that much you already know. Forgetting all scraps of rumour, his opinions were confirmed by the post-mortem, which was conducted by most experienced authorities. As a result of this confirmation, the Palace of Justice has decided to issue what is termed a commission of enquiry, of which I have been placed in charge. I dislike upsetting people with clumsy questioning and I will try to keep this to a minimum. If there is anything particular I wish to know I will come and ask. I am here to satisfy myself about this death.'

The two women looked at each other with narrowed eyes.

'Have I understood?' she began. 'You are convinced, are you – as far as your knowledge goes – that Bernhard's death was not an accident?'

'I did not say that. Not natural. It could have been an accident, though this at present seems improbable.'

'You don't think he killed himself?' shocked.

'I don't think anything at all.'

'Yes you do – you think it was a semi-accident – that somebody perhaps quarrelled with him, pushed him or hit him, so that he fell under the horse, and that anybody who did that would be frightened to admit it – that's it, isn't it?' She was a lot more downright than the other had been.

'I repeat' – the cavalry colonel to subordinate; what-I-have-said-I-have-said – 'I have no hypothetical explanations.'

'Well – what can I say? – we will help you in any way we can, naturally. Saskia, has the Commissaris been offered some coffee or anything?'

'He had a glass of wine.'

'Which I haven't yet paid for.'

'But please. Would you care for another? Or anything else? Sherry? Whisky?'

'Nothing, thanks.'

'Can we ... ?' She shrugged helplessly. 'Is there anything we can do?'

'Just the usual conventional questions – doubtless seeming useless and stupid – but you understand I am compelled to ask them. Who ran the financial side of the business?'

'I did – and do. If Bernhard wanted money he wrote a cheque.'

'He had life insurance?'

'Yes.'

'In your favour, naturally. Better give me the name of the company. You might be well advised to leave them out of it for the time being. Now had he had words with anyone recently? A quarrel?'

'No.'

'No bad blood either, existing from a longer date, with any neighbour or business acquaintance?'

'No.'

'He had words constantly with me,' put in Saskia, 'we lived at daggers drawn.'

'I wasn't thinking of little domestic disagreements,' politely.

'Sorry – it was a rather misplaced effort at humour.'

'That's understandable.'

'She's embarrassed,' said Marguerite firmly, 'because they used to bicker. There's nothing at all. Bernhard was liked by everybody – he was very easy and friendly, and,' smiling slightly, 'if there was anything unpleasant, like a complaint, or someone querying an account, he simply left me to deal with it. He was rather a coward that way.' Van der Valk had to smile himself this time.

'Quite a human trait – most men are the same. Men who like arguments are generally aggressive in several ways, and there's generally a good reason.'

'He wasn't aggressive – he liked things comfortable and the sun to be shining.'

'That was just the point,' said Saskia, 'he was a big baby – we may as well be frank – and if he had tantrums it was because he couldn't find his slippers. Marguerite indulged him too much.' She had the airy, commonsense voice of an elementary-school teacher talking about quite a likeable but spoilt small child. Who is married to whom around here, thought Van der Valk.

'A personal question, if you will allow it – was your marriage with him always smooth? I am thinking of his relations with other women.'

Both women laughed slightly, in a way neither malicious nor bitter, but more amused than anything.

'He was inclined to stroke and pat a bit if he thought he could get away with it – waitresses, even customers. Harmless. You might find people to claim he was a sort of Don Juan and it would be total nonsense – you know how people can exaggerate.'

They were both showing signs of loosening tension, which, thought Van der Valk, was a very good thing.

'Masculine vanity,' he said laughing. 'Another human trait. I will ask if I may for another glass of wine, after all.'

'But of course,' said Saskia. 'I'll get it at once.' Marguerite kicked her shoes off carelessly on the rug.

'Sas, if you're going down be a love and get me my house shoes – sorry,' airy-apologetic aside, to him, 'please forgive my manners, but these are tight.' It seemed a bit studied. As though to emphasize how relaxed and untroubled she was. The other woman picked them up at once – hm, handy about the house, and encouraging Madam to be lazy.

Was it acting? They were certainly much more at their ease. They didn't believe anybody had hit Bernhard. And they didn't miss him much, it would seem. What was it Francis had said, 'Bernhard is expendable – nothing he did they couldn't do as well.'

What appeared to have worried them the most was deciding how long the restaurant should stay closed.

She seemed to be reading his thoughts.

'You must be thinking me cold-blooded. That is not altogether true, I must say – I was very unhappy and upset indeed. I've got over the shock a bit – but we'd been together ten years. We didn't perhaps have a very strong emotional bond – what people call a marriage of convenience, I suppose – that's what I find most marriages are, though – affection, of course . . . I have to learn to live without him, and I must start now. I'm speaking very frankly – you won't take that amiss, I hope.'

Saskia came back with the glass of wine and a little silver dish of sponge fingers, with a sharpish glance at Marguerite as though anything she might have missed would be there to read. Van der Valk turned down biscuits but accepted a cigar.

It did all sound very normal – weren't people's lives generally a tiny bit more complex? Plenty of women who live comfortably and pleasantly with husbands, out of habit . . . didn't love them, didn't have any very ferocious grievances. Even if there is affection, doesn't one have grievances that will corrode after a while? This wasn't a discontented woman, though. Healthy and active, life full of interest, no awkward encumbrances, mm, appetizing-looking, comfortable and juicy. Was it that simple?

'Why did he take up riding? He was in good health, but he was, of course, overweight.'

'Overweight!' said Saskia. 'He was getting really gross!'

'I was against it,' said the wife. 'I thought it much too strenuous – but he seemed set on it.'

'You ride yourself?'

'Oh yes – not regularly; I haven't the time. Saskia does the house-keeping, and there are the girls of course, and the women in the kitchen who help Ted – but the paperwork! Perhaps twice a week.'

'And you, Miss Groenveld?' politely.

'Me, no, thank you very much, I'm frightened of horses. I prefer a good walk.'

'You have a closing day, I suppose.'

'Yes, Tuesdays – the hotel in Lisse closes Mondays. We generally go to Amsterdam for shopping and so on. Bernhard went to the town regularly for his round – the abattoir, the markets and so on, keep people happy.'

'You know just what he did each time.'

'Certainly,' disregarding any hint of irony.

'I get a very settled, peaceful picture.'

'Oh yes. We live a very even life. The manège brings most of the excitement round here. The gang there come here for lunch a lot – perhaps Bernhard felt left out of all the talk going on about horses and riding – he hated people talking about things and not being able to put in his word.'

'Well,' said Van der Valk with a beaming smile, 'I must be getting on.'

'If there should be something – that I didn't know about– you'll tell me, I hope?' She was stumbling, a thing she wasn't accustomed to.

'Nothing will be done behind your back,' solemnly. She seemed satisfied. It had been an innocent kind of remark, or would ingenuous be a better word?

In the bar was a youngish man with a cup of coffee. Dark-haired, pale-skinned, with a greenish-grey terylene suit and a white shirt that made him look paler still. A portfolio propped on the chair beside him helped tell Van der Valk that this must be the painter. He had heard rumours, it would seem, for he looked curiously, then dropped his eyes and picked his cup up with indifference and a faint knowing grin. Van der Valk stared back with big peaceful cowlike eyes and went on out leaving him to go on being knowing.

Ten past eleven; Doctor Maartens should have finished his morning surgery. The house, a pleasant trim villa with clipped privet hedges, gnomes on the lawn busy with scarlet amanitas, and a brass plate less highly polished only than the windows, looked attractive in the sunlight that had struggled through ragged cloud. The privet gleamed with diamond raindrops; Consulting Room Round to the Side, said a pointing finger painted on a wooden board, so he pealed the front door bell. A slim woman, pretty in a mousy way, opened after a long pause and said, 'Surely it's not too difficult to follow clearly printed notices – it's too late for surgery hours anyway.' She had a harassed look and a piece of paper in her hand with medical scribbles on it.

He stayed silent, which made her look at him; she became confused and said, 'I'm so sorry, I took you for a patient, and my husband told me to expect you. They will come too late and peal away happily here.'

Maartens was in his surgery with the phone tucked into his collarbone, having a luxurious cigarette.

'Come in, come in – I'm sorry, a ridiculous tangle – schoolchildren's polio vaccinations,' apologetically. 'The town hall has made a nonsense. . . . What?' into the phone, swinging his revolving chair nervously to and fro ' . . . I've said and I repeat– that list is the one for February. . . . That's ridiculous; you've mislaid it somewhere in the wrong file. . . . Quite so, but giving vaccinations is my job, and sending out notifications to parents is yours. . . . I know it's a great deal of trouble, but you must realize there's little point in calling up over fifty children that already had their top-up shots in February. . . . I'm sorry, I'm very busy, goodbye. . . . Oof!' stabbing the cigarette into an ashtray that matched the kind of desk pen-set doctors get from pharmaceutical companies as a friendly hint after passing their finals. Doctor Maartens' had a little calendar built in, so that he would be grateful to be reminded daily that Rosenblatt and Sohn in Stuttgart make the best pill.

'Delighted to see you – no, not a bit – just my round as usual this afternoon.'

'I have to tell you that the man was clonked all right. Haversma – you know Haversma?'

'Very slightly.'

'I had confidence in you, naturally – you won't feel injured by my saying that Haversma has had a lot of legal – medico-legal – experience.'

'Of course I'm not injured – the unsupported opinion of a country hick isn't Spilsbury. What did he think it was hit him?'

'A curved metal thing with a blunted edge – but you wouldn't need to do anything elaborate like tying sticks to horseshoes – twenty simple household tools or garden implements. An old billhook – a stirrup . . . '

'Something that could have been picked up on the spur of the moment.'

'Quite, but you're going too fast. All I have to do is know why.'

'I'd be fascinated to know how you thought of going about that. Anything but simple, I'd have thought.'

Van der Valk had to go cautiously – he didn't want a young idealistic doctor rearing up and worrying about his professional oath.

'Might be very simple – people do just up and hit suddenly, quite often, and then you quite often find them standing there with the poker in their hand, wondering what came over them. Or they go themselves to the police. That hasn't happened. It's not going to happen. Somebody had a reason – maybe a good reason, which we don't know. That person banked on the large probability that it would be seen as an accident. Plenty of possibilities. He was over-weight and had a congested look, so he might have got dizzy and fallen off, or even collapsed from some sudden effort like doing up the saddle. Or he was bending and lurched clumsily into the horse. Whatever happened, he hurt it or startled it, so that it lashed out and clipped him. I haven't looked at any statistics – distrust them anyway – so I don't know how likely such things are. The point is that an ordinary person would accept it as likely.'

'You want to know why I didn't,' slowly. 'What cast the little seed of doubt? I don't know myself, exactly. It's true that anybody would have accepted the accident – I would myself. Just that I'd given him quite a thorough check not three months ago, when he took this riding up. He came after some pushing from his wife, with moans about his liver, and I gave him a lecture on alcohol – but he had an amazing constitution! Anyone else would have had cirrhosis – think of the horrors waiting for the man who abuses eating and drinking to that extent – and his tension and cholesterol figures were virtually normal! Healthy as a Tyrolean wood-chopper. Oh, he had some slight congestions . . . but heart and lungs – a channel swimmer.

'What's more, I don't believe in the clumsiness theory either. I can understand Francis putting it forward – someone from a town, nervous of horses and making a horse nervous, fair enough. But this chap – when he was a child his father had carthorses, and he was saying Wo and Shtiddy to them when he was five years old. Nobody's going to tell me he was that awkward – Francis says anyway it was a thirteen-year-old Hanoverian with a placid temperament.'

'You're doing my homework for me,' said Van der Valk.

'Haversma's findings confirm mine, do they? And that leaves you with the hypothesis of a criminal in our midst? And now you've got to catch him.'

'That's how it goes in the book. I don't believe in criminals much.'

'You don't believe in the book?'

'What about your big eater and drinker that defies convention? People are like that. People who ought by all accounts to be criminals and aren't. Other people who obviously aren't – and commit crimes . . . '

'Now come. Criminals exist.'

'Oh, I'm not talking about squalid crimes. Though even then . . . '

'But there is a criminal type, surely.' Doctor Maartens was rather shocked. 'Without any metaphysical nonsense – I mean the fellow distorted right from the start – bad home, unlucky childhood, wet the bed and so on, twists of environment, the whole lot fixed and crystallized by an early prison sentence.'

'That is just what I don't like,' said Van der Valk gloomily. 'Wet the bed – anxiety symptom. Bad home – or over-rigid home. Early delinquency – and so on. All neatly pigeon-holed. Tick where applicable, strike out where not applicable – form-filling!'

'But there must be some standards, man, by which you decide. And anyway, it's not decided finally – that's the precise function of the assize court.'

'Yes – and there's two sorts of assize courts, or if you like two systems. Ours, where everything is cut and dried beforehand, and the English kind, where everything relevant is suppressed because of "prejudicing the accused".'

'A criminal is a criminal and must be judged accordingly,' said Maartens primly.

'Quite so. Always provided he is a criminal. The assize court is admirably equipped to handle anyone who is a criminal and singularly inept with anyone who isn't.'

'This is an interesting point of view you're advancing' – Maartens was evidently taken aback by the aggressiveness of the other's words – 'but I don't quite see what you're getting at.'

'Briefly, that Fischer was killed – we're ready to accept that. By whom? It's pretty plain that it was somebody who knew him

53

fairly well. Somebody who realized that it would very likely be taken for an accident – and perhaps worked that out beforehand. Somebody who knew his way around the riding-school and would pass there relatively unnoticed. Which leaves me in an unenviable position.'

It was coat-trailing, but this trick of pretending to drop confidences was Van der Valk's way, always had been, and he hadn't done too badly with it sometimes. It depended on whether the other person had a streak of innocence and frankness – he thought Maartens had.

'Why? It sounds to me as though it would narrow your field of enquiry a lot – and that is a help, surely.' It had worked – he had taken another cigarette and lit it; he was hooked . . .

'Nine-tenths of our work is straightforward. Straightforward crime, first, committed for gain by professional criminals, who take a calculated risk – housebreaking, frauds, and so on. Then the crimes committed by young men who want to assert themselves, ranging from the simple ones who want to be tough to the neurotic ones who want not to be failures. Put together they make the majority – the bread-and-butter business.

'Next category are the loonies. They're difficult for the courts, but easy for us. Nearly all psychopath in varying degrees. The humiliated, the downtrodden and the solitary, the ones who want to get their name in the paper and employ press-cutting agencies. The misfits.

'Last, most difficult – and happily the rarest, though still unpleasantly common – the bourgeois crimes. Family crimes. The most respectable families have little scabrous secrets, which they will cover up to their last breath. It looks like that type, here. They are often the most unsympathetic, the most treacherous, the meanest and pettiest of criminals. One starts with a bias. To break it down, to get some tangible proof that can be presented to a court, is very hard indeed, and one resorts occasionally to pretty ignoble expedients. The only way of getting them, often, is to blacken them systematically. Make out everything they think and do as criminal. Persuade oneself that they are cold-blooded, wicked, scheming poisoners. And they aren't, you know. They're mostly frightened people – even pathetic. If one knew something of their inner lives it would be easier to avoid pigeonholing them as the foulest of criminals.'

'But they are criminals – by your own admission the worst and the most dangerous.'

'Not always.'

'But we come back to the original point,' warmly. 'That is the function of the court to decide.'

'The court goes along the rails laid down in the instruction. It's rare that any totally new spectacular fact comes to light in a court. The prosecutor's dossier is built on that of the instructing magistrate – here in Holland above all, because it's one and the same person. The lines taken by the instruction follow the police enquiry – it's inevitable. If the police devote themselves to proving a criminal guilty – and the harder it is the more effort they put into it – the court will inevitably tread the same path. I want to avoid that – I want to find out all I can about these people, and that means things they won't tell me. One of the sources I want to reach is you. The family doctor.'

'Infringes my oath.'

'That's right. You don't get justice without infringing laws, and that's twenty years' experience in one sentence.'

'You're asking to look at my confidential files.' A difficult character, this. 'I suppose you're right to say that justice is a vague ideal, unprecise and difficult to attain. It's still the job of the court. Not that I approve of the ridiculous situations one finds in America and England, with the prosecution introducing experts, and the defence countering with others intended to refute them. No – the court has to observe, to test – to hurry nothing.' He put his palms together, placing them under his nose, and rocked to and fro in the effort to be exact as he wished his assize court to be exact. 'To be merciful, in short. Not to base a judgement on the opinion of one, even – but two, three, independently, separately – with no bias towards prosecution or defence. Mandated by the court – under oath to observe and state the truth.'

Oh dear, thought Van der Valk, he is an innocent!

'Would you accept such a role?' smoothly.

'I would if I were asked – I'm not likely to be thought sufficiently qualified.'

'And it's exactly what I'm asking you. I don't ask to see your confidential files – I want your opinions, based on clinical observation. You know,' drily, 'I have a fairly broad experience of assize courts. I'm conscious of the responsibility I take. I don't want to prejudge anybody, to pigeonhole them as criminals. I'm asking this if you like as one doctor to another. We're under oath too, you know.'

Maartens put his elbows so violently upon the desk he had to lift them off to rub them.

'I'll tell you what I can. Now?'

'Tonight if you don't mind – after dinner if you're free.'

'Very well – but why?'

'I'm not trying to be all broadminded and give you time to reconsider,' grinning in a villainous way. 'It's simply that it's time for lunch, you've your visits to make at two, and your wife will not be at all pleased with me.'

'Good grief,' said Maartens, unwinding suddenly, 'I hadn't noticed.'

You should have been a prosecutor, thought Van der Valk, closing the gate with his stick.

Outside, the sun was shining, for a change.

He had rather a good lunch, in the White Horse. It was busy when he arrived, and he had to share a table with a solid Dutch gentleman who kept his glasses on and his briefcase open on the chair beside him, and worked his way steadily through course after course of food and paper, never getting mustard on the wrong slice, a thing that compelled Van der Valk's admiration. Over on one side a little group of noisy regulars in riding breeches were already at the dessert stage – he guessed that if latecomers came clamouring for table space these would be expected to drink up their coffee and shove off to make room.

There was no ridiculous head waiter; it was Marguerite in a black jersey frock who walked from table to table, plainly knowing what she was talking about. For her he was not the police officer, quite a lordly one, who had that morning been asking personal questions about her late husband, but a customer like another, whom she could judge from appearances as the type to order a bottle of wine and the more expensive dishes. He admired this firm compartmented mind.

'There is a nice roast rib – not too red; a real pink. Horseradish, potato pancakes – some spinach? Or calves' liver – with almonds and sultanas.' No mention of stew! Solid, good cooking, simply and well done, and not at all out of place since the place was packed with Germans who had been to the bulb fields.

Saskia was behind the bar, giving the orders through the hatch-way, checking the dishes as they came against the written slips, serving drinks and coffee, keeping a sharp eye on the two girls. 'Fill the glasses up over there, and get some more bread. Can't you see he wants mustard?' – there were as many kinds of mustard as one got in Munich.

Marguerite moved quickly from table to table, talking but never for too long, deftly selling people the expensive extras, being firm with a man who appeared towing a gigantic dog. 'Of course we will find him a beef bone, but I'm afraid he must be left outside.' He admired the way she did it. Perhaps not an intelligent woman, or not in the conventional sense, but she had practical intelligence.

'Have you had a pleasant lunch?'

'All you said it would be. But without your husband it must be a considerable strain, isn't it? Suppose your cook got a dose of flu or something?'

'The women are competent, and we have an old cook who can't face it day after day, but comes in to help us over holiday weekends and so on. I can't help feeling that you exaggerate the amount of work poor Bernhard actually did – he spent most of the day at that table over there.' It was an ordinary table for four, in the extreme corner, made a little more awkward than the others by the big tank of tropical fish, a little more undesirable by the door at the side through to cloakrooms. Papa, Mama, and two children, from Dortmund, were whaling into the potato pancakes with un-diminished appetite.

'The gossips are rather aggrieved,' said Marguerite smiling, 'but they won't be put off coming in to play cards in the evening, which is no harm because then, you see, there are far fewer people. Aren't you having coffee? What about a glass of cognac?'

It was said in such a friendly way that he genuinely thought she was offering it him and said 'If you insist' politely – so that he was quite disgruntled when it duly appeared on the bill. She had out-smarted him – he was amused by this, once the momentary pang of paying for it had passed.

Down the road, back in the village of Warmond opposite the chill little row of shops, was a poorer, humbler kind of hotel. An ordinary Dutch café really, where they have a few rooms, and 'do you a meal'. Tomato soup, pork chops or steak, fried-egg-and-ham sandwiches. Van der Valk had eaten too often in humbler days at these tables not to know exactly. . . . Tinned peas or tinned beans; fruit salad with ice-cream or just ice-cream. . . . But he went in because he wanted to phone Arlette, and had not wished to do so within reach of that Groenveld woman, who certainly had an uncanny talent for keeping her ears pricked.

A few Dutch transitories were chewing on chops in front of glasses of beer – the humbler kind of travellers, whose expense accounts were carefully scrutinized! And a few family parties who had gone out for the day to the bulb fields because it was Grannie's birthday or some such reason: unassuming people who would know instinctively that they would only feel out of place under Marguerite's eye – not to speak of the prices!

On his way to the phone his eye was caught by the painter, eating quietly away in the corner at a table by himself and reading the paper. He was eating a homely Dutch meal of beef stew, with boiled potatoes and apple sauce, doubtless what the café owner had himself. He must eat here every day – very likely lived here. Van der Valk's interest was sharpened by the chap seeming more interesting than most of the people who haunted the riding-school.

It was a coinbox phone and he was disgusted at how much small change he had to dig out and feed into its maw before he could get hold of his wife only twelve kilometres away, but he preferred that, and being stuck in a stuffy cubby-hole smelling of dust and disinfectant next to the men's lavatory, to having people listen while he talked to his wife. The little nickel 'dubbeltjes' tinkled musically and he scrabbled for more.

'There you are. All quiet on your front? Yes, I had lunch in the White Horse – not bad at all. Yes, very dear, but worth it for the interest, huh? I'll be spending the whole day out here, even part of the evening.' He heard the door from the café open with a noisy creak and lowered his voice, going on in French. 'No no, just that I'm using a public phone. So you won't be uneasy, and you'll keep me some supper if I should be held up? – try and find a cos lettuce. Yes, a rare bird, I know. 'Bye.' He stepped out and found the painter innocently buttoning his trousers. And that was perhaps a little too much coincidence – he decided that he would try and find time for a nice chat with this painter.

The riding-school was perhaps seven hundred metres up a narrow bumpy road between trees, which would make quite a pleasant walk, but he took the deux-chevaux because the leg would be painful enough from fatigue, by the end of the day. Pottering round fields and stable-yards. The weather was cold and windy – the sun hadn't lasted, of course. . . . The rain was holding off still – would be there tonight, no doubt.

In front of the manège a pretty large group of cars was parked already, just the kind he had expected. 'Second cars' – Mini-Coopers and little Triumphs bought for the women. He left the deux-chevaux provokingly next to a decidedly gaudy scarlet Giulietta and noticed that pressure of work had not stopped the very-important-business-men bringing the 'first cars' either – a Bentley, two Mercedes 220s and two DS 21 Citroens . . .

He did not go in at the front this time, but round the side, where there was a strong smell of horse and a good deal of activity amid which he passed quite unnoticed. Perhaps it was his clothes – he would be put down as one of a horsy set, not perhaps their own, but kin. Buying a horse, maybe. . . . Three men in bowler hats and white trenchcoats reaching to the tops of their boots, all with clipped moustaches and commanding voices, did not as much as glance at him. He passed the girl Els, who looked askance but kept her trap shut.

There were several buildings in a cluster at the back – stables, he told himself, harness rooms and – er – harness rooms, and paths led out both ways past the big roofed-over exercise ring, roughly gravelled, cut about by hoofs and boots, with patches of mud and hacked grass. Here Bernhard had been found – yes, it was as he had thought, looking back – a blank wall, and the overhang of a roof, hid one here from the windows of the house. On the far side was a belt of trees through which one could – if one wished – pick a way through roots and sodden branches back to the parking place in front. Before him was another clump of firs, and paths leading both ways around it into the fields. He walked on and looked. Yes, left was the way to go hacking out across country in the direction of the White Horse. Cows grazed; in a few fields green corn was sprouting. And to the right were the fields where they practised jumping, and painted obstacles of different heights and sorts stood about for you to spill yourself over.

Between the path and the wall of the exercise ring was a strip of rough grass and weeds; between the path and the trees was a bigger patch, thirty metres long perhaps, twenty wide. A variety of junk was slung in corners – it was just a waste patch of empty ground, serving for nothing in particular. A place where a horse coming in from the fields might stand for a minute cropping, the reins loose, twitching flies off his sweaty skin, while the rider stopped to gossip, or went perhaps across the yard round the corner in search of a stable-boy. Perhaps from time to time beginners learned here to go through elementary movements, how to mount, to dismount, how to walk a horse around, perhaps how to trot. He supposed there would be no room for more elaborate manoeuvres, and that it would be in the exercise ring that they would learn to change legs with the off fore leading, or whatever it was. He knew nothing about horses, and cared as little, and what was more felt disinclined to learn. It would get very rapidly as technical and wound in jargon as cars, which bored him equally – he asked nothing but that the wretched object should go when he pressed the button . . .

He poked about in the grass verge with his stick. It was scythed from time to time; Francis kept his premises carefully, and would certainly take pains that rats should not breed, but junk accumulated terribly fast, and apart from the usual toffee-papers slung there by badly-brought-up children there were unlikely objects like a decaying tomato box with a moist and musty sack folded in it, the remnants of a worn-out woollen saddle-lining, and a rusty golf club. He stopped to stare at this carefully, and even lifted it before putting it back in the whitened track it had left in the grass. He didn't want any technical staff out here; it wasn't his style. . . . He went on poking, suspecting himself of wasting time, and after covering the whole length he had found an old enamel saucepan, chipped, the handle broken off, and an oval metal affair with zig-zag holes punched in it that puzzled him for some time before he recognized it as a potato-masher. . . . Further on he found an old-fashioned round weight, half-kilo size, iron with a faint film of rust. It had crushed but not whitened the grass beneath it – going by that and the rust, it had not been there long. Mm, he remembered seeing a weighing machine in the stable-yard somewhere, and went in search of it. Yes, there it was; a thing doubtless much used around here, where they were always weighing themselves and their saddles; it was important somehow. But this was of a much more modern pattern, using no weights but a graduated metal arm, one sliding counterpoise for kilos, one for fractions of a kilo . . .

He found Francis in the exercise ring, under an echoing roof that magnified and distorted a welter of horsy sounds.

'Ah, hallo. Anything I can do for you?'

'Did you ever have another weighing machine – the kind with weights?'

'Still do – use it for checkin' sacks of feed; grain and so on. Has it any importance?'

'None at all. I found a weight, and I saw that the machine has a sliding scale, and wondered what a weight would be doing here.'

'Where?'

'Outside,' vaguely.

'Happens constantly. Machine's in the store where we keep grain, but people keep on usin' weights for doorstops or whatnot, very tiresome of them. Can I be of any service to you?' Plainly he was busy, and anxious to get rid of this tedious visitor, with his gabble about weights.

'No, thanks. How far is the White Horse, across the fields that way?'

'About a kilometre and a half, I suppose. Make a pleasant little walk if you don't mind gettin' your boots dirty. Marguerite comes round the road with the car. Bernhard did too – too lazy to walk. So am I, come to that. See you later, perhaps.'

'Whenever you like.'

He went back round his corner – nobody had passed him for a good quarter of an hour, he noticed. He got a magnifying glass out of his pocket and examined both the golf club and the weight carefully. There was nothing to see. Why should there be? That they should be there proved nothing at all. Of course there need not be anything. The golf club had rather too sharp an edge, he thought, but he wasn't very taken with the golf club anyway. It made no difference that he could see whether Bernhard had been hit by somebody he knew well (equate possibly with trusted) or less well (equate with distrusted if you cared to but he didn't) – if he saw you standing there with a golf club in your hand, it looked either lunatic or sinister. Since the evidence seemed to point to Bernhard's having got off the horse – and he hadn't got off complaisantly to make hitting him easier . . .

Whereas this weight . . . You had it in your hand and it hardly showed. Should anyone meet you walking round the corner there was nothing to catch the eye. If you put it into a largish handkerchief – or scarf – and held that by the corners you had a good weapon, didn't you, that could be slid into a pocket in a second if the need arose. The need hadn't arisen, and you just chucked it away. Nobody noticed and in three days it had acquired enough rust to make it look as though it had been there a week or two. Yes, he rather liked the weight.

The afternoon of a working day is dead, in a restaurant. Hotels stay open in a somnolent way, cafés go on serving beers and ice-cream for anyone along the road that takes a fancy to stop, but a restaurant shuts its doors and sleeps. In the White Horse the girls had served Marguerite and Saskia their coffee and gone home; Ted the cook had turned his stoves out, cleared all remnants of food into the larder, and left his apron on the just-scrubbed table. The women had piled the last of the washing-up into the sink and scarpered. Saskia made herself a second cup of coffee and turned the machine off, and complete silence settled like dust upon the whole house. It threw into relief the tiny sounds of Saskia stirring a lump of sugar, the squeak of the cork that Marguerite was pushing back into Bernhard's last bottle of mirabelle, still half full, and the distant fridge motor clanking to a stop.

'Maybe a drink will do me good. I've been so nervous all morning I could scream.'

'It's sort of disquieting not knowing,' agreed Saskia, in a calm, unworried voice.

'First all those mysterious hints dropped this morning – I still don't know what to make of half that – and then having him back for lunch . . . '

'I can't say I took to him personally, but I think he's relatively harmless.'

'It's silly to say harmless. They go on digging and digging at people, listening to every sort of silly gossip – how can one feel safe?'

'We could try and have a discreet word with Mr Mije and see whether he couldn't be choked off, possibly?'

'I don't think so – he's a separate department. Anyway he said he'd got instructions from the Officer of Justice – Mr Mije couldn't do anything about that.'

'Well there's no use in worrying.'

'I only wish I knew what that stupid Maartens has fixed in his head.'

'Still, he's a doctor – they have to be discreet – the professional secret. It would be much more Francis that I'd be uneasy about – he's always such a loose talker.'

'Marion I feel sure I can rely on. And I'm convinced, you know, there's nothing in it really. But if that awful man comes back I don't know what I mightn't say.'

'Listen, darling,' said Saskia, 'you're tired and overwrought. He said, after all, that the funeral can go ahead, and there'll be an end of it as far as the gossip is concerned.'

'I'll have to change and go and see those funeral people.'

'Tomorrow's closing day – you can go and do that then. It would be foolish to do that now when you're overtired. I've a much better idea.'

'Oh, Sas, no.'

'But it'll do you good – think how it will rest you. You can have a nice sleep and you don't have to come down this evening at all – there are only six bookings, so far.'

'But Sas, we shouldn't – especially now.'

'Don't be such a goose – I'm only saying that you need to unwind. I'll give you a really nice hot bath and then you'll already feel miles better – you'll see. You can be lovely and lazy – you don't have to do a thing. And this evening I'll bring you your supper up and you can have it nice and quietly.'

'You don't think he'll ask the girls questions, do you, and that they'll blurt out heaven knows what?'

'The girls don't have a clue,' firmly.

Van der Valk had got bored with peregrinations round the back yard. He had seen things for himself. Any person not a total stranger would melt into the landscape around here. You could be seen by twenty people, noticed by three and remembered by none. You could be somebody arriving in a car, promenading on a horse, having a stroll across the fields, or you could just as easily be living right here in the house.

And of course Bernhard could very well have been killed by a small boy with a catapult . . .

What was it that Maartens had fixed in his head? What had

made him so uneasy that he stuck his neck out? It wasn't just the physical appearance of the wound, nor was it Fischer's level of general health. Something a lot more than that, to make a country doctor do something that – if he were wrong – would mean the end of his practice in that whole area of Holland . . .

Stupe – he was not walking round the back yard any more, but he hadn't stopped peregrinating inside his own skull yet! He jerked at himself: the sit-down had done his leg, which was beginning to warn him that fatigue led to pain, some good, and in front of him there was a cup of coffee that had gone cold, which hadn't improved it, and heaven knew it was in no further need of disimprovement. The jerk was completed by his wife's name suddenly penetrating his mind.

'. . . haven't seen her all afternoon.' A woman's voice, speaking in French too, so that he knew immediately that this must be the famous Janine. He was turning round for a cautious eyeful – wasn't she supposed to be very pretty? – when a jovial smack landed on his shoulder and Francis' voice said, 'Ha – we have a surprise for you.' Well – it was certainly as stupid to pretend he was not there – everyone here knew who he was – as to draw attention to him. He got to his feet.

'But I saw her little car outside.'

'She stayed home to gather grass for her rabbits – let me present her husband.'

He turned round with an amiably polite face and had to adjust his eyes to something that only came up to his shoulder – a pretty woman, yes, but one of the miniature ones, a tiny bit of thistle-down. Without knowing why, he was surprised – Arlette had never said she was a tiny one, had she? The beautifully cut breeches, amusing as they were, did not really suit her type: a cashmere sweater showed off elegant breasts as well as splendid hair. The all-black get-up was fetching but she was the kind of woman that would not look her best in sports clothes. He wondered why she was looking astonished.

'Enchanté, Madame,' kissing the hand, though it was a long way down.

'Oh – you talk French.'

'Learned from my wife.'

'I was just asking – isn't she here with you?'

'I'm afraid not – I borrowed her car.'

64

'You – you ride too?' Francis, who obviously found her a good joke, was enjoying the scene.

' 'Fraid not. I happened to be here – I have the pleasure of knowing Francis here slightly and was having a look at his domain.'

'The Inspector Calls.' Francis guffawed at his own pleasantry.

'You're the Commissaire de Police – Arlette – I'm sorry, I mean your wife – told me, I remember.' She seemed very shy and embarrassed.

'Is that alarming?' A tremendous beauty, sure enough, but the rather whining voice and this startled fawn act lessened her attractions. Not so much shy, perhaps, as ill at ease and defensive. She was looking for an excuse now to get away from him.

'I'm sorry I can't stop – I've quite a long drive – it was just that seeing the car I wondered why I hadn't seen . . . ' She let it trail off and fidgeted.

'Must get out of that slovenly habit of lettin' him hit the fence,' Francis was saying. 'I've told you often enough; you're bein' over-impetuous and lettin' him take off too soon. Not pickin' him up properly, and he feels the indecision in you. You must know the exact moment at which you want him to jump, and he'll know it too.'

'He's always in such a hurry – I try to slow him down more.'

Van der Valk gave what was supposed to be a winning smile.

'My wife speaks often of you with great enthusiasm – I've been looking forward to meeting you.' There are plenty of easy answers to this kind of silly remark, ranging from the equally conventional to the mildly flirtatious, but she wasn't playing. So defensively as to be hostile she said, 'I'm sorry not to see her – you must please give her my love – my regards,' and turning hurriedly towards Francis, 'I'm sorry, I really do have to buzz; I'm supposed to be going out tonight.' She literally ran: Van der Valk grinned.

'She's inclined to be a bit like that,' said Francis tolerantly. 'Stand-off-don't-touch-me – still, I hadn't thought she'd be like that with you, seeing your wife is the one she's big friends with. Got an inferiority complex or whatever they call it. Nice little girl really, apart from that nonsense of talkin' French all the time – people say she's affected because of that. I like her; looks like ninepence but got courage. Not afraid of any jump, even far too big for her; sticks on like a monkey, and when she does fall she falls light –

not like some of our sacks of spuds here. You're lookin' a bit peaked, old chap – leg bother you much?'

'A bit of fatigue – normal.'

'Come upstairs; have a drink to pep you up.'

'I'd like that.'

Indeed he was tired, and glad to get away from the gabble, install himself in one of the big armchairs upstairs, and have a lot of Queen Anne whisky – typically showy whisky for export to just this kind of place, he thought, sipping at it and immediately feeling better. Francis had seized on his wife's absence to have some too.

'Any conclusions? – I mean do you really believe in monkey-business?' conspiratorially.

He had known well enough that solicitude about his fatigue was really curiosity.

'Not a lot. Doesn't do to have conclusions. He didn't hit himself. Which leaves a pretty wide field – anyone might have strolled past and clonked him.'

'Clonked him what with?'

'There's any amount of odd junk lying around. That coke furnace – the boilerhouse door in the yard was standing open – about twelve kinds of poker standing about.'

'Damn careless stable-boys.' Francis did his Weygand act, producing a monocle from the watch-pocket of his breeches, fixing it in his face and staring at nothing before letting it fall back in his palm. 'Doesn't sound like much, though, does it? A vague theory still, I mean to say. No real evidence – "pièces de conviction", what. Must say I'm obliged to you for keeping so quiet. Thought there'd be a lot of chaps tramplin' about – pressmen too, most likely. Seen none of them – don't want to either.'

'Might be some for the funeral.'

'Funeral, mm. Everyone'll go. Lookin' sad and pious. You too, no doubt.' The first sign of spitefulness he had seen. 'Lookin' for people to show signs of guilty confusion.'

'All I've got is an interrogatory commission, you know. Nobody says there have to be signs of guilty confusion. I don't even interrogate anyone – you notice? Just myself.'

'Too complicated for me – too much self-interrogation about, these days.'

Van der Valk decided to change this conversation, which showed every sign of being aimless.

'I saw what looked like your painter in the village – having lunch in the pub.'

Francis, still ruffled by his own self-interrogations, grunted, swallowed whisky jerkily, remembered his manners, and said, 'Dickie? Talented chap. Yes, he lives in that pub. Seems to suit him well enough – dog's life I'd call it.'

'He make a living?'

Rather a crafty grin appeared on the fierce military countenance.

'You'd be surprised. He makes these series of kind of huntin' prints. Etchin' – sells them too. And these other things, what the devil is it you call them?'

'Lithograph?'

'Knew there was grease in it somewhere,' obscurely. 'Rapid sort of chalk drawings – a good eye for a horse, don't know how he does it. I offered to get him up on a horse but he wouldn't, said he was scared, don't understand that because he's no more scared than I am. With that kind of love for the animal you're not scared out of ignorance, that makes no sense.' Francis evidently had admiration for this odd talent.

'No, Dickie looks as poor as a rat on an oiltanker but he makes a livin' all right. Done portraits of some of our industry wives here too – don't care much for them myself but he gets two and a half thousand for them!'

'But why does he live here?'

'He explained it all to me one day – he's carved out a sort of reputation with horses; a sort of signature, I suppose – what these art wogs recognize him by. Marion bought those two portraits from him – saw to it, though, he gave her a discount! Mark you, he's a pleasant chap; quiet, retiring, doesn't get on my nerves – and in a way it's an attraction – pleases the people to have an artist about sketchin'.'

Ah – that was it – he saw now the reason for approval.

'I see.' The door at the end opened and Marion drifted in, with a vase of flowers. She had a different set of tweeds today, in more of the brilliant colours that seemed to be her style: this time turquoise and sea green, and a wonderful kind of Tyrian purple. She smiled as she drifted over towards them.

'Why, good day to you, Mr Van der Valk – delighted to see you again.'

'He's been trottin' about all afternoon,' said Francis – impossible to tell whether the tone were sarcastic approval or only mockery. 'Got pretty tired, so I suggested he rest his leg a bit away from the wear and tear. Look after him will you, Marion? – I've got to go and see to a few things.' He stood up, stamped a bit around in his boots as though they were tight, went 'Ha' a few times vaguely, and finally said, 'Be seein' you,' to nobody in particular before stumping off noisily.

The woman paid no attention, but went on drifting round the room arranging her flowers, clipping stalks afresh, pinching off dead blooms, performing that feminine rite that Van der Valk defined as 'plumping up the cushions'. Her movements were gentle and silent; she seemed not to notice his presence. He watched her quietly, which she was perfectly conscious of without getting flummoxed. 'Have some more whisky.'

He had already had one large one too many, but was ready to punish his insides for the sake of professional relations. A bit like a business man in a tax-deductible restaurant, ordering oysters which he rather hates, but they impress the customers.

'That sounds very attractive,' in a lazy voice which he could see did not take her in. She did not hurry herself, swept her trimmings into a piece of florist's paper, screwed it up to throw in the paper-basket and said, 'I think I'd like one too,' comfortably.

There were plenty of openings, but he chose the classic one of showing interest in clothes, which never does any harm.

'I'm very struck by your suits. Where do you get those marvellous materials?'

'Oh, oh,' laughing, 'that's a great secret but you're a detective of course. One or two houses in London have them – they come from Ireland. They're too thick and loose to tailor and they aren't as easy to cut as they look.'

'They suit you remarkably,' stretching out his leg in a make-yourself-at-home way.

'Thank you – but the fact is they don't look good on – how d'you put it? – sturdy women. And I'm not sturdy,' with calm.

After complimenting them, embarrass them.

'Ah, that's why you tell me – they certainly wouldn't suit my wife,' Arlette would have been very cross to hear herself described as sturdy but she wasn't here . . .

'Your wife looks very nice indeed as she is,' with poise. She had prepared the drinks by now, in a way he did not care for, with lots of ice-cubes and Perrier water – that tiresome French habit – but he took a swig with enthusiasm along with her – he rather liked this woman. She was much too upper to say cheers, or prosit, or any other vulgar slogans.

'This death,' calmly, sitting down with her long thin legs sideways and taking a packet of Player's Number Three from her jacket pocket with a little gold lighter. 'It has made me think a good deal, and I wonder whether my thoughts come anywhere near the ideas you must surely be beginning to assemble. I rather gather you're convinced there was no accident. . . . I saw you outside a couple of times this afternoon. It struck me that you were looking for something that he might have been hit with.'

'So I was,' lazily. 'It passed the time.'

This, as he intended, did jolt her a little.

'Pass the time?'

'Hundreds of possible weapons. Hundreds of possible hands to hold them. Hundreds of possible reasons for clonking people with them.'

'I see. An embarrassment of riches?'

'Exactly. Tell me about your ideas.' Oh, she had got the point all right, that he wasn't sitting there listening to tale-bearing just on account of whisky . . .

'No, I haven't any ideas. Except that I agree that somebody sloshed him, if I may be allowed the word. In fact I thought so the moment I heard about it, on Saturday, before you or anybody else arrived on the scene.'

'You didn't voice any suspicions?'

'There wouldn't have been much point in making myself that unpopular,' blandly. He laughed.

'Francis would have been furious.'

'He's too polite to say so outright, but he thinks you're making a perfect fool of yourself.'

'He's not the first.'

She took little sips of her whisky, turning him round and studying him from different angles, not yet quite sure how he was reacting to her.

'Men will never face unpleasant facts,' she said at last. 'Francis even less than most. If Bernhard had suddenly been filled with bullets he would have been quite unperturbed – he would have seen it as a cowboy from a television serial whose horse had somehow strayed on to our premises.' This amused him.

'You're quite right to laugh but it's true for all that – he's a great television addict; often pretends headaches and stomach-aches and assorted fatigues to sneak away from the job and have a nice sit-down here all alone in front of the set. He hates reality, and he genuinely sees this occurrence, dreadful as it is, as not quite real, largely because it might turn out unpleasant. I'm telling you this only to help you make allowances if he's abrupt or even rude one of these days. He's capable of pretending not to see you when you walk right past him. The novelty tickled him at first, you see. A cowboy bites the dust – and lo, the sheriff arrives pronto.'

'But you see things slightly differently.'

'I have to, you see. Otherwise it would all be a game of toy soldiers around here, except of course when one of the horses has something wrong with it – then everybody has kittens. No, Mr Van der Valk, even when you say you're here just to pass the time, I don't treat your presence here as a joke.'

'You're perfectly right, it isn't. Very well, Mevrouw La Touche, tell me why you thought straight away that fat Bernhard had been sloshed.'

'He wasn't a stupid man. I didn't believe that he would do anything so silly.'

'What was your opinion of his character?'

'Most people, I believe, found him a delightful person – I'll be perfectly frank and tell you I didn't care for him at all. Nor have I really ever understood what Marguerite saw in him, but I assume that he showed her different sides of his personality.'

'You like her?'

'I'm fond of her, even – so is everybody else, I would say; she's a likeable person. And he was a phony. He was good at his job, it appeared.'

'It only appeared?' he prodded – she seemed reluctant to say more.

'I mean he never did any work – she did it all. I see what's in your mind – that Francis is much the same; besides he's fond of telling people I do everything, but in fact he's the mainspring of this place. I do things he's no good at, like getting out sets of figures for the accountant. Whereas fat Bernhard was absolutely dispensable.'

Francis' phrase. He might have got it from her. She might have got it from him. What mattered was that the tone was different. Francis La Touche did not care about fat Bernhard much one way or the other, but to Marion La Touche he was not an attractive memory, and she had not been over-displeased at his being sloshed.

'You mentioned different sides of his personality.'

'It worked all right with most people. Everybody sang his praises, how full of charm he was, how well he played the mine-host part. I can only say he struck me always as a sly nasty fellow, a bootlicker, always on the make, and a sharp eye for other people's little weaknesses and failures – not above turning that to account, either.'

'Was he a blackmailer, Mevrouw La Touche?'

It did not disconcert her; neither the direct question, nor the tone of suave disbelief, nor the candid blue gaze that had led other people to think Van der Valk an oafish fellow. She clinked the remains of her ice-blocks round the tall cut-crystal glass and drank the watery results leisurely.

'I wouldn't have been a bit surprised. Don't conclude that he's ever seen me as a likely prospect.'

'Would you say that you noticed a lot of what went on around you?'

'I distinguish between life and television, yes.'

'And did Bernhard have affairs with other women?'

She smiled a little loftily.

'It's not as easy as all that – we are a very respectable neighbourhood. I'd put it that he was a peeper up skirts. Big globular lecherous eyes. If that ever amounted to anything – I doubt it. Marguerite wouldn't have stood for being humiliated – and he hadn't the stuffing to risk a fight with her – he knew how indispensable she was, all right.'

'While we're on the subject,' drawled Van der Valk, 'is Francis inclined to play games with his steeplechase girls?'

'Opportunity for blackmail, you mean?' coolly. She laughed out loud, but not in an embarrassed way. 'He gets rampageous every now and then. I – how to describe it? – channel his urges?'

'Really? How d'you go about that?' She got serious, at his tone, at once.

'You aren't the kind of policeman that runs about looking for hairs and special kinds of dust much, are you?'

'I have respect for laboratory men – they solve the crosswords better than I do. I don't disdain them by any means – myself I'm not very gifted in that direction.'

'I think I understand,' thoughtfully, taking another cigarette and lighting it without waiting coquettishly for him to do so. 'You ask what seem such silly questions – like might Bernhard have blackmailed Francis? If he had, obviously I'd lie about it. You aren't interested in these answers – but you're trying to understand people – is that it? That's very good. I suppose, but however far you get there's always more to understand. People are very complex.'

'I don't believe that all the world's problems can be solved by psychoanalysis. And in every crime there's a neat answer waiting somewhere to be dug up – no, I don't believe that either. In every man there are several men – at least one unbalanced. You don't have to be an authority about Bernhard. But you're well placed to be an authority on Francis.'

'He's getting a bit middle-aged – he's fifty-seven – and I'm forty-seven. He's a bit crotchety sometimes, fusses about draughts and his bronchitis, goes about eating pills. And sometimes he can be quite bouncingly youthful.'

'But don't start being enigmatic now – a child could tell me that much.'

She looked at him, put the cigarette down, sighed, and came abruptly to a decision.

'This may startle you. I'm not in the habit of publicizing my private life. But you're going to poke – well, perhaps you'll give me credit for not having fenced with you.'

She got up and walked jerkily to and fro for a minute, and suddenly said 'Look' with an effort that plainly cost her pain. She stopped, turned half away from him, and in an awkward, hurried gesture pulled one side of her skirt up. Between the top of her stocking and some poised-and-gracious sea-green underclothes was a red line about a centimetre across, fading but still bright red on her thin pale thigh.

She was quite right, it did startle him; he tried not to let his voice show it.

'I see. Thank you.' She dropped the skirt and turned to face him, a little hot and ruffled.

'I act on the assumption that you're a man who has seen something of the world. And now come with me a moment, please.' She led him into a bedroom across the landing which he would have liked to observe a bit, but he had no time: she marched him straight across the room, went on her knees in a surprisingly graceful and easy movement, and opened a cupboard beside the bed. She came up with a handful of books and dumped them on the harlequin silk bed cover.

'Take a look.' While he was taking a look she walked back into the living-room, retrieved her cigarette, came back and stood looking out of the window. Faint horsy sounds drifted up from outside. Van der Valk sat comfortably on the bed, spread the literature around him, and was delighted. It was all quite conventional – *Tales of Boccaccio*, unexpurgated *Arabian Nights*, Restif de la Bretonne of course. Not pornography. Complicated fornications prefaced by tremendous beatings, with very good coloured illustrations: witty, rococo, full of verve, almost all funny. There was a Choderlos de Laclos that showed a more formal and eighteenth-century impudence, as well as more imagination than Vadim had managed . . .

The last was *Histoire d'O*. He had it himself – so did everybody. Not with illustrations. It wasn't pornographic, but he thought it a most unpleasant book. 'Since she enjoys it,' Arlette had said with disgust, 'why doesn't she go and do it instead of boring and revolting me writing about it?' It was more succinct and therefore better than his own reaction. The visual imagination of the early scenes at Roissy was the best part, and so the illustrator had found.

'And a woman is supposed to have written that!' said Marion.

He handed them back and she put them away.

'Harmless,' he said.

'Yes. I wanted to show you. My husband doesn't reach over and paw women, you'll notice. In fact you might now be less surprised to hear that he has a lot of old-fashioned respect for women. His upbringing – and his character. That act of saying crude things to customers – and hitting things with whips – it is an act, Mr Van der Valk, and that is all it is.'

'You've helped me a lot,' he said, meaning it. 'I won't wear out your hospitality any further.' He picked up his stick, adjusted an imaginary tweed cap, twisted an imaginary moustache, and said, 'Amusin' idea, what, bein' able to look under people's clothes.'

She smiled tolerantly, as though convinced of the essential childishness and small-boy nastiness – vicious you could not call it – of all men.

'Better still if one could lift up the faces and see what was underneath.'

'More of a problem, what?' banging the stick on the floor with hearty cavalry good humour. They both laughed and he left her, still with the smile that was very nearly contemptuous round the edges of her mouth.

The rest had done him good and so had the whisky. He wasn't advancing: he wasn't even marking time – he knew that well enough, or what did experience serve for? It was always the same. One went backwards inevitably in the first half, and one had to learn not to be discouraged by it. The more one got to know, the more one guessed at what one didn't know and wasn't likely to find out, neither. Oh mother, the grammar, thought Van der Valk, and cheered himself up with the gentleman who split infinitives, by god, so they would stay split . . .

He parked outside the café and walked in, causing not perhaps a stir, but fixed stares and heavy breathing. Why? he wondered. Anyone can walk into a café – is not the admirable English name for the place a public house? Why is it a closed shop, containing a closed society, hostile, rigid?

Four rustic youths were playing pool on the billiard table, two oul'wans were in a glassy gin-haze in the corner; a middle-aged man was treating his wife to blackcurrant and toying with a beer at the counter while he gossiped with the landlord. All looked at Van der Valk as though this wasn't the place for him. No painter to be seen.

'Mr Thing in? The painter: I don't know his name.' Francis had talked about Dickie – in Amsterdam he would have asked for Dickie – it was his own fault; he himself had created this barrier.

'Mr Six,' said the landlord in a chilly way, as though not knowing the name was what he had expected all along from people like that. He studied Van der Valk from head to foot with care. 'You're the commissaire of police, right?'

There seemed little point in either denying it or admitting it . . .

'I'm interested in paintings,' blandly.

'He's upstairs – in his room. I suppose you can go up – no, I'll show you the way.' Not out of respect. Not, presumably, because he might pinch the spoons if left to himself. But he was an intruder, an irritant, the pepper in the cream cheese.

'Very good of you.'

A passage led two ways from the landing. One way was the living quarters of the landlord: a child's playpen stood folded against the wall and on a kitchen chair was a bundle of clothes, just off the line. waiting to be ironed. Signs of life . . . The other half of the passage was bare, clean, cold. Five bedrooms and a bathroom – the doors stood ajar to stop them getting stuffy. The end room was the painter's, the nicest because the biggest, the one next to the bathroom, the one with two windows. The landlord tapped; a voice inside said 'Binnen' without enthusiasm.

'Somebody to see you, Mr Six.'

He had expected a litter if not a smell of turpentine – he didn't know why; the accumulation of casual debris one associated with artists. Nothing of the sort; certainly there was a sheet of cartridge paper pinned to a pearwood board, a few brushes in a jam-jar, a rag showing smears of watercolour, but the room was tidy, bare, almost prissy. The bed was neat, no clothes had been left to lie about, and indeed nothing said the room was occupied by a bird of more than one night's passage except a few books in a row on top of the commode and an extra table in the best of the light, with a bottle of indian ink standing on it.

The young man was sitting in the one cane armchair near the window, a needle in his hand, darning the worn elbow of a pullover, his other hand inside the sleeve, holding an old-fashioned wooden 'mushroom'. He seemed to be doing it pretty well. He didn't get up, and showed no excitement at his visitor.

'Since you're in there's no point in saying come in. Sit down by all means – if you don't mind the kitchen chair.' Van der Valk smiled politely, reached out with his stick, hooked the kitchen chair, dragged it along the floor, making a horrible noise, at which the young man stuck a finger ostentatiously in his ear, and sat on it. Neither said anything for quite a long time, but Van der Valk was more accustomed to this conversational gambit, which is like the game children play, making faces at each other and betting who will be the first to laugh.

'You're the commissaire of police – I know about you. Saw you around this afternoon. Not surprised to see you – I thought you'd be running after me sooner or later.'

'Why?'

'Why, the fellow asks. I'm always round the manège, you'll want to know whether I've seen anything, heard anything, that kind of crap. I've met police before. Did fat Fischer fall or was he pushed? The second reason is of course what the hell is an artist doing here, so under pretext of hush-hush panic about Fatty you come trotting here to satisfy your bloody disgusting curiosity.'

The voice was flat, monotone. There was a trace of a rough accent in the Dutch that sounded like Rotterdam – one could not be sure, because there was another accent added, something foreign that did not quite ring true and puzzled Van der Valk. Now eighteen months ago, he thought, I would have kicked the chair out from underneath this pavement-chalker and told him to show his papers quick before he got his ears boxed.

'Something funny?'

'Oh I was amused at the thought of how lucky you are and how little notion you have of it but that's quite unimportant,' pleasantly. 'Both your guesses are good.'

'All right, go ahead and ask your halfwit questions – I don't mind. As I say, I was expecting it.' He took up the darning again, putting the 'mushroom' carefully in place and continuing an elegant basketwork as neat as a housewife's.

Looked about twenty-five, but he might be older. Thin and pale – those first impressions were confirmed, but a handsome boy too; good features, classic nose, magnificent black eyebrows. The white shirt was open-necked, but the tie hung on the towel-rail by the wash-basin. The hands were thin and bony, with clean well-kept nails. Along with the intelligence and the aggressive tone went a careful, shabby respectability that was somehow disconcerting.

'You don't work here?'

'Partly – why?'

'I know nothing about the techniques you use, but isn't the

76

material big and awkward? Copper engraving, or litho – don't you need tools, materials, chemicals?'

'Can't have that here. Mr Maag – the landlord – wouldn't have that, so I keep it in a shed behind the stables which isn't used – Francis lets me keep all my material there; makes me pay him for it though, even if he's got no use for the space himself. Trust Marion to watch the pennies.'

'You don't like her?'

'Sure I like her. She's no different to anyone else – they all watch pennies: more they've got the better they watch them. You take a look at that private-yacht gang some time. I laugh my head off at the poor miserable little bastards – turn a quarter over three times before giving it to the stableboy – count the change from a cup of coffee.'

'Is that wrong?'

'Who said anything about wrong? – do the same myself if I were in their shoes, no doubt. Having money changes people, makes them frightened.'

'You've lived in France, maybe?'

'Sure. I'm half French.' He sounded proud of it, too. 'I've lived there – three years. Go back tomorrow if I could. What makes you ask?'

'Something in your voice. I've lived there myself.'

'What the hell you doing here, then?'

'I like it here too. You don't agree?'

'Agree . . . ?' It seemed to be a silly word.

'Nothing to stop you living in France, I should imagine.'

'Too goddam dear – you take me for a lousy beatnik or something? I've had all that – going without food, sleeping on benches, all that. I've had enough of it – you wouldn't understand.'

'No?'

A look of open contempt – no, not contempt: there was envy in it too. Derision was the word, perhaps.

'No.'

'Do tell me. I should have thought,' innocent, 'that it would go quite smoothly once you got accustomed to your hair being itchy.'

'You – you've never spent the night in a tramp's shelter – you've never been chased off a bench by police.'

'They do that, in Paris?'

'They don't stop to look if you're washed or not.'

'But you liked it there?'

'Know anything about painting?' with a false politeness.

'No.'

'You surprise me. You're a painter and you go to Paris. You do neo-expressionism, or neo-realism, or neo-whatever-you-like, it makes no odds, there's a hundred thousand of you. You might even be good, you'd still be up against the machine, that takes one in a hundred, among the good and the bad alike, sells their pictures, gives them space on the wall and in the press, and might even make them a living if they're patient enough and stubborn enough – pretty poor lookout for the other ninety-nine. Ninety-eight of them are lousy anyway, they've all got names like Szabo and Soapsudski, nobody can tell them apart, and the ninety-ninth, who happens to be good, gets drowned in the dungheap. So you try to make yourself different – the bad ones just copy whatever style happens to be in the wind. But if you're any good you have your own line and you can't force it. So you look for something else characteristic, like a subject – something you can be recognized by. Butterflies! – that's Cock. Rotted tree-stumps – that's Prick.'

Van der Valk listened with exemplary patience. If you can just get them to talk about themselves they are quite prepared to stop being monosyllabic.

'So you do horses.'

'I like horses. Very few people can do them. I'm one. I understand them.'

'It seems illogical that you should be scared to get up on them.'

'Who told you that?'

'Why, Francis.' The young man was thrown out of his stride.

'You don't paint a thing you're sitting on.'

'Why not? Géricault did.' Not that Van der Valk knew anything about Géricault, whom indeed he generally got confused with Delacroix. He had read Aragon's *Semaine Sainte* though. . . . He was surprised at the young man's seeming too confused to see this.

'He was in the army,' he said lamely, 'not a suburban manège. There's all the difference. I'm a good painter and I know it.'

'And even Francis can see that.'

'Francis wouldn't know Rubens from Kokoschka but he does know horses.' He laid aside the neatly finished darn, wound up his card of wool with care, and realized that he had been manoeuvred into sounding defensive.

'It's no good trying to pump me about art. You wouldn't understand in a thousand years, so don't waste your breath. Stick to your job, like asking me if Bernhard really fell off the horse.'

'Did he?'

'I'd say no, since you ask me, but I wouldn't know why nor how. I was right there working in the shed, and I had more to do than pop out to watch Fatty exercising. I was minding my business and I didn't even know a thing about it till after they called the doctor. I came out for a coffee then and asked what all the fuss was about.'

He had at last been allowed to deliver his carefully rehearsed speech. There was probably more of it but that was enough . . .

'Yes. You going to go back to Paris?'

'I've been here six months – if I stay another six, I'll have plenty of work for a dealer I know, and I'll have money what's more to live in a decent place and hang on while he's selling them – as long as it takes. No little bits of charity in advance. You never get anywhere if you give the impression you're hard up for it, waiting for it with your hand held out. You've got to say you don't give a bugger if they take it or not – it's too good for them anyway.'

'You can make quite a fair living selling stuff here, huh?'

'I stay alive.'

'I saw the portraits in Francis La Touche's living-room.'

'That! I've done some soppy stuff for a few of the old bags. I work carefully, and I use decent materials, and you don't know what that costs. Anybody can dribble paint out of a tube on to brown paper.'

'But you don't have much expenses.'

'You think the empty stomach downstairs gives me this room for free?'

'Very interesting,' heartily, getting up.

'You got any more to ask me? I don't want you coming messing about afterwards while I'm working – I don't like being interrupted.'

'I've got nothing to ask you – since you saw nothing and knew nothing, why should I? If I think of anything I want to ask you – any time, any place – I will. Write that on a little label and paste it on your sleeve, so you won't forget that.'

'Police! – all the bloody same: just give them an office and a medal.'

'Where do you come from, by the way?' half out of the door. The young man was staring ostentatiously out of the window, being deeply interested in the odd car passing.

'Rotterdam,' without turning round; 'if it's any of your business.'

He went on watching out of the window for some time after Van der Valk had gone. When he saw the little cream-coloured deux-chevaux, his eye followed it with sudden interest. There was no reason why he should not recognize it, thought Van der Valk straightening the mirror: he must have seen Arlette at the manège often enough.

People in Holland eat their supper early. The wives have it on the table for when their husbands get home from work, and here there is a class distinction to be noticed. Working men still take sandwiches to eat on the building site in the lunch break, and when they come home they expect to find a big pot of boiled potatoes and the classic stew with lots of gravy. But bourgeois Holland 'eats warm at midday'; at six o'clock it is a cold meal and all the wife has to do is make the tea.

Van der Valk's childhood had covered the depression years of the early thirties, and though his father had been a master crafts-man, a carpenter with a tiny shop of his own, and though there had always been a massive pot of stew at midday, his supper had been bread and cheese and cocoa. And nowadays – his wife came from the department of the Var – he got soup and not tea at supper-time! But he knew the routine – backwards; he had been in so many of these houses . . .

The table laid with sliced bread – two or three sorts. The margarine in a glass dish, and one or two kinds of sausage and cheese laid out in the neat thin slices that have been cut at the shop. Jam, and at least one other sweetstuff to put on the bread after the traditional one-with-sausage-and-one-with-cheese. Perhaps little mice – little sugary pellets like hundreds and thousands. Choco-late vermicelli, or powdered sugar with an anis flavour, called stamped mice. It is sprinkled with a teaspoon on buttered bread which is then cut in little squares and eaten with a knife and fork. Laughable enough to the ignorant foreigner, but it is Holland.

Van der Valk was not in the least surprised to find that this was just what Doctor Maartens got for supper.

'I'm too early.'

'Not a bit. Sorry it hasn't been cleared away – the telephone! It's the daily girl's day off – my wife begs you to excuse her.'

'You excuse *me*.'

'Shall we go back to my room?' He had lit a pipe and was puffing attractive clouds of smoke – English tobacco. Why is English pipe tobacco so nice and the cigarettes so nasty, wondered Van der Valk, and why in France is it the other way about?

It was six-thirty, and he deserved a cigar. There is no nonsense about Dutch cigars. They are well made, cheap, and exist in every possible size and quality. Ask for a Cuban cigar in a restaurant in England and one understands this in a painful way. Come to that, buy cheap cigars in France or Germany . . .

Doctor Maartens did not seem daunted by the length of his working day. He settled himself comfortably, puffed to keep his pipe going, and shook a matchbox to be sure he wouldn't run short of fire for when he forgot to puff.

'I've looked at my files, you know, on these various people you mentioned, but it's all very banal, very unexciting. I realize that what you're after is the kind of thing people tell doctors in between the blood group and the urine test, but there's things there I couldn't repeat, you know, even to you. Stuff told in confidence, not particularly relevant to any medical aspect.'

'None of that matters. I need to have another person's impressions of these people. Can be as blurred, as disconnected, as vague as you like. You live here. You see these people both on a professional and an unprofessional level. If I go to the local town hall, the local gendarmerie, I get all the information I want that can go into pigeonholes. I come to you for the stuff that doesn't go into any files. That's all.'

'I'll tell you anything I can.'

'Tell me why you think Marguerite married a chap like Bernhard.'

Maartens looked at him a moment as though he thought his leg was being pulled, then said, 'I see.' He meditated for a moment over his pipe.

'She comes from a poor family, you know.'

'Her father was a tramdriver – pigeonhole in town hall.'

'Bernhard had not got much money when she married him, but she certainly saw the possibilities in that business.'

'She likes money?'

'I'd say she liked the nice things you can buy with money. She has a rather naïve appreciation of luxury, perhaps. You see it in her house, her clothes. . . . She loves spending money, gets more pleasure out of that than many people. She enjoys life, lives it with gusto.'

'Very healthy.'

'Oh, sound as a bell. Takes lots of exercise, eats lots of fruit – well balanced. Thought herself too fat; I told her not to be absurd. She had a tendency to go in at one time for these ridiculous diets they find in tomfool women's magazines.'

'Know anything about the circumstances in which she married him?'

'I was only just qualified at the time – not an awful lot. The place was his father's – who was Austrian, or Bavarian – I never saw him. During the war – well, it was natural that they should be on comfortable terms with their own countrymen.' He was picking his words. These times are still not spoken of freely, without embarrassment, in Holland – one can never be quite sure how the other person thinks of them.

'I don't imply that they were involved in any crimes or anything.'

'If they were there'd be a record of it,' drily.

'They were a bit persecuted though, afterwards, I rather think.'

'There'd certainly be no record of that,' even more drily. He got a slight smile.

'I seem to recall that the place was not confiscated but was closed for a while. The old man died – couldn't face the various troubles. Bernhard inherited a messy state of affairs. The local talk – I certainly don't guarantee its accuracy – was that Marguerite persuaded the Groenveld woman, who had money of her own, to invest in it. I can tell you one thing – she told me in confidence but it'll be on file. . . . Her family were National Socialist sympathizers.'

'It is on file.'

'I don't hold it against her – she was a child at the time. What is she now – forty?'

'And Bernhard?'

'I can't tell you much about him, you know,' a bit hurriedly. 'He didn't haunt my doors – type of chap who thought he'd live for ever. Physiologically, he wasn't far wrong. He came the once for a checkup, after his wife got on to him. But he didn't tell me anything – closed sort of a chap.'

'Any marital troubles?'

'Never complained to me about them, that's all I can say,' cheerfully. 'Doesn't mean much – some do, some don't – some who don't have worries and inhibitions easily detected – others don't – simple as that. She asked for pills, which I gave her – usual pills.'

'She didn't want a child?'

'She said once to me that quite apart from business demands she didn't believe she'd make a good mother.'

'Odd remark.'

'Plenty of women don't make good mothers. If they realize it, so much the better.'

'What about the Groenveld woman?'

'She didn't ask for any pills,' Maartens' turn to be dry. 'Unmarried and contented that way. Well balanced – health very good on the whole. Bit of trouble with varicose veins – I told her to put a high stool behind the bar and take plenty of walks – surgery's not much good in my experience. Some slight glandular imbalance. Worried a bit about growth of hair – that kind of thing. I won't bother you with that,' firmly, 'it can't possibly be relevant.'

'A normal household with no tensions.'

'As far as my knowledge goes – yes.'

'Tell me something about Francis.'

'Ha,' laughing. Doctor Maartens sounded relieved that the subject had been changed. 'I know plenty about him – not that he isn't really a common type of patient. Has a new symptom about once a week; he calls me constantly. He comes from an aristocratic kind of family, you may know – but impoverished. Town hall files?'

'Certainly,' laughing.

'You've done your share of homework, I notice. Oh, I approve, you're doing your job, and in a very conscientious manner. If I didn't approve I wouldn't be talking to you, would I?'

'There might not have been any crime at all. But if there was it's a murder. I've got to find out.'

'Well, I only mentioned it because he has aristocratic symptoms,' smiling. 'Cardiac flutters, awful pains here and there – thinks he's gout – he hasn't. Thinks he's angina – it's a false one. Half of it comes from worrying himself about it. There's not all that much wrong with him. A bit arthritic – I treat him for that – a bit diabetic – ditto – he does need care. He's one of those people that really need a court physician around them to fiddle with them, reassure them.'

Van der Valk liked this. It showed he had been right and that Doctor Maartens' observations, however reticent – however guarded – were worth having.

'He loves it if I suggest new pills, a new régime, a recently discovered treatment. Needs constant changes – yellow pills after meals instead of red pills with meals: even if the principle is identical he feels better – till next time. He's a compulsive fusser. Bound up perhaps with that blustering manner and that bawling at people – he needs to reassure himself constantly, of his strength, his virility, his this and that. You wouldn't call it psychological disturbance in any way because he instinctively finds adjustments and compensations. Physically he shouldn't drink or smoke but psychologically they're both good for him and the one thing balances the other, see? I frighten him into going easy on both but I would never forbid either.'

No – he wasn't a fool either.

'He sometimes beats his wife.'

This went over well, and would have, Van der Valk hoped, the desired effect.

'You know that?' very surprised and surprised into showing it. 'How?'

'She told me.'

'Ah.' A pause. 'Interesting woman – most complex perhaps of this group we've been discussing.'

'Yes.'

'She feels that people dislike her, and suffers from that. Suffers from being too thin, about which she's selfconscious: she stuffs herself with cream and then feels guilty – lot of little nervous worries. She needs more calm – has compulsions to be on the go all the while. One of her children turned out wrong, which hurt her a lot – you know all this?'

'I know the children exist. There exist some confused notes on the boy, which I could make no sense of – an enquiry that was botched – there was some question of a criminal charge but it was never pressed. I've been wondering about them.'

'I don't know anything about that, and whatever I can tell you is common knowledge and no particular secret. There are two; both grown up, of course. The boy fought all the time with Francis, who is impatient and authoritarian as you know – Marion has learned long ago how to handle that but with the boy it came to open conflict; they ended up hitting each other and the boy was flung out ... I know nothing of any criminal charge, though I have heard he's in South America and has got into scrapes there ... that might be just gossip. Marion doesn't mention it. The girl made a goodish marriage – some horsebreeder in Ireland: everything went rosily there, which throws any misdeeds of the boy's into even higher relief, hm?'

He started to relight his pipe. Not bad, thought Van der Valk; not bad at all.

'This trouble with the boy – recent history?'

'A twelvemonth perhaps. The girl comes twice a year to stay; I've had her here for banal complaints a couple of times. Sharp, clever girl, rather unsympathetic. Boy was intelligent but not clever. Had a talent for rubbing people up the wrong way, but with immense charm when he wished – I secretly rather liked him.'

Van der Valk chewed the ballpoint pen with which he had been writing little notes. He had a very slick one these days, silver-mounted. The rubbishy plastic things he used to buy half a dozen at a time were not adequate to a Commissaire's standing, but this one, he noticed – which cost twelve gulden instead of thirty cents – was inefficient. But alas, one had not the courage to throw it away.

'Murders,' dreamily, 'often remain undiscovered, largely because they're never even suspected. A doctor signs a certificate without questioning it or thinking to. You didn't.'

'I would have accepted an accident – but I would want to know what caused it and how,' unhappily.

He was plainly being evasive. Van der Valk tried to balance the ballpoint on his finger – beastly thing, it wouldn't. He decided in the end not to press Maartens too hard – not, at any rate, for the moment. A magistrate might decide differently, but that was not for him to decide ...

'A question is raised.' The ballpoint fell on the floor. 'Damn. I take a rough look at the group of people seeming nearest to the dead man – you helping me. Any of them could have killed him: what's more there's motivation sticking out all over the shop. Very discouraging.'

Maartens was looking shocked.

'You make it sound like a story, where one is led to believe in all the characters' guilt, one after another. Fiction!' with contempt. 'Few people are capable of killing.'

'Anybody is – given a favourable climate. People kill others all the time, often in atrocious ways, without feeling in the least bothered. In wartime one generalizes the climate by astute use of propaganda that you'd think would deceive nobody – but it does. Other things can produce the climate temporarily – things appearing, often, pretty insignificant. You might have them in your file there. Recognizing them is another matter.'

Maartens looked unhappy.

'I'll leave you to a few less professional occupations.'

'Delighted to be of any use,' politely, accompanying him to the door.

Dickie had put on his freshly darned pullover, and a raincoat. It was an English raincoat he had got second-hand from Francis, who had taken a dislike to it for some unaccountable reason although it was almost new. Dickie was taller than Francis, but it had been cut to come low on the La Touche leg, and it covered his own knees adequately. He wasn't proud: besides, he liked it. A snob thing; it amused him to disguise himself as a snob.

He felt competent in it, and comfortable. . . . A trenchcoat model with a big high collar, a sort of umbrella that buttoned down over the shoulders, enormous pockets, great leather buttons like a half walnut-shell – that was a raincoat. Not like these modern rags that came to the middle of your thigh, and wouldn't keep out a damp sponge. He liked everything about it: the stiff canvassy texture, the brass eyelets for ventilation, the rubbery smell inside the fleece-cotton lining; the corseted feeling, belted well in; the sheltered, bullet-proof idea, like Humphrey Bogart, you got when you turned the collar up.

He got the seven o'clock bus into the town. He nearly always did – a relaxation. There was no more to do or to see in the town at night than there was in the village – Dutch provincial towns! – but for that very reason it was rich in cinemas, and he enjoyed the

86

cinema. Because of the students there was even an art/experiment place in a basement, where one saw the younger French and Italian directors' work – the ones of his generation, the ones he felt at home with, who talked his language. . . . In these cinemas, Dickie felt almost that he was engaging in a conversation, that he was taking part. And someone he could talk with was what he felt the lack of most here.

Waiting at the bus stop, amid the horseplay of half a dozen young yokels pretending to disregard the other little cluster of local girls, their huge piggy-catchers' calves bulging above absurdly high heels, Dickie in the raincoat felt like a judge at a jumping competition. All he needed was a bowler hat. Ah, and an English accent, and that he hadn't. Every time he talked he gave himself away. He spoke French when he could – people found that natural enough in an artist . . . half-French . . . who had lived in France. He sounded better than Janine! She was pally with that bloody policeman's wife, a woman he avoided. Stupid not to have guessed at once that it might be that French cow's husband: still, the moment he had seen that deux-chevaux the bell had rung all right.

How he had hated that policeman! People like that were always the same – fellow probably came out of a back street in Amsterdam no better than the dock quarter he had been born in himself. Because he was a stinking commissaire he had to go dressing up, arsing round the manège as though he had been born in a country house, sucking up to the riding crowd – like the wife, one of these French women that looked all right in a black leather jacket with their feet up on the bar of a Solex, since that was where they belonged, but just looked ludicrous in breeches on a horse.

Snobs were all the same. Francis was a hypocrite – he pretended to despise bourgeois women but he was married to one, liked it, and lost no opportunity of kissing their big toes. Dickie smiled and climbed on the bus secure in his raincoat and the knowledge that he would not do such things. Consenting to paint their stupid portraits for money was not the same.

He had a tremendous advantage over them, with their cars and their houses with big green lawns, their cocktail parties and their clothes from London. He had eyes and they didn't. He could see through the lot as though they were glass – how long had it taken him to rumble that Bernhard? Not that he was going to let on: let that fool of a policeman work at it. He enjoyed painting their portraits really because he felt such metres faster than they would ever be. He knew how to paint them – just as they liked to see themselves. gay, daring, adventurous. Pick their pockets and set them down on a hillside in Turkey and they would just lie down and sob!

He didn't need any gold money-clip; he'd come up himself and was proud as hell of it. He hadn't even been to an art school, but he'd known how to get himself apprenticed to a printer at the very start. He'd learned litho and copper plate technique, and at night he'd learned some draughtsmanship, and he'd gone to museums and looked and looked and looked. He had remarkable eyes. And now he was really beginning to get somewhere and he resented it, having some cheesy police inspector have the power to question him, drag out into the light that he'd been born in a slum in Rotterdam and had never learned to talk English properly. He knew dirty words in English!

He used them all on the innocent Van der Valk and felt better. It was raining, and the bus windows got those blurry reflections from the light that gave him pleasure – there were ways of looking at them: you had to learn how to look at light.

The snobs did not care about Bernhard. They did not understand. Neither would that fool of an inspector. They pretended to be shocked and be sure they would all turn out for the funeral with grave expressions of assumed regret. Not him! Or perhaps yes, just to watch them all wriggle.

Would Marguerite wriggle? He had been so wrong about that. There were a lot of things he still had to learn. Plenty of things were eating him, not least his love life, but he understood discipline. It could wait . . . Dickie knew how to be patient.

It wasn't late when Van der Valk got home: half past eight, just right. He was very tired, but those messy days . . . His supper stood ready on a tray, the dirty dishes were washed, the house was quiet and felt contented. His wife was waiting for him, reading Proust and eating peanuts – what a combination! One of the boys was out with a girl, gone to the cinema they had said. . . . The other was doing homework upstairs, doubtless with a transistor radio on, maths combined with jazz by people with names like Leadbelly and Coffinlips. He put his stick next to Arlette's umbrella and yawned.

'Leg hurting?'

'Rather.'

'Have a shower. By the time you're down I'll have the soup hot.'

'Yes.' He was not too discontented with this scarred, half crippled body. It had been like a car accident; changed your ideas for you so radically you almost ended up grateful for it. He looked at the body without enthusiasm, but it was flat – he had done so many exercises to re-educate it. . . . The tremendous suntan had faded, he noticed sadly. But now he was the Commissaire he could arrange his own holidays. Suntan would come again.

He had had time to think too, flat on his back for weeks on end. Yes.

He came down in his silk dressing-gown. That was really something. Van der Valk in a – lovely it was being, no, not of course rich, but damn it, less poor. At his age one enjoyed one's little comforts, what. He hoped it wasn't softening his brain, but perhaps he had a chance to test that. Meanwhile the soup was hot and the salad mixed.

'Well,' said Arlette, wallowing comfortably in cushions: at last she had a room big enough for the old-fashioned big sofa she had clung to since finding it cheap in a junkshop, the year they were married – 'tell about your day.'

'Oh, potter potter, peering and sniffing, nice chat with all concerned – Marguerite, that Groenveld woman – I'm rather curious about them. Marion – I liked her, I'm bound to say, but it might be because I got a large whisky from her just as I was feeling daunted. I even had a word with your little pal Janine – she was asking after you, couldn't understand why the car was there but you weren't.'

'She's pretty, isn't she? Rather pathetic.'

'I don't know her that well. And that painter boyo; a screwball, that one.'

'I don't know him at all. I've seen him hovering about; he's always around. But he avoids me – anybody would think my breath smelt or something. He talks to Janine. He talks French, I know.

'French like these tomatoes. He comes from Rotterdam and has an accent thicker than the harbour water. Speaks a bit phony-pidgin, like Maurice Chevalier.'

'I don't see that it's any worse than all those women,' said Arlette, 'all pretending they were at school at Roedean.'

He got out of bed next morning in a bad humour, a symptom she recognized as coming from anger with himself, translated into discontent with everything and generally expressed first as tetchiness about food.

'This egg is stale.'

'Not as fresh as it might be, I agree.'

'Governments! Everything must be weighed, measured, peered at, x-rayed, vaccinated, rubber stamped and entered on a form in triplicate. By the time it has looked to see that all the eggs are fresh it is obvious to the meanest intelligence – but not, of course, to them – that the egg is no longer fresh.' Poor Arlette, who had given him an egg as a treat, after a hard day yesterday. . .

'Now I get a thing that looks like an abstract painting, and is about as eatable.'

'Oh give it to me then and I'll eat it.' Why did he have to go on and on ? Sighing, she knew that he would go on and on. If it hadn't been the egg it would have been coffee . . .

'Surely I've asked often enough for eggs to be bought on the black market.' It was not as scandalous as it sounded in the mouth of a respectable government servant, for it was one of her expressions. Dairy produce in Holland is all subject to a tangle of regulation that reduces it to the same mean and villainous mediocrity, but it is possible, if one knows an intelligent farmer, to get fresh eggs and even milk with cream on – if he is unusually courageous: leaving cream on the milk is rank poujadism, sabotage, treasonable.

'There's only one thing worse,' knocking about crossly looking for a notebook that was already in his pocket, 'and that's cheese wrapped in plastic.' Damn it, now he was telling her! Long-suffering women . . .

In the office the bad mood continued. A plodding report with a spelling mistake in it was pushed pettishly to the other side of the desk and everybody in his jurisdiction decided quickly that he had the plague and must be put in quarantine. The telephone girl was instructed to be tactful with her switchboard, and a shopkeeper who came with a tale about a smooth gentleman with no money and a phony Diners Club card was told abruptly that it served him right.

Van der Valk got up crossly to turn the central heating off. Damned April – yesterday it had been freezing and today it was warm, but not with a nice sunny warmth: a moist, grey fuggy warmth that did nobody any good. He opened the window, went back to get his chair knocking his stick to the floor on the way, left it lying and sat by the window where he could put his elbows on the nasty metal sill and gaze at a soggy cornflakes carton floating in the canal – pigs!

He didn't have to make a written report to the Officer of Justice, but he had to put order in his mind. It was no good going to the Palais and making an impassioned speech about cheese wrapped in plastic. He knew by now exactly what was written in his note-book; that no longer helped. Sighing self-pityingly he went and got another fresh sheet of paper – four or five had gone into the basket already.

'Bernhard was expendable. Everybody says what a nice fellow he was and nobody means it.

'Strong characters dominate their husbands. The effect upon Francis is there to be seen, but the effect on Bernhard isn't.

'Marion goes to pains to tell me how Francis copes with her, even the ways that are humiliating to herself. Is she telling me that Bernhard too had ways of asserting himself against that peculiar alliance – is it lesbian? – of the women in his house?

'The atmosphere of snobbery, the determined social climbing that everybody goes in for – that all creates tension. Marion is from upper-class milieu. Marguerite, as the good doctor was at pains to tell me, isn't.

'Should I recommend the Officer of Justice to send for Maartens and overrule this professional-secret lark? Since the fellow plainly knows something but what it is he's not going to say. He drew our attention to a happening he knew quite well was a criminal act. That, in his eyes, is quite enough to fulfil his responsibilities.

'What do all these people see in a riding-school? Marguerite, afflicted with a vulgar husband and a rather middle-class enterprise like a restaurant, sees it as an occupation to put her standing beyond doubt. It is also good publicity for the business – a kernel of regular customers is held this way.

'The girl Janine does it because she wants to be somebody after being nobody, presumably. It would be interesting to talk to her husband.

'Arlette does it for the sheer enjoyment of being able to indulge in an expensive pleasure. She would never admit it but she has a snobbish streak as well. So nice to be no longer poor. Secretly, perhaps, she has that in common with Janine.

'And Bernhard – what did he see? Seems a sudden transition from drinking and gossiping with the butchers and market-gardeners, the circle with which by all accounts he was always content. Why did he want all of a sudden to get on closer terms with the horsy crowd? There is a slight smell of blackmail about that move.'

Suddenly he thought he saw the light; it happened with a jerk, as though a pin had been stuck in his bottom. The good silver-mounted ballpoint escaped from his fingers, fell out of the window, and landed with a crash on the worn brick pavement twelve metres below. He looked out of the window, horrified.

He realized then that he was delighted to be rid of it. He wasn't going down for it himself. And he certainly wasn't going to pick the phone up and say, 'I'm afraid I've dropped my pen out of the window . . . !' He was rid of it and it was a weight off his heart.

Hadn't he been just the same as Mrs Sawdust or whatever her name was, the one Arlette disliked, with the three diamond rings? He didn't ride horses – but he dressed up as though he did. He had adopted silly clothes and a silly voice, because he felt ashamed of not being able to walk properly any more, because he missed running downstairs. . . . He was a pretentious phony, and that made it impossible to understand these people.

He banged out to the lavatory, where he gazed at himself in a cheap and nasty wash-basin mirror, lit by an odious daylight-neon tube.

He had been born in the Ferdinand Bol Straat. His father had been a cabinet-maker. No, he had been a carpenter. He hadn't been an artist; he had made good unmechanical reproductions of period furniture, but a good half of his business had been fixing the legs of rickety chairs for the neighbours, and he hadn't been above it, either.

He had grown up, himself, in the depression. Natural enough to insist now on having no margarine in the house – not that he ran much risk of that with Arlette. He had been like that always, even when he was a struggling, harassed little inspector of police. It was his character. But it wasn't his character to pretend he had been born in a country house, like Marion, or Francis.

Hadn't he turned into exactly the kind of policeman he had watched with contempt his whole life, the kind that keeps his fingers clean in a nice office, that prefers to talk about breeding dogs to doing work on Diners Club cards?

Credit cards were the curse of Europe these days, offices had had to buy electronic machines to come up in time with the right answer on current credit rating for Freddy Weiss from Milwaukee. Van der Valk washed his face, undid his tie, and walked out into the office, where the duty inspector sat gloomily typing.

'You've got the description of this fellow. He'll have moved on – they don't try the trick twice in a town this size. I'm not having any leg work. Their head office is in Paris – details of card on telex to them, description, number of card and photostat of signature to Central Recherche; they'll handle Jewellers' Protection Company. Note for co-ordination and file copy to archive. I want somebody to go out and buy me a packet of Gitanes with no filter.' What was it Arlette said – 'The day you become bourgeois is the day you switch from Gauloises to Gitanes.' Everybody was looking at him in a bemused way.

'The tobacco-shop on the corner doesn't have them; try the one in the market-place. I've no money, but just show your credit card. Willy, you come in here with me, I want you to get the man in the car by this evening – the one who offers people lifts. Type a minute to Mr Mije asking for four women agents whom we'll disguise as hitch-hikers – you know, rucksack, tennis shoes and woolly socks. I might have work for you tomorrow, so get a move on.' The telephone rang. 'It's about the working permits for those Swedes – the Consulate is on the line – oh, it's you, sir: I'm sorry to have bothered you.' 'I'll talk to them – put it through to my office.' As he went back in he heard the brigadier on 'reception' say to Willy, 'Must have had himself psychoanalysed.'

He arrived home in a horrid jolly mood that Arlette recognized as remorse for being nasty this morning about eggs.

'Haven't we still some of that Spanish Pernod left?'

'Afraid not – just ordinary boring French.' It was an improvement at least on the gloomy-gus act, and she did not make a fuss about his drinking, as well as smoking, at midday.

'Make two tomatoes, there's a good girl.' Feeling fussed, she made two Pernods with a drop of grenadine in, a drink thought highly of in the Department of the Var which normally he condemned as revolting.

'What's come over you to be obstreperous?'

'I want to be nostalgic for sunshine. I want to be smitten with an April blindness. I thought I'd give you pleasure. And I think I know why I've been making such a balls of this riding-school nonsense. That's a tiny bit too pink – my god, what a revolting colour it is.'

'You don't notice though when the sun is shining.'

'I don't care – it makes a change from Vittel water. Were you thinking of going riding this afternoon?'

'I hadn't thought. There's nothing stopping me, I suppose.'

'Ring up Janine – I'm thinking of coming with you and I'd like to meet her.'

'Didn't you say you'd met her?'

'I did – alarmed her rather. This time she's going to meet a different person and I'll be interested in her reactions.'

'I'll give her a ring.'

'Ask if her husband's at home this afternoon but don't say why. I want to see him.'

'You want to take the little duck then, on to the coast?'

'No, I'll get her to give me a lift. I intend to seduce her.'

'You're going to regret drinking that stuff,' with disapproval.

'What's for dinner?'

'Risotto.'

'Goody. In that case no.'

'What no?'

'No I'm not going to regret drinking it,' blandly.

'Where's your stick?'

'I left it in the office. I'm going to try going without it for a few days. Doesn't do to have a stick. Like having a sword between you and your wife in bed, like that imbecile Lohengrin.' He is certainly slightly drunk, thought Arlette, secretly pleased. He had seemed to her to have become so very ponderous sometimes since being promoted that she had thought rather sadly that the wound had abolished all frivolity as well as activity. Seducing

94

Janine now – some hope – better not ask what that is in aid of.

The rice had left-over ham and chicken in it, enlivened with smoked eel.

'Why no prawns?' with his mouth full.

'Prawns as well as eel is too expensive. Anyway they're deep-freeze – all colour and no flavour.'

'Remember that one last year on the coast – the one you put the langouste in.'

'I remember the langouste vividly – the beast cost thirty francs the kilo.' She poured Vittel water into a glass and pushed it across to him. Women! he thought, drinking it obediently. The incredible strength of women. She had made no remarks about his clothes, which were things he hadn't had on for two years: a suède jacket with a knitted collar, an orange shirt. . . . He was both irritated and pleased at her silence. She had understood. Women . . .

He drove the deux-chevaux, which was hers, but she disliked driving when with him: it made her nervous, she said. Women . . .

He was surprised at how expert Arlette was with a horse. He had thought vaguely that she would be a chronic faller-off and felt obscurely humiliated by her controlling the monstrous brute: now he would have approached it with great caution and protective clothing – perhaps an asbestos suit, with a little window to look through. Nasty dangerous radio-active beasts, horses.

She went out into the fields, he following at a respectful distance, and started jumping over obstacles, which made her rather sweaty and dishevelled, with hair falling all over the place. He glanced about apprehensively to see whether any mocking eyes were taking in these antics, since she was plainly showing off.

'It looks extremely high.'

'Are you sure you're not showing off?'

'My god, woman, I don't want you with a broken collarbone.'

This series of squeaking noises made her furious, not unnaturally.

'Keep quiet, you bloody old nannygoat, there's no more risk than diving off a one-metre springboard.' Mortified, he looked round again but there was no audience. Most of the riding-school adepts were staid souls, less given to tittuping about. His own presence was unremarkable. Anyone in the house, to be sure, might be studying his demeanour at leisure with a pair of binoculars.

Arlette did eleven jumps without falling off.

'There's Janine,' she said suddenly. A horse was being galloped the other side of the field by a girl with blonde hair, in breeches and a sweater like Arlette's but both black, which made a dramatic impression. He had noticed this the day before, but this time he was amused by it. Arlette, in a dark yellow sweater and ordinary fawn breeches, made a conventional figure by contrast. She was quietening the horse to stillness by talking to it in a private jargon: she was quite evidently seeking to impress him. She stood up in the stirrups, waved, and went 'Yoohoo'; Zorro came cantering towards them.

'Does she always wear black?'

'Always – rather sweet, don't you think?'

Janine pulled the horse in, but the animal caracoled about in a twitchy way, making Van der Valk keep prudently behind his wife. He could see that the horse was a splendid animal, a bright chestnut this one, now shiny with sweat. Mm, he felt quite ready to believe in Bernhard Fischer having been massacred without any human being called on to lend a hand. That was just the point – he was a city boy, who had seen the horses used to pull brewers' wagons, and those used by the mounted police. He looked at these animals with much the kind of eye people in the eighteen-nineties had had for motor-cars. Whereas Fischer had been a country lad ... Maartens was quite right; you did not get injured by a horse unless you were afraid of it.

Both women got off, and shook hands in a sloppy French way. The two abominable beasts twitched their ears, sidled nervously towards each other, pretending to bite, and stamped their huge iron feet in a most menacing fashion ...

'Quiet,' said Arlette, giving hers a resounding smack upon its great moist flank. The horse obeyed instantly; he had to laugh at himself a little ...

'You haven't met my husband, Nine. He came out with me to-day to admire.'

'Salut,' she said in a rough way, as though extremely shy. Then she looked at him sharply, as though not quite believing what she saw. 'Did I meet you yesterday? Or am I wrong?' He was enchanted; she was quite as surprised as he hoped, and being so obvious about it.

'We didn't really see each other.'

'You had a stick.'

'That is when I march about on parade,' imitating a colonel inspecting a guard of honour. She laughed, plainly relieved – he was human after all.

'I don't think I'd have recognized you.'

'We only met for a second, and I was being polite and formal with Francis.' She approved of this too, he was glad to see.

'I hate it rather when people are polite and formal – they're generally being toffee-nosed. Arlette never is and that's what I like about her. Are you, duck?' Her French was really music-hall, sounding like a butcher's wife in Marcinelle. He had a quick look to see how his wife reacted to being called duck, and found her quite unperturbed.

'Warm, isn't it, for all it's cloudy? Napoleon got into a sweat.'

'We'll walk them back. You can't just let them stand about like a car,' added Arlette to her humble escort. 'They get chilled and you have to keep moving.'

'Oh.'

Janine was accustomed to being familiar and easy with his wife, but was made uneasy by his presence. She kept wanting to talk and deciding against it, glancing at him, unsure how he might take the sort of conversation the women had being all girls together. She was not yet reassured: he might turn back into the orderly officer and say 'Any complaints?' from one minute to the next. He decided to be vulgar since that looked the way to put her at her ease and she had not hesitated to call him toffee-nose to his face ...

'First time I've seen this jumping. I'm most interested but it looks a damaging business. Don't you get kind of bruised around the crutch?' He was rewarded with a small happy scream.

'My crutch, as you so charmingly call it,' began Arlette balefully, 'is well protected, thank you for your concern. Inside my breeches I have padding and woolly knickers, so you may feel at ease; it risks no damage.' She had not yet caught on. 'Ask Janine how she is padded – she'll be delighted to explain in detail.'

'Wretch!' Explosion of giggles. 'I've nylon pants but I'm padded too – I'm too bony!'

'Black ones?' – the jovial customer, making familiar jokes with the butcher's wife across the dog's dinner.

'Always black ones,' playing up. Arlette knew him too well to be taken in for long, and shot him a sharp look which Janine caught and promptly misinterpreted. 'We must abandon this fascinating subject – I want to stay friends with your wife.' The coquetry was stupid but nice – she was perhaps too innocent to be anything but nice. Had not Arlette remarked how vulnerable the girl was?

'I'd be interested in meeting your husband.'

'Well, that's easy enough.'

'How about this afternoon?' She was taken aback.

'Oh yes. I believe he's busy with something – I mean, that doesn't mean anything,' clumsily. 'Did you want to see him?'

'Big bike fan.' She had looked disquieted a moment. 'Big Poupou fan but I like them all.' Her face cleared and she laughed. 'Allez France.' This slogan was unexpected in a Dutch police inspector – even Arlette's husband. 'Oh yes, I learned that last year at Courchevel – we were there for the winter championships.'

Arlette was keeping silent, rather embarrassed, hoping he wasn't overdoing it.

'Oh, you ski?'

'Not me – I was convalescent after this,' patting his hip negligently. 'Arlette's the sporting one. And the children, of course. Have you children, Madame?'

'No,' overhastily.

'I might go out to the coast then. I'll leave the two of you to your games. Shall I take the car then, darling?'

'You'll have to, won't you,' in a chilly tone. She thought he was being a bit mean.

'You've only got Lette's car? But how will she get back? I can drive you if you really want to meet Rob. We can give you tea.'

'That's very kind of you but I'll have to get back too, you know.'

'But I can give you a lift – that's no trouble.' It sounded over-eager even to her. 'Rob will drive you back in the Ferrari.'

'But weren't you going to have coffee or something? – what d'you usually do – go to the White Horse?'

'No – not much,' abruptly. 'I've been out since two anyhow.'

She is a phenomenon, he thought. Nothing to do with being keen on me all of a sudden! But she's mighty curious to hear anything I have to say to Rob. And she has a lot of confidence in Arlette, who is cute enough to see through all this, and knows I'm not just belting off for the afternoon because of the black undies!

Good for her! She was smiling sunnily as though nothing could have pleased her more.

'Yes, you drive him, Janine. Don't let him drink too much; it isn't good for him.' They had reached the stables, passing the spot where Fat Fischer had an accident without thought or comment. 'I'll see to Napoleon – you two go on. Be home for supper, darling.'

'Yes of course.'

The BMW coupé was an impressive affair, less vulgar and chemical inside than a Mercedes, a roomy thing but light and nervous enough to suit a woman. It was fitted in a grandiose way with thermometers and tachometers and chronometers – even an altitude meter as well as conventional things like radios and rev-counters. She looked very good in it and contrary to expectation she drove well, with brio but tact, knowing how to humour nincompoops in Volkswagens that got aggressive when passed.

'You drive very well.'

'Rob says that too. He taught me, so he is very critical and parti-cular, but I do drive well, I know. I can even drive the Ferrari! But it's not much fun here – no real open road. Holland's too small.'

'You don't like it here?'

'I hate it,' with so much heat as to surprise him. Not venom really, because she is too nice to be capable of real venom – but heat . . .

'You'd be more at home in France, wouldn't you – or even Belgium?'

She was pleased at his being perceptive.

'Oh yes! The trouble is Rob isn't. He wanted to try things here. I kept saying – but he over-ruled me – oh well, he's the boss. I suppose it's too late to get things changed now.'

'He's changed his mind since?'

'I don't know – maybe,' braking for a crossroad and accelerating away with no jerk. She used the low gears well. Arlette would have braked nearly to a stop and gone on still in third, but of course with a deux-chevaux . . .

'I'm glad Arlette's made friends with you – being lonely some-times as she is. She doesn't make friends easily.' For a moment he thought he had been too crude, but she was concentrating on a lorry.

'Nor do I.'

'Being a foreigner of course, it's understandable.'

'I'm not exactly a foreigner – but anyone is among the rich – unless you've got their kind of money.'

'I would have thought your husband, uh, hadn't done badly.'

'You don't understand,' seriously, so that he wanted to grin, 'it's not what you make, it's the way that you make it. Bikes are not good enough for the nose-turner-uppers. As though they were any better than thieves,' changing down into third with a roar from the motor. They were in the sand-dunes now, a well-built road but annoyingly kinky and bendy, curving between the rimrocks and scarps of grass-tussocked sand, with spinneys of dark pine crouched between. Brambles grew at the sides of the road, beyond the bicycle track. It had got much hotter, and the sun could be seen through a pearly curtain of cloud that gave the atmosphere an August stuffiness. It is always warm in the dunes, for the sand holds the sun's warmth, and one is sheltered from the wind. The top of the car was down – it was pleasant driving with this extremely pretty girl, a summery glow on her peach-like skin.

'Are they so disgraceful, then?' laughing.

'You'd be surprised.' Perhaps she had forgotten he was a policeman – her tone was so serious. He wondered if he could ask her to be a bit more specific!

'I thought you were one of them yesterday – I'm sorry; I was a bit rude. But I hate their guts, you see.'

'I was born in the Ferdinand Bol Straat in Amsterdam.'

'I was born in a stinking village between the cow and the cabbage,' not laughing, 'and compared to that the Ferdinand Bol is the Avenue d'Iéna.'

'You got out of it, though.'

'Yes, by luck. And how did you? Brains, no doubt. With brains one can always get out. I haven't any. Even Rob knows how stupid I am, though he pretends not to notice. Lette – your wife – she notices but she – she laughs at me – but not nastily. She's nice.'

One of the disadvantages of this coast is that you cannot see the ocean before you reach it. Instead of being perched above sea level the coast is tucked below it. You have to climb a little hill before you see anything at all, though of course you can smell the sea before you come to it.

He had been 'bland' of course. He knew all about the 'stinking village' but no need to tell her that the underling he had sent to the town hall had come up with the background of the whole manège. A fine thing, the town hall; not only are births-deaths-and-marriages on file in this most Dutch of institutions, but wonderful heaps of information useless to anybody but a nosy policeman. (Just so does one see the rag-and-bone man, wheeling his cart piled with rusty bedsprings, an old pram wheel, squashed cardboard cartons. That a man should toil, pushing that cart . . . That a man can live, and even be happy . . . Yet the sordid stink of burning rubber, the Stygian flames and pits announce the alchemist, and Dickens spoke of the 'Golden' Dustman.) Applications for a building licence, claim for unemployment benefit, religious and political opinions, changes of address over any-period-longer-than-three-weeks – the policeman can find gold in this, and a ridiculous annotation in an absurd file might fill him with the joy of the clochard finding a worn-out aluminium saucepan.

Amusing, her compulsive blurting way.

The car whisked through the sanded bricky streets of a Dutch sea-side town, turned on to the sea-boulevard, off it again, on to a large open space paved with apoplexy-purple breezeblocks, and slid into the white-painted slot next to the hotel entrance, where a France-blue marquee with gold lettering sheltered the doorway from wind and rubber-edged automatic doors played sentry against sand. Inside the dunes it had been windless: here the wind, an invisible sower, launched graceful skittish arabesques of silvery dust upon the barren parking lot. The north-westerly blows upon this coast like the mistral; alas, it brings not the fine weather but more rain. The ruffled seawater showed a few whitecaps on a churned steel-grey mud, like corpses stuck in barbed wire, here and there upon a Flanders battlefield. It was much too early for holidaying, but it is never too early for robust Germans happy to exchange the chemical vapours of Gelsenkirchen for the bracing breezes of the North Sea, and there were quite a few cars on the parking-place with Westphalian plates.

Janine, rather proudly, was showing him through a hall elegant with rubber parquet and fibreglass furniture, with a girl at the switchboard behind a muted teak-veneer reception desk.

'Find my husband will you? – tell him I'm back and I've brought someone – and ask one of the boys to send up tea for three.' Her Dutch was as Flemish-sounding as her French, as though she had found haven from the cow and the cabbage in suburban Liège.

'All right,' said the switchboard girl indifferently, not quite insolently, with an accent designed to show that she came from The Hague. Janine walked him over towards the lift: standing close beside him pressing buttons she muttered 'saucy bitch' meant for him to hear.

The flat at the top of the hotel was very comfortable if you liked being horizontal, with a lot of modern art.

'Those your choice?'

'No – Rob's; he likes art. I don't know anything about it; I just read women's magazines.' Another grievance – she was a mass of over-sensitive surfaces. He turned tactfully to the trophies: mm, a Dauphiné Libéré and a Paris–Roubaix: he had not known or had forgotten that the boy had been that good. The icy soaking rain and the greasy bone-jarring cobblestones of the 'Hell of the North' and the dusty horrors of barren limestone under a pitiless June sun – not what the French called a 'salon runner', no.

She had gone to change, and he was surprised meditating by Rob coming in unheard and saying over his shoulder, 'They say champagne tastes good out of silver but give me Perrier.' Van der Valk held a hand out grinning.

'A collection! How many litres of champagne would one get in these?'

'Never a Tour though, a Giro, a Vuelta – never even a Paris–Nice. Second once . . . you French?'

'No – I didn't think – I was talking French with your wife.'

'Ah, you're a friend of Janine's?'

'My wife is – I was with her at the manège and mentioned I was a bike fan – your wife kindly invited me to come back and meet you.' Being bland again.

'Has she ordered tea? – sit down; have a cigarette.' Kingsize Americans and blonds in the two halves of a silver box.

'She spoke to the phone girl.'

'Then it'll be up – or I'll want to know why,' smiling. 'One advantage of having a hotel – there are precious few. Rather have a cup made by my wife, myself, out of a cracked pot – tastes better! You ride, do you?'

'No – except bicycles.' That got a smile with warmth in it. Good-looking fellow. Athletes, with their monstrous overdeveloped chests and thighs, making them look like bowlegged dwarfs, look ludicrous in tweed suits, but Rob didn't. Despite the look of physical splendour and the hard disciplined control that was evident, he showed signs of tension: he had a nervous trick of gnawing at the side of his thumb, worrying it with square perfect teeth.

'In business?' abruptly.

'I'm a commissaire of police – not this district: inland.' This casually-allowed-to-fall remark caused no stir; Zwemmer nodded idly.

'Not much time for things like horses, I 'spect – like me.'

'I sneak an hour off to look at something like that,' flipping a thumb at the shelves of silver.

'Supposed to be impressive, but I've never yet seen anyone impressed – people are bored, or jealous, or contemptuous, or think it's showing-off. They'd pinch them though, if they got the chance.' It was not bitter or cynical; just that experience had taught him that mankind is like that.

'What do they mean to you?'

'A lot. All the moments when I was ready to give up and fall off, and went on like a fool without knowing why.'

'That's enough.'

'There's nothing dimmer than a champ the moment he's retired and there's nothing left of him but those.'

'And when you're still champ?'

Zwemmer's eyes came round slowly: dark angry battlefield grey, like the North Sea on a windy day.

'Being champ is a thing only the other champs know about. For every one fellow that likes you, or admires you – wants you to win – there are ten hoping you'll be whacked, humiliated. And twenty who don't care, but get a kick out of hoping you'll slip on a banana skin. Get a puncture and miss a breakaway, they'll say with joy you're finished and they'd known so all along. Win and they say the race was pulled crooked by money. You learn to use your elbows. Good training for business – I've worked as hard building this place up as I did to win those. You don't get much out of it. Television interviews by chaps who've forgotten your name the week after. Money, of course. Flowers. Silver cup with champagne.'

Janine arrived at the same moment as the tea, and with comparable grandezza: one scarcely knew which to look at first.

Human beings are more interesting than objects (Van der Valk had little liking for new-wave novelists); she had a black crêpe frock, much too dressy both for her and for the occasion, with a diamond star and a lot of noisy perfume, a touched-up bouffant hairstyle and shiny shoes so high in the heel that she looked about to perform a vertical take-off.

The tea was overdone as well: it was stainless steel with a brushed finish to make it look more silvery, in angular Scandinavian shapes. Ranged in rows on an enormous oval dish, like cocktail canapés, were the Dutch 'thé complet' accessories – the more dear the hotel the more there were of them and here there were eleven, which is high on the haunch. Little sippets of buttered toast and tiny three-cornered sandwiches. Glacés fours. Dry petits fours. Fan wafers stuffed with whipped cream. Tiny meatballs breadcrumbed and deep fried. Little chicken croquettes, ditto. Plain chocolate in shiny naked napolitaines, and milk chocolate in oblong pastilles, wrapped in silver paper and covered with a tiny reproduction of a famous Dutch painting, like so many miniature cigarette-cards.

The tea of course was ordinary hotel-tea, in a bag.

It struck Van der Valk as he waded happily through these absurd goodies that Rob and Janine were like the tea – ill at ease in pretentious frames – and likely to taste better out of a cracked pot on the kitchen table, made from a homely barrel of rainwater in the yard of a Brabant farmhouse.

Rob ate sparingly. One mustard-and-cress sandwich, one macaroon, one napolitaine, one cup of tea. His eating was slow and careful, without spitting, talking or crumb-dropping, with a large white linen handkerchief handy: paper napkins are nasty things. When he had finished he just looked meditative. He did not smoke, though he pushed his silver box forward. When he did speak his voice was soft. His French was good, slow and a bit awkward, without Janine's vulgar argot. Van der Valk liked him.

He liked Janine too, who was eating everything in sight, hungry after her ride, from the buttered toast to the whipped cream – she ate all three of these, explaining that she was too thin. She ate, too, all the pretty little pictures, since the men were only competing for bitter chocolate. She put lemon in her tea, blew on the cup to cool it, and drank it in an aggressive, noisy manner. She dripped a spot of butter on her frock, said 'merde', and scrubbed at it with a lace hanky. She even ate the little meatballs.

'I love these,' laughing. 'When I was little, getting one of these out of the automat was the biggest luxury I knew. They never taste as good now as those used to, but I hope each time I'll get the old feeling back.' Rob looked bored; he had probably heard this remark several times.

She talked a lot, and very sweepingly – perhaps she had made up her mind to show Van der Valk that she was not alarmed by him, even that she could confide in him.

'Those women, who even wear a corset under riding breeches, trying to hide their big soft bottoms rolling around the saddle – they're the ones who get on my tits.' Rob looked sharply, but Van der Valk had to laugh, and that was reassuring.

'Bernhard – the tub of tripe. I'm not surprised the horse gave him a crafty kick – I'd do the same, if I was a horse.'

Rob was looking indifferent, perhaps even a long way away in thought, as though there were no use frowning at Janine or kicking her under the table. One had to take her as she was – Van der Valk could not be sure he was listening. She chattered on – had she really not heard that he was enquiring into something not-quite-catholic about that death? Or was she acting?

'He thought himself a hell of a chap, you know, owning that restaurant. Why, it's not worth a quarter of what this is, now. But because his father had it before him he forgot that he was just a big cowboy from Bavaria. And his breath – always stinking of stale drink.'

He would have liked to ask how she knew, but Rob came out of the woods in front of him.

'You shouldn't talk like that – the fellow's dead, after all.' She shrank a little, though the tone was not snubbing.

'Do you know his wife at all?' asked Van der Valk smoothly, as though just being tactful.

'A bit. She's all right really, even if she puts on airs. She laughs and she's natural and she makes jokes. That one that lives with her gets on my nerves – sour bitch. And talk about an old hen with its chick – "Aren't you cold, darling? Hadn't you better put on your cardigan? – I've got it here for you" ' – in an absurd prissy, thin-lipped voice that was not at all the calm softspoken tones of the maligned Saskia.

Janine was not prissy. Her mouth in the little triangular face was wide, curly, and her lipstick was all over her teacup, a thing

Van der Valk loathed in women. But he still found her sympathetic – she had been snubbed so heavily and often. Even had Arlette not told him it was clear to see in all these over-loud, over-crude gestures and phrases. A nice girl. And Rob was a nice boy. He put his teacup down in a leave-taking way.

'I must be getting back.'

Rob dropped the sleepy look and said, 'Janine drove you over, if I understood. I'll drive you back.' There was no protest made about this; he had wanted to get Rob to himself awhile. And had Rob any inkling of that?

'I shall hope to see some more of you,' politely to Janine. She smiled quite confidently, as though this was not such a disagreeable notion any longer. Rob was looking from one to the other, his head cocked a scrap in a birdy way. He was jingling something in his trouser pocket, thinking: he brought it out and twirled it on his finger – a keyring on a leather tab. He seemed not quite satisfied, as though surprised that the conversation should finish so soon. After all these banalities – was there then no further purpose in this visit? But Van der Valk seemed quite content.

'Thank you for a wonderful tea.'

'Give my love to Lette.'

'Of course.'

The Ferrari was black with black leather: austere, with no superfluous accessories. Rob handled it as though it were a silk glove; it backed up without a jolt, turned lightly with no lurch or grind, and flashed out on to the road with a low growl, slipping through the gears with a noise like a little girl swallowing icecream. Inside there was warmth, fresh air, and no draught; it was a hardtop model and he commented on this.

'Cabriolets are all right for the look of things,' gently. 'Janine wanted one so I gave it her. But however good they are there's always something that doesn't work.' Silence, behind which the motor could be heard faintly. 'I take it,' slowly, 'that what you're really doing is enquiring into Fischer's death.' It wasn't a question.

'You think I'm not satisfied with it? Or just that I shouldn't be?'

'I've no idea. I heard that someone wasn't satisfied. I thought maybe that was gossip, but police commissaires in my experience don't just stroll about and drop in for cups of tea with no purpose but to pass time. I simply put two and two together – was that wrong?'

'No. It's true. I'm not satisfied.'

Rob didn't ask what this could possibly have to do with him. In a voice as relaxed as his driving style he said, 'I knew him slightly. And his wife.'

'How was that?'

'He was in the same business, not very far away – that kind of nodding acquaintance one has. I've met him at markets, Restaurant Association meetings, that kind of thing.'

'Not a bad place – have you been there perhaps?'

'No, never, though one does go to other places occasionally – window-shopping, and sometimes good ideas can be picked up – but his place was off my circuit – not on the way to anywhere particularly. I've heard about it naturally, and I've seen photos. Janine's been there once or twice I believe with the horse. Well-run place by all accounts, but Fischer knew his job.'

'Some people have given me the impression that he did nothing much but leave it to his wife.'

'I don't know either of them that well.'

'She's a good business woman, judging on what I see and hear – I've only met her once.'

'More to a restaurant than that – it's a personal business. I'd say that it showed his individuality, his character if you like. Janine told me he was always there talking to everyone, and I've heard the same from other people. I don't do that myself – I show myself as little as possible, because that buttering up the customer is something you can't stop once you start, but I dare say he enjoyed it – matter of taste.'

'I had lunch there yesterday – her efficiency certainly impressed me.'

'I've no doubt. She's an automatic, professional glad-hander.'

'You don't like her?'

'From what I've seen of her, no.' Van der Valk, with his little silver pick held in Rob's mouth, breathed on his little looking-glass and polished it on his overall. But Rob stayed perfectly relaxed.

'You liked him better?'

'If you like – you knew where you stood with him,' with composure. The car speeded up, held delicately by strong brown hands

– heavy coarse hands, but very clean, with square shiny nails and a narrow wedding ring. It was slipping now through the streets of the town, flexible and muscular as a trout in a stream.

'Second to the right. The house with the green shutters – you can leave the car here.'

'I must be getting back.'

Van der Valk smiled. 'Come on in. I came to make your acquaintance, not to drink tea.'

Rob got out without any useless words, and allowed himself to be shown into the living-room with no protest. Van der Valk went into the kitchen, got some ice-cubes, made two powerful Pernods in tumblers. Arlette was not back yet, seemingly. When he brought them in Rob was looking at an eighteenth-century print – the old walled town, with little men throwing things on the heads of assaulting Spaniards: he was not looking wistful, though, as if wishing he had some boiling oil handy himself.

'Nice thing.'

'You like pictures?'

'Very much.' He smiled a bit bleakly when he saw the drink. 'I hardly drink, but I'll take that.'

'A hot, dusty summer's day in Béziers.'

Rob appeared to like this idea, drank, and some of the armoured look went out of his face.

'It's all off the record,' comfortably. 'You're in my house – we're just chatting idly. I didn't want your wife to feel embarrassed at my asking a lot of nosy questions.'

'Fair enough,' Rob shrugged. 'But what would I know likely to be of any use to the police?'

'Ach, it's these legends about the police. Facts, we're only interested in facts, yap all the little doggies. There's nothing duller than facts and there aren't enough of them anyway. It's not gossip I want, it's ideas. Ideas are stronger than dollars, as they say in Moscow. I want your opinions, biased or not, I don't care. That's why I wanted to see you alone, so that you didn't feel bound to be guarded. Tell me what you really thought of Bernhard – you might not think it but it's of value.'

Another shrug, another little drink, some more thought.

'Well for what it's worth . . . I thought him a parasite, always sucking from anything and anyone around him. I wasn't friendly with him, didn't even know him well, but he had this trick of being your greatest pal for just as long as you were there. Moment he saw you he'd come scuttling over, all thick and warm and matey, full of malicious gossip. You never met him?'

'Never even saw him, alas,' with regret.

'He'd the kind of eyes that are for ever in the corners of the room scavenging, while he's talking to you. Octopus.'

'And her? I've met her briefly, but what interested me was that everybody likes her or seems to, and I got the impression that you don't.'

Rob's face said clearly that all this liking or not-liking was stupid and pointless – what did liking a person mean?

'She's very charming – in fact she was just the opposite. You know what the trick is? She fixes you with big eyes, and gives you a notion that everything you say and do is of enormous importance. She simply can't take her eyes off you, you're so interesting and fascinating – it's a clever technique.'

'You're a good judge of terrain,' smiling.

'On the road,' gently, 'they give the riders these little maps. So many kilometres, such a hill so long with such a percentage of climb. It doesn't do to put too much trust in those little maps. One rule I learned the hard way – always reconnoitre beforehand the road you're going to ride on. These women – phoney as an Italian route chart. All that crowd are – they're not natural. Even physically – work out how much they spend on arranging their faces and figures, all that complicated machinery – paint and varnish – keep a family of four in comfort – even their hair is phoney.' The voice stayed soft and unexcited. It was just a fact of life, like finding a road surface with sharp gravel after you had been led to expect blacktop.

'I see that the atmosphere of riding-schools doesn't appeal to you greatly.'

'I can understand a cowboy: I've had some myself. Sweat and dust, callouses even through your gloves and the seat of your pants, leg muscles so you can't walk any more and get along like a duck. But riding-schools . . . ' He gave a brief laugh and drank some more Pernod. 'Good, this.' Van der Valk offered him a French cigarette, which he looked at a minute carefully to see if it wore a wig, then put in his mouth. 'Yes, I will if I may.'

'What you have to say may seem unimportant, and for all I know is unimportant – but it interests me.'

'You seem a straight enough chap' – the grey eyes were fixed on him. 'And Janine likes your wife – I know that. I don't have the pleasure of knowing her – but it makes a difference. You know what she says? – that your wife is kind to her! Sounds daft, doesn't it? – like a kiddy at school.'

'You've met some of these riding-school types?'

'I've never been there, but don't forget I run a restaurant too. I don't go over to customers much, is-everything-all-right, that crap. I want to know it's all right – I can do that without asking them! But I know that gang all right. They come to my place, and they've loud voices.'

'Francis too?'

Rob's sombre face – perhaps it was the Pernod – had an expression that was a bit sly, and at the same time innocent, as though it were making him boyish.

'A rider – you get used to studying faces; they tell you a lot. Not just who's feeling the pinch, but who's going to stick no matter what, who's planning something pretty soon – who's in a conspiracy. And the managers, in the cars . . . La Touche does a bit of his horse-coping in my place – the food's good, and he likes it. When the wife's with him he pretends he mustn't eat because it's bad for his health. When she's not he stuffs like a hog.' He knocked ash into a clean ashtray, which he studied as though it were a glass in which Francis' face might appear. 'Janine's told me a lot too. He's all right with her – that's because she's pretty. Men like that have a soft spot for a pretty girl. He doesn't notice human beings much, I reckon – like a picture by Stubbs.'

'Like what?' Van der Valk was taken aback despite himself.

Rob, betrayed by Pernod, drank some more, embarrassed.

'Well, I know a bit about pictures – not much – I've no education. He was some English fellow painted horses – well, the people are there in the picture too, but they're just there to fill it up, sort of. Don't seem to mean much to him – horse is what counts. I sort of see La Touche like that a bit.'

Full of surprises – who would have thought it? He remembered the pictures – 'Rob buys them,' Janine had said. He hadn't looked at them properly and was angry with himself – he hated missing opportunities like that.

'Have another drink.'

'One's enough, thanks. Two'd spoil it.' He drank up the watery

110

dregs of his own, dodging half-melted ice-cubes. He liked this fellow. Resourceful; he had been poor, and knew how to handle that, and now he was rich, and knew how to handle that, too. . . . His wife, very possibly, was the hole in these fortifications. It was a risk to ask, a risk he had to take.

'What's the matter with Janine?' casually. 'She doesn't seem to get much fun out of things.'

The face, relaxed and easy, got hard and heavy again instantly. He looked attentively at Van der Valk who was lighting a cigar with a lot of concentration. Still, he answered.

'She's a hell of a girl,' challengingly. 'Poor or rich she's been with me one hundred per cent, all the way. Never looked at another man and never would. And she likes being rich – why wouldn't she? I wanted to give her the earth. Mad keen on that horse: eager as mustard, goes out there nearly every day.'

'She drives that car really well, too. But she seems to have grievances.'

'Going on about the rich, you mean? Talking Belgian?'

'Yes.'

'You're a policeman – you ought to know people do funny things, but there's often a really simple innocent explanation.'

'Yes.'

'Janine can't have a baby. She was sick, and in hospital they said she mustn't try any more,' with embarrassment, that made him more sympathetic. 'She'd had miscarriages. She was pretty downcast. Lucky that year I was world champion – maybe because of that. Things go that way.'

'What do you make, if you're champion?' curiously.

'As long as you go on winning things! – around four hundred thousand a year.'

Wow! He had expected a good round sum . . .

'It cheered her up?'

'I wanted her to see that one can go on having a good time, especially if one's rich.'

The door opened and Arlette came in, still in a sort of glow from her afternoon. She was like that – everything she did she put a lot into. Thought, zest, enjoyment, even knitting or cooking cabbage. She hated missing any fun.

She was a bit tousled, and looked good. The hours on a horse had slimmed and hardened her; she had lost that pudgy look she was beginning to get. Her fairly nondescript straight dark-blonde hair had gold lights from the open air; she was whistling.

'This is my wife.' They had been speaking Dutch but he switched into French; he wanted to see how Rob got on with Arlette. He had got up politely at once; he kissed her hand nicely, a bit shyly.

'I'm really glad to meet you, Madame. Janine talks a lot about you – she admires you a lot!'

'I admire her a lot,' said Arlette with warmth, 'she's afraid of nothing. I'm very fond of her. She's easily the person I like best out there.'

'I think without you she'd be pretty lonely. She doesn't find it easy to mix with people. She's got a real friend in you and believe me, I appreciate that a lot.' The words were sincere, but awkward, which struck Van der Valk. The fellow was so good with other men. Was he like that with all women? Or was it French women? Surely he didn't suspect her of being a bit over-sophisticated for a simple Dutch lad?

'Why don't you sit down again,' said Arlette happily, 'and we'll all have a drink?'

'I'd like that a lot – but I'd better go, really; Janine'll be wondering what's happened to me.'

'Give her a phone-call. Pity she's not with you.'

'No, I won't, thanks very much, really. But I hope she'll bring you out to the coast – any time. I mean that.'

'I'd love to,' said Arlette, throwing her gloves at the table in the corner.

Odd, thought Van der Valk after the Ferrari had slithered off. He enjoys her, obviously, but equally obviously he doesn't feel at ease with her.

Marguerite Fischer was decidedly nervous, a thing she was un-accustomed to; it made her irritable and snappy. This funeral was sticking in her throat: Saskia had been so sarcastic, so – so cynical . . . It was terribly difficult to know what to do: important that initiative should not leave her.

The undertaker wanted nothing better than that she should leave it all to him: he made more money that way. People like that, thought Marguerite, have it too easy in business; they are ac-customed to tearful and helpless widows who haven't a clue. They are over-ready to spring into the breach and arrange everything

112

with their loathsomely obtrusive tact. Marguerite refused point-blank to be tearful, although she had plenty of good reasons for being so, because it simply wasn't in her character. Nor would she ever admit to not having a clue, under any circumstances. But there were so many obstacles. . . . Saskia. The undertaker. Her sister Jo. Her sister Jo's husband, the butcher from The Hague. Oh damn, damn, damn. . . . That wasn't a very nice thing to say with one's husband awaiting burial, Marguerite told herself severely. She must pull herself together, and face the future with equanimity. Ian: the future belonged to Ian.

Under ordinary conditions she would have known exactly what to do. Funerals were part of life, and one knew exactly and in detail how they should be conducted. But first Bernhard had died – awful, to think that she had sometimes imagined that happening – in an odd sort of way, obscured at once by a cloud of gossip – most unpleasant. Then they had taken him off to the hospital for a post-mortem, which always meant something beastly. She had always liked Maartens, and now he had let her down really badly. Who could stand up to that official questioning and suspicion and using phrases nobody understood? – and that horrid feeling that authority will decide, all heartless and inhuman as it is, leaving you helpless, not knowing. . . . And now on top of everything this awful police commissaire, soft-voiced, soft-footed, saying all sorts of things in a way you could twist to mean everything. Beastly man. . . . The thunderclouded, blood-dark word homicide hung about choking her, like a poisonous vapour. Marguerite was not a woman of much imagination, but she found herself thinking of carbon dioxide – or was it monoxide?

And Ian – what about Ian? Tell him? – or not to tell him? He had an official position, he couldn't be mixed up with such things. He would be very angry. He might even decide that his judgement had been wrong.

Oh that policeman – he had said too much and left too much unsaid, and that had been what had caused her nerves to give way this afternoon – that lunch had never ended. She had had to turn to Saskia – who else was there?

She felt better on Tuesday morning, at first. It had been a comfort to have Saskia sleep with her – it had helped obliterate the other figure, who had been used to snore, with a strong fume of alcohol. She had got used to both, but at what a price.

She hoped to heaven that worried as she was she hadn't talked in her sleep or anything. Saskia was so sharp, and so suspicious.

At least the policeman had given permission for the funeral – otherwise she would only have had the official note in the post this morning, and that would have meant at least one more day wasted.

She had been crisp and businesslike yesterday evening with the undertaker. The bath and the rest had done her good, and restored her courage: after a cup of tea at four she had driven over again.

'Quite all right, dear lady. In confidence, it is by no means the first time I have dealt with such a situation. A post-mortem means nothing, dear no. I will arrange the formalities with the University Hospital. You do realize – all aspects to a perfectly natural state. . . . Now the ceremony itself; when were you planning that? For what day?'

'As soon as may be. Wednesday, if possible.'

'Mm, dear lady, mm – it could just barely be done, I suppose,' dubious and discouraging. 'We would, I fear, need twenty-four hours at the very least, to produce, hm, a good effect. It depends on the hospital – what they have done – where were you thinking of having the bier? At your home? Of course our premises are at your disposal. Many families prefer the respects to be paid at our resting-place – we are so exceptionally well equipped for a bier that has real dignity . . . solemnity . . . But dear lady, have you thought of the cards – the notifications?'

'There aren't going to be any cards. It's not too late to put a notice in tomorrow's papers.'

'Yes yes, I see. I do realize that the occasion is, hm, an exception to what is generally – but won't the warning be extremely, hm, brief?'

She had thought this one out.

'I think that's all to the good. Less publicity. I want to keep this strictly private. Very few people will be attending, probably.'

'I see,' with disappointment. 'Very well, dear lady. And the bier – from our premises?'

'No. From the house. I'm closing the restaurant all day. Bring – uh, bring it at nine in the morning. We will have the funeral at eleven. That will be plenty of time.'

'It is short, very short,' he mourned. 'I do fully completely understand – thoroughly highly approve – your feelings do you the greatest best credit – but very short. We would not like to think that any service we can provide had been, hm, scraped.'

'Yes. Will you arrange to – start at once?'

'It is already quite late.' The word 'overtime' was looming on the horizon, and he was arranging a tactful phrase to wrap it up in. Marquerite, a business woman who knew all about overtime, saw it coming.

'I will understand if you are put to extra expense – as long as you have it all properly itemized for me to see.' He cheered up.

'Rest assured, dear lady – assured – that no pains shall be spared. No pains – we are very well equipped.'

Newspaper offices were less trouble. It may be too late to advertise your second-hand car, but newspapers stretch points for deaths, especially in the provinces – if they want to stay in business. On Tuesday, notices duly appeared.

'Mevrouw Fischer-De Kimpe regrets to announce the sudden death in a tragic accident of her dearly beloved husband Bernhard Fischer, owner-manager of the restaurant "The White Horse", Warmond-Lisse. In the circumstances the funeral will take place in strict privacy on Wednesday, April 27th. The last respects may be paid between 9 and 11 a.m. on this day. You are kindly asked to send no flowers, and to observe the family's wish for simplicity and privacy.'

According to subeditorial fantasies the morning paper in The Hague and the evening paper in Haarlem added little comments of their own.

Mr Bernhard Fischer, whose sudden death is elsewhere announced in our columns was one of the best-known restaurateurs in Holland, and our readers will be grieved to learn of his fatal accident. The late Heer Fischer had made the "White Horse" one of the best-known meeting-places in the country for visitors to this famous region, and was known throughout Europe for his friendly hospitality as well as his unmatched skill in culinary matters. To Mevrouw Fischer we present our deep respect and sorrowing sympathies.

(See news columns p. 9, and advertisement columns, p. 13.)

Van der Valk turned obediently to page nine.

Mr Bernhard Fischer, the well-known restaurateur, whose obituary notice will be found on p. 2 of this edition, met his death in tragic and untimely circumstances over the weekend. While out riding, a sport he had recently taken up, it is presumed that he dismounted to adjust the harness. Frightened or disquieted, possibly by a low-flying jet, his mount lashed out and by unhappy coincidence struck the rider on the head, causing instant death. The accident was discovered within minutes by passers by, but all efforts to reanimate the unfortunate victim proved fruitless.

(See p. 5 – 'Supersonic bang – Minister studies further complaints.')

Van der Valk, who had invented the low-flying jet and was rather proud of it, felt contented. No mention of the manège, or of Doctor Maartens' reticences, everything beautifully vague and no awkwardnesses. Since this had taken no more than eight or nine phone-calls, it wasn't bad at all.

A 'box' in the advertisement columns stated that the 'White Horse' would be closed on Wednesday, April 27th, for the whole day, on account of bereavement.

'Do you have to go to this funeral?' asked Arlette.

'Certainly. In full cavalry regalia – accompanying you.'

'You mean I have to go? – but it says private.'

'Private simply means discreet. We mingle with the patrons of the manège – you'll find they'll turn out in force.'

'But why you?'

'Inspector Maigret always goes to funerals, which are pregnant with significance: on this occasion I incline to agree.'

'Very well,' resignedly. 'Is a black two-piece all right?'

'Quite all right. And my clergyman suit.'

The whole of Tuesday had been a headache to Marguerite. She had deliberately kept the restaurant open in the interests of normality; now she wished she hadn't. For every normal German that hadn't read the local papers there were two Morbid Marias looking for attention, and Saskia had been annoying. The telephone never stopped ringing with barbaric expressions of conventional condolence concealing a wish to get things straight. (Nobody had noticed an aeroplane, but then one didn't notice aeroplanes these days. If that policeman Maggie Sebregt mentioned had been sensible enough to check up on aeroplanes – now one thought of it nothing was more likely: those horrible jets, darling, that frighten all the animals, and me, too . . . well, perhaps he was of some use after all. With which Marguerite, who knew nothing about any aeroplane, had to agree.)

There had been the President of the Hotel and Catering Association, and the editor of the *Hotel Keepers' Weekly* – both fussy and ponderous. And Saskia had gone on and on.

'Why not have the whole thing done from the undertaker's as they suggested? He has a suitable place, the thing is properly organized, and people don't so intrude on you; you have some protection from gossip and spying eyes.'

'I'm sorry, Sas, that's a thing I couldn't do. He was my husband after all, this was his place, here he lived; here he has a right to die. Anyway' – she had paid her tribute to the decencies, and could afford now a bit of the disillusionment that had been creeping up on her – 'if we had it there we'd be likely to find people saying we'd no heart, etcetera, and that we were ashamed to bring him here – afraid to show him even. There might not even be wanting people to whisper that I'd been glad to have him dead.' She thought – hoped – that Saskia knew nothing about Ian, but there were other people, she knew, who did.

'There are never people wanting – even to hint that you'd killed him,' expressing downright, that dreadful outspoken way Saskia had, a thought Marguerite had had but not dared put into words.

'Yes, but shut up, Sas, do.'

Jo had been just as annoying – even more so – in the opposite direction. She was Marguerite's only sister, three years older than her, and had at last found something to lay down the law about to that stubborn girl. Had she not arranged the funeral of their father three years ago, in circumstances of splendour? She had wormed out about Doctor Maartens – and got in a fine fume about it – but Commissaire Van der Valk had been suppressed.

'It's outrageous, that's all I can say, outrageous. So hole and corner – such things just aren't done. And such a well-known man.'

She had detested Bernhard for being a well-known man. It was just sheer accident that a restaurant-owner should be better-known than a butcher.

'The restaurant should have been closed the moment you heard of his death, and kept shut till after the funeral. We should have made a really fine laying-out room, where people could come and pay their respects properly – a well-known man like that. Disgusting. You seem to have lost all your proper feelings, that's all I can say.'

The husband – the prosperous butcher – agreed, and said so. Marguerite could not help thinking how he had refused to deal with Bernhard.

'No no, Margie, that's no way to do business. I'm your brother-in-law, right? – and then you make an arrangement, and there's too much gets taken on trust, and things get into an embarrassing situation. Suppose you queried a bill or something – why, I'd be bound to accept your word for it, wouldn't I now? And an order that size – you know how it is, these restaurant managers – a butcher who gets that size order from a place, now they expect him to drop an envelope each time he delivers, isn't it, with a kickback. Now I wouldn't know what Bernhard would be suggesting but I . . .'

Compromising on the funeral, trying to keep both sides happy, she had succeeded in discontenting everybody. The one thing she could feel grateful for was that the few rather-lost-sight-of relations Bernhard had had in Germany weren't coming. She had telegraphed news of the death on Saturday, but, being a village, they hadn't had the wire till Monday morning. She had wired again on Monday evening, and a stiff reply had come on Tuesday. That the notice was too short, that they regretted, that things were crucial on the farm (they always were), that the harvest couldn't be left just now (at the end of April? – what harvest?) and that they were sure she understood. She did.

Now that Wednesday had at last arrived, she was feeling stunned, although it was still only eight o'clock. At least that odious undertaker seemed competent: she supposed that was a comfort, obscurely.

Saskia and the girls had been busy since seven. Tables had been removed and piled in the yard at the back, the restaurant judiciously dimmed with flowers and candles into an atmosphere of whispering. The bar and the goldfish tank had been kind-of-shrouded. The others had just disappeared to wash and change, leaving her in command, already in her black frock and gloves with no jewellery, looking serene and rather splendid, a dignified figure but with a nervous need to go to the lavatory every ten minutes.

At a quarter to eight the undertaker had arrived with his discreet black fleet and begun at once to buzz.

'A public room, Madam?'

'Our private rooms are upstairs – one can't expect people to troop up two flights and I wouldn't want it either.' She was stung by the note of disapproval. 'This was his room, where he was best known, where everybody remembers him.'

'And where shall we put the bier?'

It had been arranged, finally, in the familiar corner, where Bernhard had been used to sit chatting, cardplaying, pouring out glasses.... Now it was a kind of altar. No spotlights, thank heaven, but a decided feeling of stiffly-bunched-madonna-lilies. Bernhard looked as natural as though reading the vegetable-market prices in the evening paper – she felt guilty at this thought. One had to admit the fellow had done a good job – all that was lacking was a Pharaoh's gold mask ...

She felt she wanted to cry, which wouldn't have mattered since legitimate grief had warned her to put no mascara on. But she couldn't cry because she wanted to laugh as well. Bernhard in his corner – there ought to be a bottle of mirabelle and three glasses.... She rushed to the lavatory, where she laughed, cried, decided not to be hysterical, calmed herself sternly, straightened her clothes and face, and came out in time to meet Van der Valk, arriving punctually at nine o'clock and leaving Arlette in the car down the road, waiting for a group with which to mingle in a properly effaced manner. He had his midnight-blue suit on and was carrying his stick to reinforce the note.

'Good morning, Mevrouw Fischer. My profound respects and sympathies and I trust you have not been annoyed. Press?'

'Just the ordinary.'

'Have unpleasant suggestions – or hints – been made?'

'I don't know what hints could be made,' icily. 'If you mean has anyone hinted he was drunk, no. People are not as nasty as you seem to think!'

'I see. That is better than I might have feared – I'm relieved to hear it.'

'Are you still, uh, enquiring, Commissaire?'

'I am, yes, but you notice that I am very quiet about it. I don't go about cross-examining people. I have every reason to believe that when I have finally assembled all the details and the accounts of all the witnesses the authorities will be perfectly satisfied. Such things are bound to take a few days.'

'A plane made a bang and frightened the horse?' timidly.

'All these tiny details need minute examination. It was wise of you to go ahead with no loss of time.'

'Will you be wanting to talk to me, uh, any further?'

'Not today in any case,' politely. He walked over to look at the bier. 'Very good – excellent.' He didn't say what, but presumably he was impressed by the convincing look Bernhard had. After the pathology laboratory . . .

'Good morning, Commissaire.'

Saskia, with her softest voice, was standing at his elbow. 'We are not offering anything officially, but perhaps you would like a glass of sherry? Or are you here officially?' It was a pleasantly turned sarcasm – of course plenty of people are sarcastic when nervous.

'An unofficial drink, in an unofficial moment – with pleasure.'

'If you don't mind coming through to the back.'

Through the door, between the kitchen and the cloakrooms, was a fair-sized hallway. The stairs led up to the living quarters, and a passage led through to the scullery and store-room doors. A restaurant table had been set against the wall, covered with a white cloth, and laid with sherry and port and a tray of glasses. From this vantage point he could observe the undertaker in the grateful role of chef de protocole and the arrival, scattered but growing thicker, of the people who come to a 'Private' funeral, only a few of whom were smuggled through by Saskia for a ritual glass. Cooks, stiff in Sunday suits, a delegation from the Hotel and Catering Association (which got sherry), the local burgomaster and councillors (who preferred port – sweeter), Bernhard's cronies, looking no deader than he did – they got a dignified handshake from Marguerite and a sort of bow from Saskia, as though from an open carriage. Wholesale butchers and greengrocers. Rob, in a dark suit, very polite and formal. Most people, after saying the right words, melted out to the carpark, embarrassed by Bernhard's nose sticking out in a jovial, faintly alcoholic manner.

At the end arrived Francis La Touche, shepherding his horsy

band. He was very good, bowing over Marguerite's hand and saying in a clear military tone, 'I am greatly saddened, this occasion touches me personally and deeply, and I speak for all of us when I ask permission to extend my heartfelt sorrow and regrets,' which made the mumblings of butcher sound unusually lame and lengthy. Van der Valk, hovering, could not quite hear what Marion said: her voice was too low.

Janine had not accompanied Rob. She was perhaps in the group of those who did not know the family and had not been invited, but who would come to the churchyard. Not a churchyard, thought Van der Valk. A cemetery. Churchyards in Holland are thought of as slightly insanitary inventions.

He was – both professionally and personally – unsentimental about dead people, and believed in being earthy on the subject of rotting to flowers and fruit. He detested hygienic cemeteries, polished granite with gold lettering, marble noticeboards, little metal plaques saying dogs and prams were not allowed. One can be an English Protestant or a French Catholic, he thought, but one is short, to the point, and one does not take portentousness as a substitute for nobility. It was Arlette's influence that had shaped him – she was a great enthusiast of country churchyards. 'A wooden cross,' she said, 'and if your children like, a sandstone slab.' You that are born of woman, he was saying to himself now in this abominable municipal cemetery, are a breath and a whisper before you descend into the soil that will, we hope, nourish an apple tree. You are the breath of flutes at evening time, the little curl of whitish foam on the sand. He thought he would be quite contented to be thrown overboard at sea – it showed more confidence. Committed to the deep – he liked that word 'committed'. God would know how to disentangle the bones from the sea bottom. He would rather be in the ossuary at Verdun than in Père Lachaise between Marshals.

This now – petty smallness and pretension – undertakers had recently decided to suppress the hole in the ground, pretending it was not there. Cypress branches had been arranged to screen the infamous with an ingenious fan, a cunning mechanical invention was added that poised the coffin above this prudish cache-sexe, and at the crucial moment the chef de protocole pressed a button. No men with ropes: you sank silently from sight, the fan bending to admit you to Abraham's bosom and – this was the really expert touch – springing back into place: not only was there no hole – there wasn't even a coffin! The old and noble custom of throwing handfuls of soil had long been suppressed as unhygienic.

He almost laughed, and hurt his nose suppressing it. Victor Hugo! The Mother Superior, in *Les Miserables*, who has a cunning plan for putting dead nuns in the crypt, a thing frowned on by the administration.

'God subordinated to a commissaire of police,' she fumes. 'What a century!'

That was him! Seeing that everything went off hygienically. Seeing to it that the administration was satisfied . . .

Just before pressing his ignominious button, the undertaker lifted his voice unctuously.

'Does anyone desire to say a few words?'

Marguerite stood still and stony. A few butchers stirred uneasily, led by the brother-in-law from The Hague. Francis stood in an attitude of military petrification, with a slight sniff: funerals without ceremonial shots, flags, and the Last Post, were a very poor affair. Marion wore a faint knowing smile, like a child with a secret that the others are begging it to tell. Saskia Groenveld had a face of beatific content, flights-of-angels-wing-thee, and Arlette was concealing boredom really extremely poorly. Just behind her, looking as though she should be holding to the older, taller woman's skirt, Janine was snuffling in a silly little hanky. He wondered why. Was it one of her conventions to sob at funerals? Or was she snivelling for something else, more permanently lost? His eye travelled round a ring of butchers, liquid of eye as humanely killed calves, and was struck by the painter, in his dim everyday greyish-green suit, armoured in his contempt for such goings-on. He would not have thought that the painter might deign to attend a funeral, surely a bourgeois attitude. Still, there he was, his face designed to tell anyone curious enough to look that he was not there in spirit.

Marguerite had her eyes fixed on the coffin with steady severity, as though determined not to miss the vanishing trick. The Rope Trick Inverted, thought Van der Valk. We want no little Indian boys; we want a live and faintly sweaty Bernhard in his white jacket to come climbing out from behind the cypress-branch fan and invite everyone back for the apéritif.

The President of the Catering Association would dearly have

loved to say a few words, but had waited too long for someone with prior claims – he was too late; the head mute pressed the hoojah and a fruity eulogy sank into the womb of lost opportunity.

Perfect, thought Van der Valk. He bowed to Marguerite, cut his wife adroitly out of the ruck, and ran away as quickly as dignity and his stick would allow. The motor of the deux-chevaux raced noisily, but was masked by many much more expensive motors doing the same thing in their politer way.

'Why do you think nobody had the courage to say the few words?' asked Arlette.

'Perhaps in the clinch, now that they are really rid of him at last, words would have been otiose,' with relish.

'For a person presumed to have been so universally liked, though, wasn't it a scrap pointed?'

'I feel fairly certain that there wasn't a soul there that didn't detest him. . . . Have you ever been to a cremation?' She hadn't, and what was more she never would. He had – professionally.

'It is only worse than that performance in that you don't even get a breath of fresh air. Not even a smell of earth and leaves. A sort of desiccated drowning, asphyxiation in an odour of atheist piety.'

'When you die,' said Arlette happily, 'I will be there to finish you off. Women are always tougher than men.'

'You won't commit suttee?'

'What is suttee?'

'Widows' self-immolation, on a pyre.'

'Penses-tu,' greatly shocked. He laughed.

'What will you do?'

'Put you in a little boat and pour whisky all over before striking a match and giving a determined shove.'

'Lovely. What's for lunch?'

'Steak tartare – nothing to get ready. Did you notice how the sun came out suddenly?'

'Yes indeed.'

Yes indeed. That April sunlight that came out suddenly, blinding: illuminating . . .

Full of peace and good digestion, he had to go and see the Officer of Justice. He was not yet back from lunch, but, being the Commissaire, Van der Valk could wait in the empty bureau. The magistrate was a punctual person, and would certainly be back in five minutes.

He had known many of the breed. Old Slotemaker de Bruin in Amsterdam, elegant and eighteenth century, with his little digressions from law into metaphysics. Karstens, the opposite, the very worst type, the old-fashioned hanging bullying magistrate whose summing up in the courtroom never varied, who banged out a good dose of correctional training with the same emotional impartiality for robbery with breaking as for indecent exposure. (He had once, to his immense joy, overheard a barely murmured whopping indiscretion, unthinkable in an Officer of Justice . . . Old Slotemaker, passing Karstens in the passage on their way to their respective offices, half to himself, half to his 'greffier' – 'I do believe he must be a repressed homosexual . . . ') And Rodcik, thin and dry and infinitely scrupulous, more scrupulous than most presidents – and Keller the swift and cutting, the reporters' delight, with his love of colloquialism and folklore illustration.

This one was of a newer school, a youngish, ascetic man with close cropped grey-blond hair and rimless glasses that gave his bony face a boyish look, so that from some angles he looked like a young law-student, and from others like a fanatical military bishop – he was both. You could never be sure how he saw things: at times startlingly progressive and liberal, one for 'leaving the door open', he could be ruthless, a hammer of the infidel. His name was Romeijn and as Officers went he was reasonable; patient and considerate with prisoners and courteous towards the police, which was more than some . . .

'I beg your pardon, Commissaire.' A doublebreasted suit of brighter-than-legal blue, a long bony white hand, slightly moist. A non-smoker – there was something to be said for those healthy tireless old hams, smoking big cigars and thumping the table. A man of the centre, embedded uneasily at times in the Palais, a pompous Victorian building smelling of damp umbrellas and echoing to continual clerical coughing. He had a canopied brass table-lamp and a modern red-and-grey telephone, a morocco blotter whose green had dulled to black – and a goldrimmed Parker pen-set; diamond-paned mahogany bookshelves full of lawbooks bound in quarter-leather – and a Philips tape-recorder encased in chaste grained grey plastic. He had a trick while talking of taking his glasses off (which gave his face an indecent appearance), gazing blindly at the lenses, which were always perfectly clean, and rubbing at them nervously with a huge pure white hanky.

'Do sit down. You've come to tell me about this Fischer business, have you?'

'Yes, sir. He was buried this morning. I think we'll have to do some work on it. I've spent some time on the persons and places, getting to know their little ways, but it would take a whole team and thorough work – it may come to that.'

'Your conclusion?'

'That the man was killed.'

'Your premises?'

'None at all.'

Plenty of Officers of Justice on getting this answer would get all exophthalmic and flap their hands like angry pigeons, and yelp about timewasting. But Mr Romeijn stayed tranquil and said gently that perhaps it was time for him to know something about these people. Van der Valk was grateful. His idea about violent emotions, so jarring in this placid landscape of pale green and watery grey, like the belts of brilliantly coloured flowers, wouldn't do at all in this office.

'The presumption about Fischer begins with the village doctor. A youngish man but of considerable experience among these people. He chose to stir up a troublesome enquiry that would certainly harm him if it failed to produce its result. It wasn't physical evidence that really moved him, because an accident, while unlikely, remains possible. We couldn't act on that alone. I have questioned him, indirectly. He knows something, but he won't say. Possibly aspects of what he feels come under professional lipsealing, and his suspicions can't be substantiated and can't consequently in fairness be formulated. He cuts the knot by throwing veiled warnings our way, which takes the monkey off his shoulder.'

'The physical likelihood of an attack?'

'Open. The ground is reached easily by anyone whose presence at the manège would pass without comment, and that is very large. One could be seen but unremarked. The spot is not, though, overlooked either from the windows or the fields.'

Mr Romeijn had uncapped his fountain pen and begun to make notes. It was a little like a copywriter presenting an advertising campaign to a soapflakes manufacturer.

'Around this patch of ground – here are the photographs – lies a variety of natural junk – by natural I mean that it's not unexpected or incongruous. Among the rubbish an old golf club and a round iron weight. The means for an attack lay at hand.'

'Thus no presumption of planning or spontaneity.'

'No, sir.'

'Further.'

'Fischer: his wife is on friendly terms with the owners of the manège, Francis and Marion La Touche. He is if anything not. Told to take exercise by the doctor, he chooses horses. The choice seems to strike a false note. He had never shown interest in horses – he suddenly does so. I am left with a notion that he wished to provoke people – to show his importance – perhaps even his power.'

'You must support this remark.'

'He had nothing to do in the restaurant, beyond superficial appearances. There he was faced with a coalition of two women, his wife and a woman called Groenveld, of no particular age, not unattractive, of decided character.'

'What is this woman's standing in the household?'

'Manageress, but she has an investment in the business – a part owner. She helped to rescue, before the marriage, a place that had run down in the post-war atmosphere – the man was of German origin. She lives in the house and has a close relationship with the wife. It's not going too far to call it an alliance, and the man may have felt he was not master, that the alliance was hostile . . . '

'A lesbian relationship?'

'Possible. The wife, who ran the business and still does, combines energy and decision with a casual laziness in private – the other adopts a protective maternal attitude, and speaks disparagingly of the husband. Both show anxiety, tension about gossip, fear lest their even peaceful ways be disturbed.'

'He put up with all this?'

'Odd isn't it?' said Van der Valk, feeling he had made his first point.

'Go on.'

'He might have looked for authority in other spheres – naturally blackmail came to my mind. On the surface liked and hail-fellow with everyone, he aroused dislike, which everyone mentions once their confidence is gained.'

'They feel free to mention this dislike?'

'He had a reputation as a gossip, a talebearer. A collector and retailer of malicious tattle.'

'A weak man, he had pleasure in noticing and discussing the weaknesses of others?'

'One might push a hypothesis like that – a hypothesis is all it is.'

'I merely wished to test your awareness of the dangers of doing so,' said Mr Romeijn almost apologetically.

'All this circle of close acquaintances seem normal enough – Doctor Maartens was willing, guardedly, to give me a little medical background. An even-tenored, pleasant set of lives, settled, without financial worries, no obvious emotional distortions, surrounded with comforts and conveniences – it's just that which awakens my dissatisfaction. All so smooth, and they all show a state of tension. I can't say it's out of the ordinary – I just wonder.'

'A police officer – the mere fact of an investigation arouses embarrassment, worry, hostility.'

'Yes, sir.'

'You aren't satisfied?'

'No.'

Mr Romeijn looked at him for some time in silence.

'Very well. Since you wish to convince me, I presume you have more?'

'La Touche. An anxious man, with a sense of inadequacy, needing reassurance. Shouts at clients, who seem to enjoy it, carries violence a stage further in private – he beats up his wife. She told me this with a frankness intended perhaps to disarm me. She cultivates a façade of calm, poise, chic, weary sophistication.' Mr Romeijn plainly disliked this phrase; since he was quite right, Van der Valk kicked himself in the ankle.

'There is a grown-up son, who got into some trouble – there were violent scenes with the father. The boy left the country with a black-sheep label of sorts.'

'Anything on our files?'

'A charge of fraud that didn't seem terribly convincing and was later withdrawn. Cheques. There was a rather – halfhearted – enquiry.'

'Here?'

'No – Hague.'

'Are you suggesting that this charge was true but was manipulated?'

'I don't know whose name he was supposed to have written on the cheque.'

'I see.'

'A riding-school is of course a hotbed of namedropping, compulsive boasting, anxieties about status.'

'I suppose that might be so,' with distaste.

'My wife goes there. She genuinely likes horses. My status as an officer of police is sufficient to satisfy snobbery, but since she is French that scarcely interests her. She has given me some amusing lights on behaviour – one striking example of the persistent striving common to many of this group.'

'What is that?'

'A girl from a village who married a bicycle champion and has pots of money.'

A small smile stirred an austere mouth.

'I can see how that might be possible,' he murmured. 'Unacceptable on both counts.'

'The husband owns a hotel in the district, and though he did not frequent the riding-school he knew both Fischer and his wife professionally. He speaks of both with dislike. A lot of things in this circle are half felt, half seen.'

'And what, Commissaire,' incisively, 'do you suggest?'

'You gave me a commission of interrogation, sir, with some doubt. You might consider summoning the people most closely concerned, and examine subsequent statements for inconsistency,' colourless. 'The classic method – when one has anything to go on.'

'Just so. Your suppositions, Commissaire – moonshine. That is, judicial moonshine. To test and sift all this – there's no nail to hang a case on, and people have a natural distaste for accounting for their private lives – any further suggestion?'

'I would be inclined,' gingerly, 'to consider some discreet observation to see if these people have relationships we know nothing of.'

The magistrate had stiffened, as Van der Valk had known he would.

'I don't like it, as you know. We don't like that in this country. Smacks of interference with a subject's liberties. Unwarrantable sniffing and snuffling – unconstitutional.'

'A riding-school – there's something dashing and uninhibited about horses, an atmosphere Mr La Touche encourages. It is fashionable there to be outspoken and a bit daring. By the way, the customers had a habit of lunching at Fischer's restaurant, and meeting there on horseback. Fischer certainly knew many of them well.'

'You think blackmail, do you? Covert rendezvous, flirtations, extracurricular carryings on, hm?' with irony.

'I don't know what I think. But I feel convinced that somebody is banking on our impotence all round. We can't even prove this death wasn't an accident from the medical evidence, but there is no doubt in the state pathologist's mind – that is of course his unofficial opinion expressed to me in private.'

'Very well, Commissaire,' suddenly. 'I will allow this observation, holding you personally responsible.'

The fact was that in Amsterdam he had done such things constantly, without any reference to nervous juridical functionaries either. It might be unconstitutional, but if one wasn't going to sit being impotent, one had to. But here in the provinces it was another matter, and if he put his staff on to something on this scale, there would be talk. It would leak to higher spheres. He would be up shit creek, and without a paddle too.

And the magistrate had agreed – unexpectedly.

Did he – like Doctor Maartens – feel something he himself was not properly attuned to? All he could say about this whole business was that it was not quite catholic – and now he would swear that the magistrate himself had just such a phrase lodged behind his sinus somewhere.

What could it be? Inaudible transmissions came from the bourgeoisie. Janine was right and you could never be one of them unless you were born there.

'Is your staff adequate – trained, I should say – for that kind of thing?'

'No.' The magistrate showed consternation, which paid him out for 'that kind of thing'. They weren't going to open an embassy safe and photostat the contents!

'Then what do you propose to do?'

'Get a few off the retired list. I haven't enough people anyway that I can take off their normal work. And there are several advantages – more experience, more patience, more time, not fussy about union hours – and much, much more convincing.'

The magistrate was slightly cheered up by this, but Van der Valk could see him, having unwillingly agreed to the principle, searching for drawbacks of detail that would be a face-saver. Really he had given in much too quickly.

'But an expense,' querulous.

'We'd think nothing of it, sir, if it was a state visit.'

A faint smile.

'Crime is more important than a state visit, is that it?'

'Yes, sir,' soberly.

'Quite true, really,' as though to himself. 'Very well, Commissaire, I'll see what can be done. But I'm holding you personally responsible.'

As he was going out a voice called him back; not very peremptory, just enough. 'And – Van der Valk.'

'Sir?'

'Remember how it might sound in court. "The accused was taken under observation." You know, eh?'

'Yes, sir.'

He's oddly confident, thought Van der Valk, getting his leg down the flight of stone steps. I wish I were.

He was lucky; he got two of his old staff from Amsterdam, as well as two local chaps recently – but not too recently – retired and picked on their records. Solid chaps. With little cars of their own, knowing the country – and Rademaker and Hendricks, at least, could do this kind of work in their sleep and probably would.

'An easy job,' he said. 'All round the clock, and you'll be in shifts of two, but these are settled people who get eight hours' sleep and so can you. You can eat and drink as long as you keep the expenses within reason, and your petrol will be allowed of course. Use a very light hand and work from far away. No breathing down necks – I'd rather you missed fine detail than got rumbled. Remember – if you get rumbled there's a complaint. If there's a complaint it's my job. Is that quite clear?' He had added two of his regular brigade.

'Valuable experience for you two boys but I hope you haven't been reading any gangster magazines lately. This isn't a goddam tail. I'm putting a technical man on the telephone exchange who will, of course, keep track of their calls. You'll call in hourly as you get the opportunity and he'll keep you posted.'

'Are we to be disguised?' asked one of the young sub-inspectors happily, evidently enjoying the idea.

'You do anything you damn well like as long as you don't turn it into amateur theatricals. If your false moustache gets tangled in your binoculars, you've got the wrong disguise. I'm pairing each of you boys with our retired thiefcatchers here and they'll train you. You are on a motorbike or a scooter – find identities that match that. Mr Hendricks here is a silver-haired business man – what's your car, Bob?'

'Renault Ten.'

'It'll do nicely. And you, Will? I'd say myself you were an inspector on the railways.'

'Simca thousand.'

'At least it's not a Daf – but you've been warned,' with guffaws, 'if it comes to a chase we're in the Ferrari bracket. This may go on for some time and six of you to three houses. . . . Bob, you and Will think of a couple more to relieve you, and work in rotation of course. I leave the cover to you – remember it's a village, government survey might not be a bad one for this riding-school, stroll about with a theodolite and a measuring-tape.'

Mr Hendricks, who had been retired three years, was watching Van der Valk the Senior Officer with some enjoyment.

'What tactics, skipper?' out of the corner of his mouth, tough like Gravedigger Ed from the thirty-ninth precinct.

Yes, one had to think about that. Van der Valk lit a cigar, rather a good one, a courtesy present from the Officer of Justice for bright pupils. An expensive cigar; it had to be clipped with a pair of nailscissors accustomed to more plebeian use, carefully examined for scar tissue, licked like a baby with a nice mouthful of mama, and a match had to be borrowed to light it. All this was watched with proper respect by the young subordinates, patience by the locals, and cynicism by the two Amsterdammers, who had watched too many Senior Police Officers going all sensual and back-to-the-womb with large cigars in the course of their careers.

'The chappie was murdered. We're certain, but not the way the Palais has to be certain. He was a fellow who went to trouble nosing out scandal, and that is roughly your starting point. His wife is in business partnership with an older woman who has money in the business and the partnership interests me. The wife is a young woman, vigorous and spirited – more in her than meets the eye.

'La Touche – on the face of things interested in nothing but horses but you find out. The wife is classy, a woman of strong character, exercises fascination on those she meets, which goes for us too.

'Over on the coast is a hotel, small but manicured, called Le Relais du Midi. Owner you all know – Robbie Zwemmer, a boy who has invested his money wisely. His wife is a tiny blonde who likes horses more than bikes. Neither of them find our deceased friend a pleasant subject of conversation. Bob, you'll coordinate all this. Everything blow-by-blow in the little book and given the stenographer here – typed transcripts available each morning. Midnight to eight in the morning free in principle, unless you've some sort of a lead – it's a healthy habit.'

The two young policemen of the criminal brigade were listening with faintly dazed suspicion.

'What I don't quite get, skipper, is exactly what we have to hope for.'

Van der Valk knocked the ash off his cigar and looked at this imbecile.

'Nobody knows,' blandly. 'While I am in this brigade you will call me sir. Mr Hendricks here was teaching me my business when you were sucking tit, and has worn out three hundred and seventy-eight pairs of boots on the tramlines. Us stupid old bastards are wondering whether a collision in outer space will release molecular energy and start hitting you with protons and neutrons, and if you don't understand that start going to the polytechnic on your free evenings. Since you won't be having any for some time ask these gentlemen to take you under the wing till you've got your knees brown.' They looked concussed but prudently said nothing.

'We will now adjourn. Before the next lesson the peasants will go to Vietnam and study on the spot what General Giap did to General Navarre, which is a good example how to handle people who think they are brighter than you are.' A guffaw from old Rademaker, the one who looked as though he had been on the railways for thirty years. The two local inspectors made silent promises to kick the arse of their subordinates at an early date and everyone went home to lunch – non-Commissaires round to Heck's Lunch Room: rank hath its privileges, as the captain said when they asked what the fifty-seven gin bottles were doing in his cabin.

Arlette had a shin of veal. She had buttered an oblong pyrex dish, put in a sliced carrot and onion, a clove of garlic, a tiny spike of rosemary and a glass of white wine, and buttered the lid lavishly before shoving the whole thing in the oven. She was washing her spinach, which she did under the bathroom shower, when he came in and noticed a good smell.

'I would like some alcohol for my machine, please; Suze, if there is any.'

'I don't want to be an old hen, but is that a good idea?'

He looked at her in a sober way.

'No, I'm not just being exuberant. We're faced with what could be a stupid fiasco. I've nothing to go on and it will be hard work.'

'But what are you talking about?'

'Sorry – of course. I was talking about Bernhard Fischer.'

'You aren't still going on with that! You're not going to tell me anything horrible, are you?' He had always had a rule about bringing work home. It was only since he had been shot that this had changed, but after all the whole nature of his work had changed.

'I must take the lid off the veal.' She had always agreed with his rule, refusing to sit listening. 'I am not an indigestion pill, whatever the women's magazines may say.'

'There isn't anything horrible. There isn't anything at all. Did you watch Marguerite, at that funeral?' tangentially.

'Of course. You want to know what she had on?'

'In a way. How do you see her – attractive to men?'

'Are you asking me?'

'She'd enjoy that, you think? Be alive to it?'

'Be pretty inhuman if she didn't.'

'But encourage it – give way to it?' They were still shouting through the open kitchen door.

'Try her and see,' tinkling ice-blocks into glasses and banging the fridge door.

'I just don't know. I might have to do some trotting round myself tonight – and other nights. Put some cold coffee in my flask, will you, doped up a tiny scrap with whisky, and give me a few codeines in case my leg starts being silly?'

She softened at once.

'Of course I will. Here's your drink – nice for me to have an excuse for having one too.' She never drank unless he did too, saying it would be unfair. 'We've half an hour before the boys get here so I needn't put the spinach on yet. I've new potatoes – terribly expensive still – I'm sorry; go on with what you were saying.'

'Lot of vitality,' he mumbled. 'Pretty, warm, still fresh – she's not much older than you are. That peculiar laziness . . . but I don't see her being vegetably contented with that lump of a chap. She might not be unfaithful to him, but . . . I don't see her happy with an exclusive woman's world either. One has the impression the other follows her everywhere wrapping her in cocoons, but would she be happy with no more than that? She might be just indulging the laziness and love of comfort.'

'Are you thinking she's lesbian – surely not?'

'Why are you sure?'

'I don't know – I just think she would be a man's woman.'

'That's exactly what I wanted to know.'

'Perhaps both. Likes girls too. Some are like that.'

'Are they?' smiling. She blushed, almost, and wriggled a little.

'Everybody likes her – women too – that's all I meant. Take Janine now – the women hate her and she hates them. You wouldn't find her being sweety in a corner with another woman.'

'No, I see that. And Marion?'

'I've no idea. If I had to be very honest I'd say she impresses me a bit. So – so reserved.'

'Self-sufficient?'

'Is anybody self-sufficient?'

'Suppose she were threatened in some way.'

'You mean would she hit them on the head?' asked Arlette.

'That would be a very stupid question, wouldn't it?' mildly.

'You mean anybody could – I know I could.'

'I mean she'd be competent about it. Not sudden, spontaneous – like you? Or?'

'She'd think it out. Marguerite might hit out – I don't know. Are you thinking a woman killed him?'

'I'm just keeping every possibility handy. I don't want to be like General Navarre and get caught with my pants down.' She laughed with affection. He didn't go about constructing theories about people – he wasn't that stupid.

'You know that Thurber drawing – the man who looks crossly at the dog and says, "Oh why don't you go out and track something"? I love you,' she said, meaning it. 'You'll never learn.'

His turn to get as near blushing as he ever would. It had been while 'going out and tracking something' that he had got shot. By a woman, too!

'I love you,' she said again.

The veal was good. The Muscadet less good; cheap because young and acid – the grapes hadn't had enough sunshine last year – but it did him no harm.

At a quarter past two he was in his office again, occupied but not for very long by a young, pleasant, attractive, successful married couple, his brother, and her sister, who had stolen over eight thousand guldens' worth of stuff from local shops. The stuff was all in their home, except for the generous presents they had made to friends and relatives.

What made them do it? Why eight transistor radios?

Was it that the things looked so attractive, so ingeniously miniaturized, so much the toy of the times? He had sympathy with people who could not resist a toy of the times, from dear little trains that made real smoke to eighteen-year-old featherheads with big breasts (making real smoke), but his sympathy put no brake on his professional wheels. That was what prisons were for. A sharp month in a nasty prison – Dutch prisons are not nasty enough – made a suitable corrective to self-indulgence.

Murder was a different matter. Prisons were admirable for the something-for-nothing brigade, who were frightened of nothing but getting their hands dirty. Putting murderers in prison, though . . . He had had various ideas throughout his life about how to deal with murderers – he was president of a special association called 'Murderers Eponymous' – but none of them had found favour in the eyes of penal authorities. One must not forget the bishops, as the English say.

You needed to be a good actor, didn't you, to be in the criminal brigade and get on well with all the murderers? A 'good mixer' – a 'good team man'. To understand someone who had been very poor and was now rich you needed to have been the same. You needed inspectors born in the back streets, who knew what it was like to have grown up in the depression – good, you still had them

– a few! You needed modern bright young men from bourgeois families, like those two idiot boys of his, who had never seen a dead man, let alone a pretty girl who had died alone, of haemorrhage following an abortion. . . . Good, you had them – plenty of them! But how did you manage both together? A woman like Marion and a woman like Janine, who simply didn't talk the same language . . .

He would have to go disguising himself tonight – he was going to cultivate an acquaintance with Dickie the painter: that was going to be his little contribution, and he hoped that it was a good idea.

He did not, after all, need any disguise; following the painter around, even several nights in succession, was surprisingly easy.

The fellow paid little attention to his surroundings, seeming entirely wrapped in his thoughts, or his fantasies, or whatever they were. Was that it? Perhaps he had spent his days looking at things which interested him, very closely and carefully, storing himself up to the brim, soaking himself to saturation. After this he would wrap himself in his cloak and meditate on the shimmer of light over skin, or whatever. . . . Later on he would distil, but first came the process of fermentation, during which impurities and irrelevances scummed up and heaved and turned into the thick crust of rubbish that the winegrowers call 'the hat', while sediment sank, and the turbid unattractive liquid clarified, and the sugar got lighter and grew wings as it turned into alcohol. Van der Valk was amused at his analogy. Perhaps when a painter took his brushes and made the first strokes on canvas it was alchemy, the heating of the still to the seventy-eight degrees at which alcohol takes leave of sugar-and-water. When all the alcohol had gone through the still there would be a painting. So much at the start, baskets full of fruit being gathered in, all mixed with stalks and leaf, dust and insects and copper-sulphate spray, and so little, apparently, to show at the end. To the casual onlooker it was just a field and a horse and a rider, just as to the onlooker it is just an orchard. Only to the distiller is it a bottle of mirabelle instead of just a basket of plums. And perhaps these dull passive-seeming visits to cafés and cinemas, Van der Valk found himself thinking, are just a process of fermentation. For obviously Dickie was a good painter.

Nearly every evening – Van der Valk taking post in a little black

Volkswagen in the dimness that was turning to darkness at eight o'clock – the painter would climb on the bus and go to the town. Van der Valk risked sitting on the bus under his nose and he still saw nothing, wrapped up under his hat.

He would go to cafés, and drink there an apple juice or a coffee, sitting staring for long minutes, his ascetic face pale and even distinguished under the dark short hair. He did not choose cheap, poor cafés – his favourites were the two or three solid, old-fashioned meeting-places in the very centre of the town that had remained unchanged for a hundred years – heavy and ornate mahogany, plush-upholstered, and great massive plated mono-grammed ashtrays. Places where hobbly old waiters brought quiet elderly gentlemen games of dominoes or chess. No billiard tables, but music at night made by a trio of elderly flatbreasted virgins in dowdy black velvet – violin, piano, and cello, and 'The Dollar Princess' or a depressingly dainty 'Ziguenerbaron'. Van der Valk liked these places too, where you got coffee in heavy scratched little pots, and a glass of water with it, and on the big marble centre table lay *Le Monde* and *Figaro*, the *Neue Zürcher Zeitung* and the *Corriere della Sera* and the *New York Herald-Tribune* rolled round solid wooden batons, and you sat for hours over very brown cognac – did it just look browner in this heavy yellowed light that was like a Caravaggio drowned in varnish? – and gazed back at layer after layer, generation after generation of cautious con-servatism, of Dutch Forsytes cooked in their juice like Agen plums.

What did the painter see in places such as these? He spoke to nobody. He watched no games. He read no papers. Shopgirls do not come into such, and though in the big harbour towns of Hol-land there will be a few discreetly overdressed whores of ripe years, the prim university towns inland are too cautious for such goings-on. Van der Valk knew three ladies of easy virtue, all very friendly with the police, all taking a keen interest in the Stock Exchange and owning their own houses, who wouldn't have dreamed of sitting in cafés.

After finishing his drink the painter would go for a walk, along the quiet streets of evening, along the narrow canals reflecting streetlamps and neon signs in their placid ribbons of water that seemed so clean at night. He walked slowly, so that Van der Valk, hip and all, had no trouble at all in holding the thread between thumb and finger. But nothing happened. The commissaris kept it up for a week and got more and more fascinated by these pilgrimages.

During the daytime he worked steadily and it needed little detective work to keep an eye on that. He did his distilling in the little shed he rented from Francis, coming out occasionally to stretch and gaze enraptured at a tree the way he did at the huge hideous chandelier in the Café de la Bourse. Sometimes he would take a pencil and a sheet of paper and sketch something. He had an old broken-down couch in there, on which he often lay down and had a little sleep. Sometimes he would sit on a tree-stump in the corner of the field and watch the riders practising jumps with the same absent look. At slack times, when it was rainy, he often went into the house, asked for a cup of coffee, and sat reading the paper while it got cold, paying no heed to anyone. There was nothing to see, and nothing to write on bits of paper to be turned into a typed transcript by police stenographers. Once he came with a painting wrapped in brown paper, a thing done for one of the 'millionaires', and there was the usual jargon about frames and varnish and where to hang it; he seemed a competent salesman.

People had learned to pay no heed to Van der Valk. He often pottered about the riding-school, and the regulars had grown used to it. If anyone were showing signs of unease at his continued wandering around they were very small signs.

One afternoon he came upon the painter leaning over the fence, making pencil strokes upon a sheet of paper that did not seem much to do with a young horse being held by a stable-boy on a lunging rein, while Francis watched, fists on hips and his switch playing up and down slowly behind his back, like the tail of a cat watching a gluttonous big blackbird. He stood alongside the thin clean hand that sketched, got no reaction, and said, 'Tell me something about Stubbs, can you?'

Dickie did not look up, took another piece of paper, made two rapid lines that became suddenly Francis' boots and breeches, and said calmly, 'You interested in Stubbs? Remarkable! What d'you want to know?'

'I'm just getting interested in these animals, since I'm spending time out here. Stubbs is the only horse painter I've ever heard of much. And Géricault – or is it Delacroix? – I get them mixed up.'

The painter was quite accommodating, even polite.

'Not much in common. Géricault paints bones, skeletons, likes

138

horses in violent and distorted positions – rear, prance, hup, charge – clippety-clop. He was very good at anatomy and cannon-smoke. Started doing other more interesting things – died young.'

'Stubbs is English, I take it?'

'I don't know – English, American. Paints muscles, all the nerves exposed even if the skin's on. Arabs – can always tell a Stubbs horse – small delicate head, big long arched neck, very g-rr-aceful. Were six Arab stallions imported by some goddam duke to improve bloodstock. They stand there very beautiful, in fields or by houses, sometimes with a carriage. No action in particular. Sometimes there are grooms, little Moorish page-boys in fancy dress, put in just to make it more exciting and flatter the duchess.'

'No interest in people?'

'Not an awful lot. Dead right too. Where did you hear about Stubbs? Not much of a subject for police; they're too busy pinching things that belong to the poor to make it easier for the rich.'

'Some gallery, I suppose.'

'You don't see them much in galleries – most in private ownership. There are quite a few phonies though, most by some English chap called Hall, but if you know horses you can tell the difference. Now bugger off, will you – I can't breathe with other people heaving deep sighs just behind me.'

Van der Valk buggered off, obediently.

'Damned false position to be in,' Francis was complaining. 'Complain and like as not they'd think I had a bad conscience or something. If the fellow would do something I wouldn't mind as much, but that endless pottering around gets on my nerves. God knows what he sees or hears. Each time he goes off with that mysterious air I tell myself it's finished at last and then damn me if he doesn't turn up again three days later.'

'Darling, are you talking to me, or just to yourself?'

'Both of us.'

'You'll have to turn the sound down; I can't understand a thing.'

'I like this music. Look at that chap twiddlin' away at his saxophone or whatever it is.'

'I said Turn the Sound Down.'

'Well you don't have to shout at me. I think that police fellow is just wanting to taper off without losin' face. Make a dignified exit, what.'

'He thinks we've something to hide, maybe.'

'Who's got something to hide?' aggrievedly. If Marion had something to hide it was her look-out.

'Everybody's got something to hide, in his mind.'

'I'm damsure I haven't. 'Cept maybe the prices I pay in Hanover. Don't usually like that – damned hotels – but this time I'm lookin' forward to it. Stay away a week. Time I'm back, maybe the fuss will have petered out. They can't go on worryin' for ever, not about a chap like Fischer. Who cares?'

'You want me to come with you?'

'No no, you've got to stay here and keep an eye on things. I can't trust any of these people – there's talk about swamp fever again.'

'Talk . . .'

'Yes, talk – still, it's died down, hasn't it?'

'Fischer you're talking about – or swamp fever?'

'Damn it, Marion, you know perfectly well what I mean. There's another thing – I have to work like a fool for every penny and these policemen have nothing to do but stroll about. Government employees . . . I see these people are messin' about with their survey again – they did one only six months ago!'

'Maybe they got it wrong.'

'Would be just like them. Walkin' about with those red and white pickets and gettin' their sums wrong. And the taxpayer foots the bill, as usual.'

'I certainly think it would be a good idea to go to Hanover a few days early. Give you a good break. You need that. It might be better weather too – Stephen was down in Wiesbaden; he said it was lovely there – all the blossom out.'

'Blossom – what blossom? Ha – this is always a good programme.'

The 'observation' seemed to be making little progress. Francis and Marion La Touche had friends in most nights. The inner ring: a company lawyer and his wife; a paint manufacturer who cared deeply about paint, to listen to him at the office, but much more deeply about horses, to hear him at the manège. An elderly hussar colonel, with an impressive façade, like the Iron Duke, that made you wonder what there was behind: there was nothing much, except an honorary court position, Grand Ecuyer or something to the House of Orange, involving an appearance in gold-laced full fig two or three times a year: the Opening to the States General, Royal weddings, Royal birthday parties. . . . In his Grace-and-Favour quarters out at Het Loo he refused to have any television, he said, but Marion believed he really came to look at theirs. Stephen, a show-jumping rider, son of a wealthy farmer and one of the well-known faces of the European circus. A pleasant young man with fair hair and muscular athletic figure, straight and proud in snow-white stock and the velvet cap he would sweep off for a deep elegant bow, with one hand controlling the horse, caracoling in a camera-conscious manner. . . . Born to it: you couldn't imagine Robbie Zwemmer doing that. He had a sentimental attachment to Marion, but liked even better having long orgies with Francis, explaining to one another why one show-jumping champion after another had a bad style.

The group played bridge, drank tea, weak brandy punch, lemonade, ate little cakes and salted biscuits, watched the television, gossiped, discussed horses' illnesses and their own, the best ways of worming dogs, swamp fever. It was very dull.

Things were enlivened by Francis going to Hanover to buy horses. Preparations for this filled a whole week, and there was a great fuss whether he should go by plane, or by train, or by car – Francis was the type that insists on open cars, because in closed ones you Asphyxiate (he had a shabby, splendid, noisy old Borgward cabriolet, but once in it he would need many caps and scarves, and complain continually about draughts).

They did not bother following him to Germany, of course, and never knew whether he had created a whirlpool in the placid waters of the local call-girl system.

Marion stayed at home, quietly, and certainly did not misbehave herself with the handsome Stephen. She went sometimes to Amsterdam in her Mini-Cooper to buy some clothes, have her hair done, drink a cup of coffee in the Hotel Polen with an acquaintance. If she ever did anything fishy she did it in London, concluded the policemen. There was nothing slinking about any of her movements in Holland, and if Francis, enjoying his change of air, was doing any slinking in Hanover she showed neither disquiet nor curiosity.

Came a day when she put them in a great state of excitement

because she did behave furtively. She drove her little Mini-Cooper to Rotterdam and hid it, and while they skulked with bated breath she had an assignation with a young man. Disappointing when with extreme ease they found that it was the son, the one under a cloud – Van der Valk had not been able to find out just what was fishy about that half-dropped charge. . . . The young man had come from South America for business in Bremen and Danzig, and his ship had called in at Rotterdam. He showed great affection for Marion, she felt great affection for him, and all policemen present felt slightly ashamed of themselves, though they wondered whether she had encouraged Francis to stay dallying extra days in Hanover.

Marguerite, said the reports, was only faintly more interesting. There was at least more movement, and the little Renault and littler Simca had to do a lot of buzzing to keep up with her smart Fiat fifteen hundred. She had needs. Needs to fly about and buy things – a tremendous, almost neurotic quantity of things got bought, most of them serving little purpose. Not just clothes, though there was, they noticed, a need to be admired.

Miss Groenveld was generally brought along on these expeditions, apparently to serve as Chorus. And to Admire. She had decided views about clothes, and what-really-suits-you-darling. About such things as antiques, expensive bric-à-brac, not pictures or furniture, she had less to say. As for the restaurant, it ran very smoothly, and with the summer coming along business increased every day, and so did the bank account, despite the numerous punctures made in it.

'Hallo.'

'Hallo – ah, it's you, Marguerite. Very agreeable to hear your voice again.'

'You haven't been ill or anything?'

'By no means. But I did not want to seem intrusive. Anyway – the telephone . . . '

'That was very sensible; one never knows who might answer.'

'I was most distressed to hear . . . '

'Oh, Ian, you don't know the half of it. We've had the police prowling about – they held a post-mortem and everything.'

'My poor girl, how perfectly horrible for you – I am so sorry. Is there anything I can do?'

'Take me out and cheer me up, if you will.'

'Is that altogether wise – so soon . . . ?'

'It seems to have died down – they must surely be satisfied. One can't tell. There was a rumour about a bang made by a plane, but they wouldn't either confirm or deny it. The man in charge seems to be still hanging about the manège rather a lot.'

'Has he worried you?'

'No-o. Whenever I've seen him he's been polite, in a soapy sort of way. I'd like to tell you all about it really – it would be such a weight off my mind. You could advise me.'

'I don't know that my advice would be worth much in the circumstances . . . but if I can be of any service to you . . . '

'Oh yes, Ian, please.'

'Well, I'm most joyful to hear you . . . I had thought you might not wish to see any more of me.'

'Oh, Ian, don't be silly.'

'Shall we perhaps meet for dinner in the little place? Seven-thirty suit you?'

'It would be perfect. Saskia will be in the restaurant.'

'I look forward immensely to seeing you. Till then, shall we say?'

'Marvellous.'

'I've rather a nice jade figure from the Manchu Dynasty I'm looking forward to showing you.'

'How wonderful. Good-bye for now, then.'

More amusing to the police than all the shopping was Marguerite's need not only to be admired, but by a cavalier more romantic than Miss Groenveld. All unbeknown to this lady the young woman went out about twice a week, all the way to The Hague, where she met an admirer, a middle-aged gentleman to do with a British Cultural and Commercial Mission (fortunately he had private means as well). He came to their meetings gallantly bare-headed, with a carnation in his buttonhole and more in his hand for the lady. They would have dinner in a small restaurant and go dancing in a hotel. If there was a courtship it was restrained and leisurely: there was no adultery. The friendship seemed to date from some months at least before Bernhard's death – had there been, then, these discreet but not hidden gallivantings? The admirer had occasional fleshly hankerings, but was most correct about expressing them. Once or twice there were tender kisses left upon a wrist, and once on an upper arm – but that was late at night, and he had drunk quite a lot of cognac after dinner. Marguerite always behaved quite naturally. The friendship was a sentimental one, but not aggressively flirtatious, and when one got near enough to overhear the conversations were mostly about antiques – the gentleman was an amateur of porcelain plates.

Miss Groenveld stayed home and ran the restaurant efficiently on these occasions. If she made scenes when Marguerite came home they were not noisy.

There was something mildly lesbian in the relationship between them, to be sure. A bit of prowling around and peeping showed that Saskia washed and ironed all Marguerite's clothes, that they wandered in and out of bathrooms when the other was inside; they seemed to stick to separate bedrooms judging by light, and if they were a bit kissy and cuddly together, what then ? All very even; all very normal and, on paper, very unexciting.

The extreme normality and evenness of people's lives, illustrated in these reports, was underlined by Rob and Janine. They too generally had friends in at night, mostly after a party of six or seven in the restaurant. The bicycle boys: a Belgian team manager; a fizzy-lemonade king, who invested in the riders and made excellent business out of their wearing his label on their shirts and ostentatiously drinking the obnoxious product at the end of the stages (they didn't drink it – what they drank was Perrier water, but they filled their mouths and spat it out generously over anyone unlucky enough to be in range). Riders too – it was the season of the Belgian classics that come in a bunch before the Four Days of Dunkerque announce the major business of the summer season: the 'Dauphiné', the 'Midi Libre', the Giro and the Tour. Riders were picked and dropped, for the teams, politicking went on, tactics were discussed, quite a lot of this over Rob's dinner-tables and coffee-table.

Janine enjoyed these meetings; in her element, one would say, with the jargon she knew amid accents even thicker than hers was. But she seemed not to have friends of her own, and seemed often solitary in this throng. The group often had wives with them but Janine, restrained with the men and not given to backslapping, had nothing much to say to the women. Still, the group did not split into cock party and hen party, and, since the riders were in training, drank little but beer and went to bed early. Janine went to Dunkerque for the Four Days, but Rob didn't. He got offered money to comment on races for papers and radio programmes, but he was too busy with the restaurant, and turned them all down. About once every three weeks he took a weekend off, according to a formula of his own.

'I'm feeling the need – my legs are rusty.'

'What about Germany – that nice woodland the other side of Oldenburg or is it Paderborn – you know.'

'I mentioned it to Jean last night and he said they'd be down in the Ardennes for the Liège-Bastogne and why didn't I come.'

'Oh yes, I'd like that.'

'Not worried about this police nonsense still, are you, darling?'

'Why should I – nothing to do with us, after all.'

'No, of course – just that it might have upset you, I thought – not very pleasant, that cloud of gossip after the fellow died.'

'Oh I was just nervous and silly – a bit jaded after the winter. I've come round to your way of thinking – it was just curiosity brought him here, I guess. I was out with Arlette yesterday afternoon – well, she wouldn't be so friendly if there was anything – he's her husband, after all.'

'He might not tell her all his business. Nor what he was thinking.'

'If he thought that anyone had really killed Thingummy he wouldn't be letting his own wife . . . '

'I'm not bothering about it – just glad to see you aren't. All right then – Ardennes? I'll get Joey to put the bike in shape.'

All the watchers were caught bending by Rob getting up at an unearthly hour – a weekend, too . . . They were puzzled at his having left the Ferrari behind, concluded irrefutably that he was with Janine in the BMW, found this, with some trouble, two hundred kilometres away that afternoon in Limburg, and were upset to find her alone. It took some time before it sank in that Rob had done two hundred kilometres on the bike, just for the pleasure of it, for fresh air, to stop his legs rusting away.

He and Janine spent the night in a country hotel that was no more than a pub really, and went on the next day into Belgium, finishing up in Marche, where there was a hotel full of oak panelling, stuffed wild boars, and some very grandiose Burgundy, which both Rob and the police enjoyed greatly. He spent the next day asleep in Janine's car, with her driving, and one of the 'follow-up' station wagons that carry riders' spare bikes on the roof brought his back to the coast, the following week . . .

That week too there was a minuscule incident involving Janine. The bicycle circus had all gone to Brest for circuit riding against the clock, nobody was left in Holland, and the watcher had been ready to slope off, seeing them installed for a domestic evening in the flat. It must have been eleven when Janine, in trousers and a short jacket, appeared suddenly, and jumped into her car which went off with a roar, so that he had to rush for the little Simca, a thing with determined but noisy acceleration: he managed to keep within striking distance till she turned on to a main road and began driving. The road had traffic on it still, was not lit at all between towns – and there is nothing that looks so like the rear lights of a car as the rear lights of another car. He followed what turned out to be a Mercedes 230 coupé, and wished he had been given another Simca to follow – the lamps are arranged in large distinctive circles.

'I don't think it of much consequence,' said Van der Valk. 'She's the type that does take the car out for a flip at night, simply because they're restless and nervous and don't feel like sleep.'

There were no significant meetings between any of the three households, everything that passed on telephone lines was of an almost painful rectitude, and the watchers were beginning to put notes of apology into their voices when they spoke to Van der Valk. The Officer of Justice seemed to have forgotten all about it, since he never mentioned it.

Van der Valk had not even known that Mr Stomach, as the painter called his landlord in Warmond, possessed a motorbike. A placid individual, who spent his evenings in the most conventional style of a village café, dawdling about the bar, adjusting the television when it didn't need adjusting, playing billiards with his customers, drinking four or maybe five beers, fixing up the odd traveller (delayed on his way back to the city) with a meal, polishing glasses, rubbing up the chrome on the coffee-machine. When the painter, who hadn't gone to town that evening, appeared wheeling the motorbike across the pavement Van der Valk thought it must be an illusion – he was getting more than tired of his vigils, and had more than once had to eat codeines to stop his leg nagging at him. He woke up instantly.

The Volkswagen had no trouble keeping close but not too close: the motorbike was a lightweight affair, one-twenty-five c.c., with a distinctive loud noise. They headed towards the coast; for the first time in ten days Van der Valk got rid of the feeling that he had to grip his patience very tightly with both hands. The way he was doing – without realizing – to the steering-wheel.

The sand dunes behind the coast of Holland are like Chile on a map of South America, a narrow belt down from Den Helder at the northern tip to the Hook of Holland, the southern jut where the delta begins and the New Waterway runs up to Rotterdam. All along this line they are pierced at only one major point, the canalized waterway that takes ocean-going ships through from Ijmuiden to Amsterdam. Through them lead only a handful of roads, giving access to the beach resorts. A main road, lined with large villas, runs out from The Hague to Scheveningen, and another from Haarlem to Zandvoort. But most of the roads wind for solitary stretches.

The dunes are nothing exciting – a miniature Andes of fine cold silvery sand, anchored by wiry dunegrass and planted with little stands of fir. There are plenty of brambles, coarse ferns, heaths, and a few small, pretty wild flowers. Buried now in sand are the bunkers and pillboxes of Hitler's Atlantic Wall, filled with drifts where they have not been deliberately buried by the Dutch military authorities. What exactly is left is not easy to judge, for access is strictly forbidden. Indeed as a park the dunes are poor fun, barricaded against the public by a lot of barbed wire.

If you take off your hat and pay money, there are places where you can buy a ticket allowing you to follow certain paths. You discover surprises, like the little canal and the waterworks which once, wistfully long ago, supplied Amsterdam with clean sand-filtered drinking water.

You can stray off the paths into the bracken – you can even sit down and light a cigarette, but it will not be long before you are detected and expelled by one of a swarm of terrible official ogres lurking everywhere for this purpose: rude of mouth, heavy of hand, and loving to lick pencils and write everything down to your bloodgroup in a tiny vile notebook.

Of course at night one can get in, without paying, and without

being caught, either. There are weak spots in the wire. . . . In all the
seaside villages there are young men to whom a pious government
forbids smuggling and wrecking and such normal seaside pursuits,
who are forced to seek amusement from moving silently in the
dunes, and setting a wire for the occasional rabbit.

The motorbike stopped suddenly, warily, and Van der Valk had
to go sailing innocently past for over half a kilometre, well round
the next curve, before he could stop and turn the Volkswagen
round with lights doused. He got out rubbing his nose – a kilometre back they had passed, stranded vaguely on a patch of rough
grass between the bicycle track and the barbed wire, the stubby
silhouette of a little Simca, but there are many such in Holland.
He performed the feat of shutting a small car's door without
slamming it, and then had to open it all over again to get a pair
of twelve-fifty night-binoculars.

Cars parked on the road would arouse little comment for some
time at least; it was only ten, not late even here. Sooner or later a
patrolling policeman would want to know what they were doing
there. His leg no longer hurt, now that it had work to do, but he
hoped he would not have much tramping in the dunes to do, above
all with no stick. Walking, he had time to realize that in the soft
sand a stick would be useless – more trouble than the stupid leg
was.

He found the motorbike easily enough, though it was hidden in
a patch of fern. Getting through the wire was less easy; mustn't
tear his breeches, for that would make Arlette cross.

There wasn't any question of flitting from leaf to leaf like an elf,
either. He had to find patches of cover that gave a view, crouch
down, and use the glasses to sweep the shadows. Somewhere was
a moon, that had given wan light earlier after the twilight faded,
but was now drowned in the cloud that flowed overhead in dark
ragged masses. The sand was damnably cold, the fern damnably
damp, the wind damnably chilly, and his leg was a pest. He was
forty-five: to enjoy this performance one had to be young, active,
and if possible in love. There was nothing, he supposed, incom-
patible between that and having an expensive sports car, a horse,
and two mink coats.

He saw them before he found his inspector. Janine's hair had a
glimmer, a paler shadow than that of the head beside her. He
circled around, covered by wind and night sounds, making not

much more noise than a large lame rabbit that had to walk with a stick. Verbiest, the youngest of his staff, was well laid up in a tussock of dune-grass, nearer than he himself would have tried to get, but not near enough to overhear whispers. Verbiest was not startled, since he saw and heard Van der Valk over the last half-dozen metres, but he was surprised.

'How did you know, sir?'

'I've been sitting on that fellow's tail for the last fortnight,' getting his leg out from under him. 'Where's her car?'

'She came by bike.'

'You'd better get back – I don't want a lot of police busybodies wondering who the cars belong to – mine's about half a kilometre up towards the coast. Did you hear his bike?'

'Yes.'

'See where he left it?'

'Yes.'

It was an excuse. The most nosyparker of policemen would do no more than hover by a felonious car till its damned fornicating owner got back. But he felt embarrassment at Verbiest being there. One person lying there squinting through binoculars was business – two together was intolerable. He guessed that Verbiest was as glad to go as he was to see him go.

Not that they were making love or anything – they were arguing – but he had an ignominious feeling, and he wasn't going to sit shivering here waiting for it to paralyze him. As things were, it was not as wide as a barn door, but it would serve. He stood up, his leg painful, and walked forward. There was a startled movement and he stopped.

'Very sorry,' in a normal voice, 'but some explanations are owing here.'

They had got up at once, Janine standing stock-still, head hanging, caught with her hand in the jampot and much as though she had never expected anything better. The boy stood loose and in gear, like a boxer. It must have been recognition of Van der Valk – the chap with the gammy leg! – that made him lose his head and run. What use did he think that was? Not that the startled fawn lark would make Van der Valk blow any whistles – he hadn't any whistle, and didn't feel the least like yelling. He just hoped the boy would be panicked enough to run for his motorbike.

Poor Janine – she was quite numb. He took her arm gently.

'Come. I'll give you a lift – we'll go and find Rob.'

Back on the road two figures were waiting, both breathing fast.

'You take this character back to town, Verbiest. If he's obstreperous tie him up with a piece of string or something.'

'I've a pair of cuffs in the car.' The things these young policemen carried about with them!

'Very well. Lock him up; I'll see him in the morning.'

He walked down the road with Janine. She evidently expected to be handcuffed too, flung in a cell and shouted at, treated – not with brutality – certainly with callousness. She was even more scared by his quiet manner than she would have been by the handcuffs. She would have understood that – she deserved to be punished, and she was waiting for the punishments to start.

'Does Rob know you're out?' opening the car door.

'Yes.'

'He wasn't curious?'

'I often got out at night, walking, or on the bike. I've been in the dunes often at night.'

'Yes, it's nice. When there are no people.' She hung her head.

A night porter in the hotel looked with no more than faint curiosity.

'Rob will have gone to bed,' she said timidly.

'That is what you call trust,' without sarcasm, but she winced. He thumped on the bedroom door like a fireman.

'Rob? Come on out. Janine's here, nothing wrong with her, but a crisis has blown up. Van der Valk here.'

The man was startled out of deep sleep, but lost no time. He appeared almost at once, having taken just enough time to put his face under the cold tap. Not tousled, and with his mind collected. He looked from his wife to the policeman.

'I can see this isn't a joke. Sit down; tell me quietly.'

'I have to take her in, I'm afraid. I don't know how long for. My report will go tomorrow to the Officer of Justice, and the day after he'll want to see her himself. It depends on him what will happen to her – he might decide she has to be kept.'

'And what's the charge?' said Rob coolly. Janine stood biting her nails. 'You want a drink or something?'

'I'd like a glass of water if you have one.'

'Evian all right?'

'Anything. A charge . . . they haven't any meaning. I could write down homicide without necessarily suspecting she killed him. I might write suspected guilty knowledge, even complicity. But the magistrate decides what charge is actually made, if any.'

'Are you talking about Bernhard? But you can't arrest her on any charge – she knows nothing whatever about it.'

'I found her in the dunes, with a chap. I'm not accusing her of having a lover or anything – I think they were cooking up a tale together. The chap is the painter –you know, I think. I always did wonder where your interest in Stubbs came from.'

Rob stared stubbornly, a flush growing on his face, but his eyes clear and firm, looking straight into Van der Valk's.

'She knows nothing about it,' he repeated. 'This painter – I've heard of him. So what? He doesn't interest me. What Janine thought or did has no importance. If you want to arrest anyone, go ahead and arrest me. I'm more likely to have killed Fischer than she is; I know more about him than she does. You bloody police always arrest the wrong person, and you have to pick Janine – I'm not having that.'

Van der Valk drank his water slowly – it was beautifully cold. He put the glass down carefully and wiped his mouth in a vulgar way on the back of his hand.

'I'll take you too, if you insist. The more the merrier. You might have something interesting to tell me, at that. But I have to take her, you can't talk me out of that one, and that is my last word.'

A vein showed in Rob's forehead; he was getting very angry, and holding it under a thin thread of control.

'I could break your neck.'

'You could have broken Bernhard's neck. You might have, but there are reasons why I don't think you did. He might have been a blackmailer, and there's some support for the opinion that he was, but did he blackmail you? I don't think so. What for, money? He was in no particular need of money, and he would have had to account for it to his wife, who knew just what he made and what he had. And you would kill him on that account? Don't mess things up; it can't help. In the end, she may be called as a witness and no more.'

'No,' Janine broke in violently. 'Not just a witness.'

'You're not going to tell me as well it was you killed Bernhard,' deflatingly

'I knew, and I kept my mouth shut.'

'Knew what? Who killed him?'

'Knew – knew he'd been killed.'

'Ah. Dickie told you, did he? And then twisted your arm to make you keep quiet? And how did he know?'

'I don't know.'

'And why did he tell you?'

'I'd – slept with him.' Neither of the two men believed any of this.

'Rubbish,' said Rob. 'She's saying any fantasy that comes into her head, and she's saying it to protect me.'

'Why?' mildly.

'Because she knows I killed him.'

'Oh. You killed him, did you?' Van der Valk seemed impressed with this admission, and as if thinking it over. 'What with?'

'I don't even know. I didn't stop to look. Whatever it was I just threw it away. Something I picked up – he was trying to blackmail Janine. I shut his dirty mouth and I'd do it again tomorrow. Now take me in and leave her alone.'

'Very well, I'll take you in,' mild. 'Since it'll help her, I'll agree. Means sitting on the back seat of a Volkswagen.'

'You leave her here.'

'No, you bloody idiot. Stop acting the goat.'

'Rob, stop,' said Janine, and this time she did burst into tears.

Janine was left in the outside office, where the duty brigadier, at the sight of his superior officer, had slid his volume of cowboy stories under an impressive heap of forms. Van der Valk switched lights on in his office, pointed Rob to a chair, sat at the desk, opened a drawer to get paper out, and stopped suddenly dead, staring. His expensive cavalry ballpoint was sitting on the desk looking at him; some detective had recovered it from the street where it had fallen and lovingly returned it. He looked at it, put it back in his pocket, and got a cheap plastic one out of the drawer. This failed to write. He sighed and went back to the expensive one.

He wrote a few lines at the top of the paper. What a bore these things were. Name, christian name, date and place of birth, domicile and profession. He scrabbled in the drawer, looking for cigars; there weren't any, and he lit a cigarette instead.

'You want to make a statement?'

'I don't know.'

'You got some sort of story – something I'm likely to believe?'
'No.'

'All right. Unwind. The painter's here, in a cell, thinking up lies to tell, like everybody else, but he's safe in my pocket. He knew all right who killed Fischer. He heard or saw something or someone – he was in his shed affair he has there, working, about thirty metres away. And what he knows, he'll tell me. Right? Don't worry overmuch about protecting Janine. The worst that's likely to be against her is that she didn't know how to tell me what she knew.'

'And that's not too bad?'

'Of course it's not. But she was with this painter. Furtively, as though they'd agreed to meet to work out a good tale, since I was still hanging round the riding-school. I've been waiting for something of this sort.'

'You've really got him?'

'Since I tell you,' impatiently.

'Then ask away. I'll tell you what I can,' dully. His voice struck the policeman.

'You aren't really thinking she slept with him, are you?'

'I'd like to believe she wasn't, but since you ask – I'm afraid yes – she might have been.' Van der Valk was a good deal taken aback though he tried not to show it. It didn't fit in with what he thought he knew of Janine! He thought about it, putting the point of the pen on the desk, sliding his thumb and finger down it, letting it turn in his hand, and doing it again. Thinking, calling himself a fool.

'Remember when I met you first? – we were talking about the bikes. You're a champion – you've got everything. Yet you aren't quite happy with it all, might I be right? That it could have been better?'

'I was as good as it was given me to be,' blunt. 'Never in the very top rank – you've got to win a Tour – you've got to win two. And how many got there? Coppi, Bobet – you can count them on one hand.'

'I remember your using the word aristocracy – it struck me.'

'What's that got to do with it? There's isn't any aristocracy – the real one is something you're born in – you can't make it any other way.'

'Something your children can do but you can't.'

'Yes.' A slow careful look. 'I haven't got any grudge against Janine, you know.'

'You feel any grudges against someone like Francis La Touche, who is what you call born in it?'

'Why should I? I belong on a bike – that's where I look good. A few years ago I thought I'd like to play tennis, and joined a club. I just wanted to play tennis, but I got mixed up with more of these butchers that think tennis is a game for gentlemen. They wanted to get into the act. I was being lumped along with them so I gave it up.'

'And the hotel?'

'What about it?'

'You aimed it at a wealthy, snobbish group of customers – the riding-school crowd.' Rob looked at him almost pityingly for so much naïveté.

'It's a shop. As long as they're paying you money they don't find you getting above yourself. Just don't mix with them on their own ground.'

'And Janine? She was snubbed. She reacts her own way, putting on that act of "I'm only a Belgian peasant, and proud of it, and I wave it like a flag and don't care who sees it". But she went on riding. That's what one has to do, no? Pay no heed.'

'She loves horses. She wanted a horse more than she did clothes or a fur or a car or anything. She'd give it all up to keep the horse.'

'Like the painter.'

Rob stared sullenly, leaning back in the chair, his hands pushed aggressively in his pockets.

'What about the painter?'

'They've that in common. The fellow's a real artist – he loves horses more than anything. Like Francis says – horses don't cheat. Horses can mean more than human beings. What I don't understand is that Janine is a very loyal person – and not just to her horse.'

Rob took a long time answering; Van der Valk lit another cigarette.

'It was my fault,' at last, leadenly. 'I didn't see things her way. She used to come home at first and tell me about the stupid stiff women with their airs, talking all gracious and affected. I told her to stop it – it made me mad – to get out of that dump. She wouldn't, said she didn't care. That they looked on a horse like a witch on a broomstick, and she didn't give threepence for them. I thought I'd make it easier for her: if she didn't care why should I? I bought this place on the coast – a sort of challenge, see? And then she was furious I hadn't told her – she wanted to go back to France – she'd always wanted that, she said. I would have liked that too – I didn't have the nerve, and just out of obstinacy I stayed here then. I wanted to stick it out, to prove that this was my place where I belonged, that I could show them – all those ones that laughed and said I was just a peasant on a bike and would never be able to run a place like a restaurant. They liked my money, though – they rolled up their sleeves and moved in when they thought they saw how to take it away. That the money came from bikes – that didn't worry them.'

'Janine?'

'She wouldn't talk to me. Then she came – some months after. Said she'd changed her mind. Said she wanted to pack the riding-school up, sell the horse, everything. I was mad at her then – called her a coward. I was working like a bastard, and I wasn't giving up then. They were waiting to pull my shirt, give me the elbow. If I'd sold this place then I wouldn't even have got what I'd paid for it – they'd have seen to that. If I sold it now,' drily, 'I'd get double. I wouldn't let Janine stop then. She kept saying she was fed up, didn't want to go on – and she wouldn't give any reason.'

Light suddenly dawned.

'She'd met the painter.'

'I reckon so, yes. He turned up one day at the coast. Told me he'd got to know her, very silky. I never suspected a thing.'

'What did he want?'

'To make a big portrait, Janine and the horse, for a fancy price. It's his trick – he makes money that way.'

'I know.'

'I sent that notion overboard. But – well – ' defensively, angrily, 'I like painting, I've even bought a couple. I wasn't prejudiced against him – fellow has to earn his living. His stuff might be good. I gave him a drink, I said maybe I'd be interested in other stuff of his – how did you guess all this?'

'I didn't. I thought there'd been some meeting between you – a remark you made about Stubbs.'

'He told me about Stubbs. I had thought of buying a small

picture of a horse – even I could see it was good,' bitterly. 'To make it up with Janine.'

'How does Bernhard the boor from Bavaria come into the picture?'

'Don't ask me.'

'He never came near you?'

'If he had I'd have broken his neck for him, big as he was – fat slob. I would, I tell you. If I'd just known. Janine never told me.'

'The best thing you can possibly do,' said Van der Valk, jabbing the cavalry ballpoint at the air in a schoolmasterly way, 'is to go home and pretend you don't know a damn thing.'

'I stay here. I'll stand by Janine no matter what. And if she killed him I'll take whatever's coming to her.'

'You'll do what you're told,' acidly. 'This is quite enough of a ballsup without you making it worse. The moment you start hanging about, the press will draw conclusions.'

'Can I see her?'

'No.'

Rob threw him a bitter look.

'Being a champion means knowing when you're beaten as well. And not throwing a little tantrum. Just stay quiet, act normal. No matter who asks you and what, know nothing. I'll deal with any pressmen.'

Rob stood up; he had dignity. He had more to say but he turned and went out. Van der Valk arranged a few fresh sheets of paper neatly on his desk and picked up his telephone.

'Madame Zwemmer.'

A policeman in uniform held the door for Janine looking absurdly young and vulnerable in her short furry jacket and black ski-trousers. Van der Valk stood up and went for a short walk around the furniture.

'Can I sit down?' She had forgotten her French and the exaggerated accent; she spoke in the natural voice of her childhood, soft and not unattractive. The only thing wrong with her, he thought, is that she is a little peasant girl who looks like a little princess and she doesn't know how to deal with it.

'Of course – I was rude, I'm sorry.' He paced as far as the window. Nothing to be seen but darkness, a peaceful Dutch street, brick-paved, an old-fashioned ornate lamp-post of cast iron, painted a rather pretty pale blue – he had never noticed that before.

So accustomed one got to the greys and greens of Holland.

'Have a cigarette.' She looked wan, poor little wretch.

'Where's Rob?'

'I sent him home.'

'I wanted to tell him – how mean I've been.'

'I know?'

'You know?'

'A bit – not enough. You're going to help me understand. I can see why you got friendly with Dickie in the first place. But what made you see him tonight?'

'I was scared he'd tell Rob.'

'That you'd slept with him? Rob wouldn't have believed it.'

'He'd have had to. He could have proved it.'

'Prove it? How?'

'I have a tattoo. On my hip – I can't wear a bikini. Nobody knows, except Rob, and . . . it's a rose. In blue. It was done when I was young. I mean I had it done.'

'I see. Dickie threatened to do that?'

'I thought he might.'

'You mean he asked to see you? Why?'

'I don't know. He asked had you been on to me, and if I knew had you been on to Rob?'

'He's a bit of a hard boy.'

'Yes.' Simply.

'How did Bernhard find out?'

'We were in the White Horse. I was alone and I couldn't speak to Dick – he was with a whole group, chatting them up – the way he knew how. . . . I was very lonely and unhappy, and I suppose a bit jealous. I couldn't think how to approach him. Then I saw him look at me, and I wrote a note and screwed it up, and was going to just pass and slip it him, and then those women came back from the powder room and I flicked it, pretending it was a joke. But he let it fall – I don't know why. I think he was just being cruel – he is cruel, you know. I didn't dare pick it up – it would just have drawn attention. I let it lie. I thought the girls would sweep it up or drop it in an ashtray. Bernhard must have been watching. I suppose he must have picked it up.'

'He told you.'

'He came over at the manège and said he'd keep any date I cared to make – in such a greasy way – I was disgusted. I knew he must have found it.'

'He said he'd tell Rob?'

'No.'

'He just left you to draw conclusions?'

'I don't know.'

'Why not tell Rob anyway?'

'I don't know. I half thought of it. I would have. He was being awfully nice to me too, after I'd been bitchy to him. That was why I didn't, I suppose. To tell him then, that I'd got into trouble – that was all it needed, I thought. So I did nothing. I thought of telling Arlette.'

'I wish you had.'

'After – I realized that you were whatdyoucallem, investigating, I was scared to.'

'You told Dick?'

'No – I was ashamed to.'

'Did he make any reference to Bernhard having got on to him?'

'Not to me he never said a word.'

'Had you seen him – before tonight – since Bernhard was killed?'

'No. I thought it was an accident like everyone else. Then I heard some people talking, and I was frightened. I stayed away. I knew you were looking too, then. I thought I'd better be very careful. I was paralysed when you talked to me. Then I thought that was dim, and I'd better be friendly or you'd think it fishy.'

'I'd like very much to know who started the talk about it's not being an accident.'

'I don't know. I heard them whispering together. Mrs Sebregt and Mrs Elsenschot. Something like he'd been asking for a fall and the other laughed and said yes, but not just being too fat, but being too inquisitive – something like that. I was terribly frightened, I pretended I heard nothing.'

'Did it strike you that he might have picked up other notes – or overheard things – that he might have tried the same trick on with others?'

'I don't know. No, I don't think so. I thought they were talking just to be nasty to me. They were always saying little things that sounded harmless but I knew were meant for me. They are like that.'

'I know. Who did you think killed Fischer? Did you think it was Dick?'

'I thought it might have been – Rob – I thought he might have hit him, not meaning to kill him – he can be fierce, when something – when he feels he's attacked.'

'Has he ever been to the manège?'

'Not that I know of. He knew where it was.'

'The place – where Fischer got it – would seem pretty public to a stranger, wouldn't you think?'

'I suppose so, yes.'

'A dozen people might see you. You would need to know the routine of the place well to realize is was pretty safe – it isn't over-looked by a window – it's easy to come and go unnoticed. Rob wouldn't know that.'

'He wouldn't bother,' proudly. 'He'd hit out and not care.'

'You still think it might have been Rob?'

'No.'

'You think Dick would do a thing like that?'

'I don't know. I would have thought he wouldn't care that much – not enough to kill someone.'

'What did you want to do, tonight – when you went?'

'I wanted to make a clean ending. To say I'd gone wrong, but I wasn't going to go on.'

'How often did you sleep with him – once?'

'Just once.'

'Very well. Listen attentively. I'd like to leave this – finish with it, send you home. I'm certain you've told the truth. But I won't do that. I'm keeping you here till you've seen the Officer of Justice. I may question you again, speak sharply, call you a liar. I'm the Commissaire of Police, it's my job to interrogate people. Plenty would grumble – the crowd always grumbles, saying, "The police are always against the poor; they'll always stick up for the rich" – do you believe that?'

'Not now,' slowly. 'I've known it would come to this – that I'd have to swallow it.'

'You aren't wrong. The law's a fool, and unfair. You've said it all your life – so have I. But it bears down on everybody once they're involved. You and I both – we have to carry responsibility. You're not a criminal, but you might be called to suffer. I have to

159

put you through it – I'd have to do the same to my own wife. You get that?'

'Yes.'

'Come on then – I'm going to lock you up.'

He felt very tired. It had been a long day and was nearly midnight. He could do with his bed. The painter could wait till morning, couldn't he? No, he couldn't.

No no no, thought Van der Valk, swallow it boy, just like you just told Janine.

He called the 'cipier', as the old quiet policeman is called whose job is to sit in a guardroom outside a row of cells. They need to be old and quiet: it is not difficult work to lock someone up after taking away all ties, shoelaces, belts and bits of string, but it takes stability.

'Verbiest gone home?' he called through to the inspectors' room. At this time of night the criminal brigade was not ordinarily on duty at all: what did one have municipal police for? The boy had had his share of work today; Van der Valk would not blame him if he had just sloped off.

'No, sir,' came the duty brigadier's voice. 'He's gone to scrounge a cup of coffee; he didn't know whether you'd need him.' Good. The young man wanted to learn his trade. Very well, the odds were that he would get the kind of lesson that is best quickly forgotten. Buried, thought Van der Valk – tactfully buried in an obscure corner of the mind. Like morphine – a dangerous drug, but there are times when it is still useful.

'Tell him to come in and pick up a shorthand pad. And to bring me a cup of coffee too.'

A young uniformed agent brought in the painter. There had been no nibbling at his ego yet; he hadn't been wearing a tie, and he had sandals with buckles. He was in shirt-sleeves, carrying his jacket – it wasn't a cold jail.

'Sit down there.' The boy sat, paying no heed to anything, without particular ostentation or insolence, simply as though all this bureaucratic paraphernalia were a great bore, which of course it is. Verbiest came in silently with his pad and pencil.

'Sorry, sir – I was just getting . . . '

'That's all right. You don't have to take any notes till we get a pattern of question and answer; we have to get a few things straight first.'

'Tell him not to waste his time,' said the painter calmly. 'There aren't going to be any answers. I went out on the bike and met a girl with whom I had a date. Nothing illegal in that. Being in the dunes is forbidden – fine of ten gulden. You know my name and address.'

Van der Valk paid no heed, but sat on the corner of his desk and stirred his coffee.

'That's all you'll get from me – make up your mind to that. You can keep me here all night and you won't get any farther.'

Van der Valk went on paying no attention to Verbiest.

'What d'you do with the motorbike?'

'Told the boys where to find it and to put it in the van, bring it back to the owner in the morning.'

'Good.' He stayed sipping till the coffee, black and smelling good, was finished. Verbiest, after an interrogatory glance, lit a cigarette. Van der Valk put the cup down carefully, walked around and sat behind his desk, and said, 'Look at me', in a soft voice. The painter glanced at him and looked away contemptuously. He smiled in a bored way – he had seen this tactic so often.

'Verbiest.'

'Sir.'

'Put a headlock on him – choke him a bit – just till he falls un-conscious.' The painter jumped to his feet; the young inspector, a healthy football-playing boy, was a lot faster, twisted an arm up behind the back in a professional way and got his elbow crooked round the throat. He did not put any pressure on, but watched his chief, who sat polite as a cashier waiting for a cheque to be made out.

'A silly boy. Thinks I'm stupid. Thinks I'm just a cop. Thinks I'll hit him. Mistake – I want you to feel what it's like being murdered. You're a painter – an artist. Very well, I'll treat you as an artist. Choke him, Verbiest.'

The young man struggled, heaved, was helpless in the grip of a stronger heavier man, thrashed about trying to kick, got feebler, went limp, tried to scream, collapsed on the floor like a dishcloth.

'Glass of water . . . no, throw it at him. Pick him up and dump him in the chair. Stay behind him; you don't need your pencil awhile. . . . Nasty, isn't it? If he'd gone on another thirty seconds you'd have been dead. All your life still to lead, cut off by a sadistic old swine like me. Dead. That's what it's like being murdered. Look at me now.' The blueness went out of the boy's face and he got his natural sallow pallor back. He looked.

'You're not a bad artist – I've taken a look at some of your stuff. You're intelligent enough to understand what I say to you. You're all right now – unless he starts again. It leaves no mark – just cuts off the blood supply to your brain. I want you to use your brain so he won't start again unless I tell him to. That is my responsibility. An illegal act, putting pressure on a suspect. What the English – they're sweet – call aiding us in our enquiries. I commit an illegal act, that's my personal responsibility. You understand anything about the doctrine of personal responsibility? The law is based on it. Do something – anything you like – and answer for it.'

There was a hint of a return to not-caring.

'Look at me,' softly.

'Better. Stay looking at me and understand clearly. You thought I'd question you and you wouldn't answer. Then I'd get the little old psychiatrist and he'd get you out of it all right. Big mistake. In this office I'm my own psychiatrist. The world owes you a living – I know. Diminished sense of responsibility – I'll undiminish you, sonny. Divorced from reality, feelings of hostility and desire for vengeance – I know. Get an extra kick out of finding a girl in something the same situation – it won't help. You're going to learn, while here in this office, to answer for your actions.

'I know the tale you tell yourself, too. You're an artist, so the rules don't apply to you. You argue that the world is a place of total rot, inhabited by stinking bourgeois like me. Since there's a bomb, since a hundred thousand die by fire in one breath, since a million more die of famine, it doesn't matter if you kill a fellow. He's nobody – it's an artist's duty to dismiss these stupid scruples. An artist's duty to do anything he can to shock and hit and cut into the rottenness, to hit back against little scientific lunatics who sit thinking up new ways of killing people.

'You don't know me – I'm an artist too. A policeman, you think, capable of dirty tricks to fix poor little you. That's right. I could kill you this minute and fix it afterwards. You could be found three days from now, as the maggots are getting at you.

'Go ahead and spit – you'll wipe it up later. You're an innocent little lad. Been kicked off a park bench by a chap in a cape in Paris – pinched food a few times, fiddled a few shopkeepers – think you know it all. You know what it's like, finding a dead body? You ever made a painting of a dead body? Someone that's been strangled, and stayed in a closed room for a week, in summertime? I have. I've gone out of the door to vomit, before coming back to have pretty pictures made.

'Do you even know what a dead body means? You've read crime stories. A riotous game. Fellow who's killed is just a Hollywood Indian, paid to fall down. The murderer is nobody either – he's just the loser. In the old days he was a real hero, because they set the guillotine up for him at dawn, and shaved his neck and gave him a drink, and shoved a cigarette in his mouth, and a crucifix to hold. Then he said "Oh, Mummy" and they chopped him, and he dirtied his trousers while he jerked about on the plank like a frog, but the police were real tough, they'd learned not to pay any notice. All the boys in the prison lit candles for him. Heroic, huh? Well, right now you're not the hero. Choke him some more, Verbiest.'

'No.'

'Oh,' politely. 'You've changed you mind. Maybe you got a new fine idea. You make a big sobbing phoney confession, and I'm so dim I'll be delighted, and tell Mister Verbiest here to write it all busily down, and then I'll let you go, so that when you get into court you can make a big drama. The press will be there – big day! A write-up – boy, will you have a good time telling the president and thinking how you'll have your name in the paper just like a hero – five whole columns. About how you were tortured, and brainwashed, and how you were ready to sign anything, but it's not true at all, and how it was Janine killed him, or Rob, or Marion. He was blackmailing her too, wasn't he? You simply had to kill him – he was such an obnoxious fat slob anyhow.

'I'm not interested in any of that – how long you go to prison for, and whether Doctor Ganzgek thinks he can make a decent citizen of you with ten years' re-education. I'm not interested in good citizens. I'm a bad citizen; I want nothing but for you to know right now and here what it's like being chopped. Pin his arms, Verbiest.'

'You're a ham actor,' said the boy with a frightened anger.

Van der Valk was hunting in his desk drawer. He came up with a round metal weight, the old-fashioned circular disc kind, weighing five hundred grammes.

'Quite right, I'm a ham actor. Sir Henry Irving. People nowadays dismiss it all with the one word "ham", which is meant to make me sink into the ground. They forget one thing about ham actors – they had a remarkable effect on even intelligent and artistic members of the audience. My dear old mother told me that.' He put the weight on the desk and slowly took his jacket off. He rolled up his sleeve and settled the weight in his fist so that it projected edgeways between his middle fingers. He got up and walked round the desk.

'Turn him round. Hold him pinned.' He brought his fist slowly up and forwards till the metal touched the young man's temple.

'Just – there – was where fat Bernhard got it. One punch, you get it. Oh it'll show, but that's of no consequence. You struggled, you made a hysterical plunge and tripped, and you hit your head on the edge of that filing cabinet, which is metal. You've got ten seconds to live, which is more than you gave Bernhard when he got off his horse. Yell if it pleases you.'

The boy glared helplessly at the face, which was terrifying, even unaided by green light, unlike Sir Henry Irving. Even Mr Verbiest thought Van der Valk capable of it. The muscles in the bare arm tightened.

'Don't.'

Van der Valk, who was tired, limped over the other side of the room, rubbed his nose once or twice, and limped back.

'You want anything to drink – coffee, water – a cup of tea?'

'Can I have a cup of tea?' doubtful that this too might be a Tantalus act.

'Verbiest, make us all a cup of tea.' The young inspector left the room, grateful for a breathing-space.

'You had to understand, you realize? You can have all sorts of things putting pressure on you. You can be forced to do pretty near anything, but not to kill. If you kill, you weren't forced. There's your hand, your arm,' he laid his bare arm out along the desk, 'that makes the decisive movement. You could be holding a gun, a stick, a knife, a bottle of pills, a pen, a telephone – there is one gesture you make, means a man alive or a man dead. Nobody is responsible for that gesture but you. Exactly how responsible is not my job. I'm not a lawyer. What you have to do with me is finish the step you took when you hit him. Say yes. Yes I did it and I'll accept the consequences. No art without responsibility. You make a stroke on paper, your mind can be conscious, unconscious or subconscious and I don't give a damn, it's still yours and nobody can take it away from you or do it for you. Want a cigarette?'

'I don't smoke.'

The boy looked at him with a faint glimmer of something in his face - not sympathy or even respect - but there was a contact. That, thought Van der Valk, is all we need. Just to belong to the human race. Verbiest came back with tea.

'Better,' drinking it. 'Now question and answer. Goes down in the little book, he types it up, you sign it, it goes to the Officer of Justice. You're not being asked to confess any weakness or anything else. You're asked not to try and get other people to sign the pictures you paint. Right?'

The tea seemed to have put heart back into the boy. The pale, handsome face had regained its calm.

'All right.'

'Fischer got to know there was something between you and Janine, whom I may as well call by her name. He mentioned this to you?'

'He said he'd ruin me.'

'What interest could he have in that?'

'Just spite, probably. He was a spiteful type.'

'How did he propose to ruin you?'

'Said he'd tell Zwemmer to do me up.'

'You thought Zwemmer would believe him?'

'He said if he made it public Zwemmer would be forced to.'

'You believed that?'

'Not really. I was afraid he'd do something.'

'Like what?'

'He said he'd break my hands. Like you. He was a big fellow. I was afraid of him.'

'What had you done to him that he should get violent?'

'I told him he was a dirty Boche.'

'No use taking all this down,' in a resigned voice, to Verbiest.

'Why?' asked the painter, startled.

'It's all nonsense,' patiently. 'You're making it up as you go along.'

165

'I'm not,' indignantly.

'We'll see. When exactly was it you realized Fischer had a hold on Janine?'

'He told me.'

'On what occasion?'

'He came into the place I have – in Francis' shed.'

'And what were his words?'

'He said, "You're playing games with that woman. D'you want the whole neighbourhood to know?" '

'What was your answer to that?'

'I said even if it was true what did he propose to do about it, and he said he could ruin my whole life, just by a few words to Zwemmer and to Francis, who wouldn't stand for anything like that around his place.'

'And that frightened you? To that extent?'

'Yes.'

'And what was to be the price of his silence?'

'What?'

'He wasn't doing all this for fun, or because you called him a Boche. He wanted something out of it. Not money – he had plenty, and you had none. What did he want?'

'He wanted – he wanted Janine to be his mistress. He wanted me to fix it up.'

'Janine?'

'Yes.'

There was a pause. Van der Valk smiled, put his cigarette out, and said with unexpected mildness, 'All right.'

'All right?' replied the painter, startled.

'I'm tired. So are you. We've had a hard day. We'll leave this till tomorrow, when we feel fresher. Night, they say, brings counsel. Verbiest, tell the boys to fix our friend up, will you?'

The young man came back looking puzzled.

'I say, Commissaire, I don't understand this. It sounds – odd, doesn't it?' His voice was dubious; he was not sure whether he might not be talking out of turn. This amused Van der Valk.

'Very odd.'

Very odd! Understatement of the year.

'He may not have quite realized how absurd he sounded,' went on Van der Valk, thinking aloud. 'He guessed of course that I would have to take in the Zwemmer girl.'

'I can't make head or tail of it. He's a cool customer, isn't he? You can't see him murdering Fischer – what on earth would make him do it?'

'Can't see him murdering Fischer in a sordid way. . . . You're quite right; this idea of a threat is what sticks in my throat. It's fairly common knowledge – it always was – that Fischer was rather a nasty person. Several hints were made about blackmail but they never added up to what a court would call blackmail. He liked to get hold of little scraps of information, secrets if you like, that seemed slightly disgraceful. I don't mean anything criminal especially – so and so used to be in the Nazi Party, so and so, who is very rich, got his money from his mum who kept a stall in the fishmarket – more that kind of thing. He dropped these remarks in the hearing of their subjects, for the pleasure of seeing them squirm. His death seems in that context exaggerated, huh? – overdone. Listen to the scene tonight, and the kind of conclusion we're being asked to draw is that this boy and the Zwemmer woman had an affair, Fischer found out, threatened to make it public, and to suppress him they – separately or together – sloshed him.'

'Which doesn't sound very likely,' said Verbiest sensibly.

'Right, it doesn't. Suppose Fischer is as good as his word. It won't affect the painter – who cares if he has an affair with a girl, especially one all that crowd thinks little of. If it had been anybody else . . . Mrs La Touche, or the wife of a big industrialist – or my wife.'

Mr Verbiest was rather shocked at this lighthearted remark.

'Nor would it really bother her. She wanted to tell her husband and would be relieved if he knew, really. She had behaved out of a fit of pique, no more. She threw her hat in a moment of emotional depression and discouragement. Her husband would forgive her and she knows it.

'Now this boy Dickie. You heard him. He wants us to believe that he's so scared of its coming to light that he forbids her to tell, frightens her into not telling, and he's so scared of Bernhard that he kills him – or so angry that he hits him hard enough to kill him – neither the least in character. He doesn't admit killing, but neither does he deny it – he's secretly rather proud of it. Why doesn't he admit it? – he has so many defences. If Fischer really threatened him he has a good defence.'

'Could he have done it out of jealousy? If he was in love with that woman,' said Verbiest in embarrassment, 'and if Fischer made a pass at her.'

'Nothing shows he really cared twopence for her. He went for her out of vanity, because she's rich and pretty. Out of a sort of fellow-feeling, because she's an underdog too. The same feeling of an ally, someone who would understand, made her turn to him. But there's no sign of affection on his side. I conclude that since we now know of this affair, since we caught him redhanded with her, he's playing it up. Wants us to think of nothing else. A manoeuvre, to throw dust, to stop us looking somewhere else. Where? And why?'

'Could Mevrouw La Touche . . . ?'

'Yes . . . ' said Van der Valk, 'the magistrate would want to hear what she had to say. We have evidence that she has things in her life she would want to keep hidden. But that this boy Dickie should spring to the defence of the La Touche family . . . '

'He's a funny boy.'

'Self-centred boy, with a big idea of his own importance – and putting on, with that in mind, a very funny act. I want to let Janine go, too, and I don't dare till this is cleared up. . . . No use sitting here. Home you go, boy. Night brings counsel.'

He was so tired, and his leg so painful, that he needed his stick to walk the ten minutes to his house, needed it as he had not in a year. Arlette was asleep.

Night did bring counsel. Or rather Verbiest, the young inspector, brought it at eight the following morning.

'Couldn't think of anything, Chief. Broke my head over it, too.'

'Mistake. Never break your head. Forget about it. Sounds easy – nothing came to my head either.'

'I kept thinking what you said – what kind of threat Fischer could have made.'

'He wasn't a villain,' looking through the morning post with distaste and with a hopeful curiosity, as though there might be a lovely anonymous letter telling him exactly who had hit Bernhard and why. Perhaps it was Doctor Maartens, whose wife was deceiving him! 'If he wanted to be vicious it was because he felt humiliated – that's what makes people spiteful. But why feel vengeful towards the painter? What way could that boy have attacked or injured him?'

'Might he just have felt spiteful towards everyone? Suppose he discovered his wife was pally with that other chap – you know, sir, the one Mr Rademaker found? He might have wanted to be vengeful towards anyone having a love affair that was handy – the painter and Mevrouw Zwemmer, perhaps.'

'Oh fool and clown,' said Van der Valk very suddenly. Mr Verbiest thought this was him, and was alarmed.

'Quickly, boy – find me that man's name and telephone number.'

There was a bemused hustle amongst paper.

'Man's an art-lover,' said Van der Valk happily.

There were buzzes and clicks on the telephone line, the phone burred in The Hague, and Van der Valk made nervous irritable hand movements.

'Can't be gone to work yet; these people don't start before nine. Must be shaving, or in the bath, or something . . . Ah. Hallo . . . Mr Matthews? Sorry to disturb you so early. Van der Valk, Commissaire of Police. No, you don't know me. No, not from local headquarters – a matter of some importance. I would very much like to talk with you, as early as may be. No, not at your office – I can be with you in half an hour. Can you spare me fifteen minutes then before you leave? . . . Naturally. I would not, believe me, but this is likely to have weight. There are people in prison at this moment on this account. . . . No, I can't discuss that over the phone. . . . That is good of you. Very well, I'll delay you as little as may be.' He put the phone down, went off, and turned to his puzzled subordinate.

'Cooperative, luckily – diplomat. Get a car as quickly as you can.'

The main road from Amsterdam to The Hague is always busy, but rapid. It was the flow of people still going to work, in the government offices of The Hague, that held them up. Still, they were in the pleasant quarter of this pleasant town called the Way to the South Wood in half an hour, and that was good going for a Volkswagen.

A flat in a building constructed in the gloomy 'style' architecture of the nineteen twenties, a flat suitable for a middle-aged diplomatic bachelor, and an English car equally suitable – a Wolseley – standing outside. Van der Valk, in the large slow comfortable lift, realized that he was putting on his cavalry act again, with amused detachment, leaned on his stick, and prayed he was right. The door opened very promptly.

A man in a stiff dark suit, too heavy for spring, even spring in Holland. Fresh, glossy-shaved, alert face, a bit heavy, like the suit. Looking intelligent in a well-nourished, rubicund way.

'Commissaire Van der Valk. This is Inspector Verbiest.'

'Please come in.'

A very agreeable large sitting-room, with well polished English furniture and cabinets with what looked like a nice collection of antique china. Van der Valk had no time to look at it, because the first thing he saw was the thing he had hoped to see. He tried not to make his breath of relief too noisy. A picture of a woman on a horse.

'I do talk English but not very well. I notice though that you speak excellent Dutch, Mr Matthews.'

'Part of my job. Please sit down, gentlemen,' politely. 'I accept your assurance that this is important, naturally, but I am bound to point out that I have no time to waste. I am anxious to help you in any way I can, but your mention of people in prison is disturbing: you do understand that I am attached to a diplomatic mission, and I may have to refer your enquiries to my superiors, or to a person more competent in this matter than myself – and now please tell me, Mr Van der Valk, what it is I can do for you.'

'A purely personal matter, Mr Matthews, in no way interesting to the Embassy or your superiors, upon which by coincidence you are well placed to throw light.' Even in English the phrase would have sounded hopelessly pompous – but he couldn't help it. No use telling Mr Matthews that he had been born in the Ferdinand Bol Straat! This was not Janine's world, or Rob's world, or the painter's world. The nearest you got would be Francis La Touche, and even that . . . It had been the trouble all along. Two worlds . . . intertwined . . . not easy for a poor policeman to unravel.

'You are acquainted, I believe, with Madame Marguerite Fischer.'

Mr Matthews was not happy.

'I have that honour – but, really . . . '

'There is no need of protest, or embarrassment. I am acting on information received, but your private life has not been intruded upon – nor will it, necessarily. This is all quite confidential.'

'There is nothing improper about my friendship with Mevrouw Fischer.'

'Nobody suggests there is.'

'I have, I agree, asked her to divorce her husband.'

'And now that her husband is dead?'

'I hope to persuade her to do me the honour of marrying me. After, naturally, a proper lapse of time.' Spoken well, and firmly. 'Nothing, I need hardly add, in our acquaintance could injure her reputation, nor, I might say, my career.' His eyes narrowed. 'I am aware that her husband died in sudden and rather tragic circumstances – is that the object of your interest?'

'Quite shrewd of you, yes it is. Do not worry – it is very far from my mind to imagine that you had a hand in hurrying Mr Fischer into another world.'

'I should certainly hope it is,' very tartly, so that Van der Valk felt properly snubbed for a vulgar joke. 'And may I ask what the object of this visit is, exactly?' Suddenly he got in a great panic. 'You mentioned people in prison – not Mevrouw Fischer, of course?'

'No,' mildly. 'Should she be?' getting his own back.

'Please state your business in my apartment,' nastily.

'My interest is in art,' in a pleasant tone. 'There is a picture on your wall.'

'It is,' very stiff indeed, 'as you perhaps notice, a portrait of Mevrouw Fischer, with a horse. She was kind enough to give it me, as a present.'

'Was it kept a great secret?' Mildly innocent.

Of course, Mr Matthews was embarrassed. How could he have been anything else? But he kept his end up stoutly. The English have some phrase, thought Van der Valk. A straight bat? Or is it a straight wicket? The boy stood on the burning deck Playing a game of Cricket . . .

'I distinguish, Commissaire, between a natural wish to avoid any breath of indiscretion or what might be thought irregularity, and a guilty silence, or what might be so construed. I find it most unpleasant – revolting – to be compelled to keep my friendship with Mevrouw Fischer – furtive. I hope very greatly that it will not remain on that basis.'

'Quite. Look – don't worry so much. We were interested in knowing about all the friendships. We observe. But we keep discreet. This will do neither yourself nor your career the faintest harm. I simply ask – did you commission this picture – or did she?'

'She did. It was to be a surprise for me.'

'You know the artist?'

'I have never met him. I know of him. He has, I believe, done other portraits of persons who use that manège, and is regarded as quite a good modern painter.' This in the tone of someone who thinks Georges Braque is a poster artist, and doesn't want to be enlightened.

Both men, by a sort of common consent, had turned to look at the picture. It was a good one, thought Van der Valk. He's a good painter.

'Quite a good bit of work.'

'Quite fair,' agreed Mr Matthews cautiously. 'My appreciation – the value I set upon it – is high for other reasons.'

'Just so. So Madame Fischer got this idea, perhaps, at the manège, and you knew nothing about it.'

'I imagine so. A generous idea, designed for no purpose than to give me some pleasure – in which there is nothing illicit.'

'Quite so. That's all, Mr Matthews; I've finished. Very likely you will never be worried again. Your private life is no concern of the police – not in the Kingdom of the Netherlands at least,' unfairly. Matthews reared slightly and he held his hand up. 'You must bear one thing in mind. Mr Fischer died by violence, and it is my work to throw the circumstances of his death into daylight. It is conceivable that you may be mandated to appear at the Palace and asked to repeat what you have told me to the Officer of Justice. As a private opinion it is very unlikely that he will see any need, in view of your diplomatic status, to make your testimony public. That, you must understand, is for him to decide. I cannot give you any promise or assurance – I would be overstepping the bounds of my functions. Good morning, Mr Matthews, and many thanks for your frankness and lucidity.'

'There goes a sadly worried man,' he said in the car, laughing. 'They'll have all their legal experts working on it.'

Verbiest was full of admiration.

'So that was the connection.'

'Art. We knew he and the Fischer woman shared an interest in art. They buy china, silver, things like that. I didn't connect that with painting – stupid of me. Especially once we knew Dickie did

172

several portraits of customers at the manège. She took a risk, to prove her devotion. She commissioned the picture, and kept it a secret. That's what Matthews feels guilty about – he knew she paid for it secretly, and kept it utterly dark from fat Bernhard.'

'How did he find out?'

'It wouldn't surprise me,' slowly, 'to learn that the woman Groenveld found out – and told him out of jealousy. She may feel a certain rivalry with our friend Mr Matthews.'

'What really happened, do you think, though? How did it come about?'

'We'll probably never know,' slowly, staring out of the window at all the little whizzing tin boxes on their little silly wheelies. 'What's paradoxical about this job is that we've got to be interested in character, since otherwise we'd never understand anything at all. At the same time it's not our work, as you learned in training school, to worry about whys and wherefores. That is usurping the function of the magistrate. What we are given is a form, which we get people to fill in, just like every other godforsaken functionary. Are you single? Are you married? Widow/Divorced? Strike out where not applicable. What's your income, and what's your hire-purchase debt? What's your religion? Your hobbies and interests? What are your political views – Right, Centre, Left – strike out where not applicable. They don't ask your fears, your anxieties, your hopes, what you trust and cling to – but the psychiatrist does, of course.

'It's exactly like the form for filling in your income tax, for applying for a passport, for soliciting a job. One of these forms, we are supposed to pick the one that adds up to a criminal. But the really interesting things, the things that make up a character – they are too complex, too illogical, too inconsequent. Décousu. . . . They follow no laws. We have to go up against people as though they were characters in a book – oversimplified. Are you in love? – not in love? Strike out where not applicable. It's a nonsensical job.'

'Where did the threat come in?' asked Verbiest, who hadn't heard a word. Van der Valk sighed. Young – too young. Wants everything explained.

'How do I know? Fischer felt humiliated. He felt he wasn't even in charge of his own restaurant. He felt his wife slipping away from him. He felt a big stupid clumsy farmer, and that the riding-school crowd looked down on him. It makes a dangerous man, who does sudden and bizarre things. Not unlike Janine. . . . But it made him spiteful Who knows what he found out, or how? He may have felt there was something he didn't like between his wife and the Groenveld woman. He may have been told by her that his wife was overfriendly with a fellow in The Hague. Out of jealousy – maybe. He might even have been taunted with it by the painter – out of jealousy . . . we'll never know. Maybe the magistrate will.'

'But why should the painter have killed him?' persisted Verbiest. He got a sudden doubt, too late. 'Did the painter kill him?'

'Leave the door open, boy. It wasn't a squalid crime. What Maître Floriot calls an idiot crime. There was a clash involving Janine as well as Marguerite. Janine knows nothing about it at all. It seems likely the painter used her as a mask, to fox Fischer – that he deliberately let Fischer find and pick up that bit of paper Janine threw' – Verbiest didn't know what he was talking about, and he went on more or less to himself. 'Throw Fischer off the scent, maybe. . . . He had no emotional attachment to Janine. Whereas he might, in some obscure romanticized way of his own, have loved Marguerite. She sat for that painting – in secret . . .

'Fischer might have thought Dickie was his wife's lover – seems absurd to us – might not have seemed so to him. He rumbled the Janine camouflage in some way. He might have gone in a red rage to Dick and threatened to do him – Dick hinted as much. . . . He may have threatened to massacre Marguerite – how should we know? Fear, love, rage, anything, Floriot says, creates an idiot crime. One of them picked up that weight and clonked him. I wonder if Saskia knows . . . '

They were back. Van der Valk got out of the car briskly and fished for his stick.

'We have the item of information we need to open the oyster,' he was saying five minutes later in his office. 'He'll probably admit he killed Fischer, now. Five minutes' work – a short signed statement. Doesn't much matter if it's true or false. I'll take it straight over to the Palais, and the Officer will be very pleased. Get a release order in the same moment for the Zwemmer girl. A nice easy one. Anybody else and there would have been publicity. A poor little devil of a painter kills someone – that's not news. And that's the way magistrates like them. I sound cynical? – never mind. While I go over with a handwritten statement you'll see

about having the boy fingerprinted and photographed, Verbiest·
And you'll type up the procès verbal, afterwards. Now get the boy
out of his dungeon, lad; we've no time to waste.'

He was right. From then on it would only be a matter of form.
Have you ever been a member of the Communist Party? Strike out
if not applicable. Male/Female? . . .

He was home with Arlette by lunchtime. Janine had been released – Rob was waiting for her with the Ferrari and an enormous
bunch of roses. The magistrate's clerk was busy issuing sum-
monses. Marion La Touche would be asked whether Fischer had
ever held information over her head she would be glad to have kept
secret. Marguerite would be asked. Saskia Groenveld would be
asked . . . The painter would be asked . . .

Most of it would be kept secret. It would depend on the defend-
ing lawyer. They would not get away with legitimate self-defence,
but they would manage large, impressive extenuating circumstances. Nobody liked people like Bernhard, even if no money was
ever demanded. They are reminded of their own little secret
weaknesses, and feel uncomfortable – and pick on the handiest
goat to drive into the desert. Poor Bernhard. He was dead, so he
would get systematically blackened by a defence lawyer.

It was Friday. Tomorrow May the First, Fête de Travail. On
the balcony of the Kremlin they would be saluting, in fur hats. In
France they would be going to the races. In prison they would be
thinking.

Arlette had made mayonnaise. She had hake, a lettuce salad, an
early cucumber, spring onions, raw grated carrots, the famous
tasteless Dutch tomatoes. They had a glass of white wine waiting
for the boys, and he told her about the painter. She only said two
things. One was, 'Poor Janine. She'll get over it. Do her good,
maybe. Shall I invite them to dinner?'

The other was, 'What a fertile, fruitful, months-long source of
gossip this is going to provide for that awful Maggie Sebregt.'

Nicolas Freeling

THE WIDOW

'Van der Valk's widow, Arlette, steps into her dead husband's shoes, and trips over herself, irresistibly' – *Yorkshire Post*

After the death of her husband, the late Piet van der Valk, life gets boring for his widow, Arlette. So she chooses to remarry, a decision which spurs her into setting herself up as an advisory agency.

Clients, though, bring with them not merely their own problems but also danger and threats upon her own life . . .

The background is Strasbourg – a regional capital with unusual riches and resonance which attracts the best from both France and Germany. And it is into this city of crossroads that Nicolas Freeling launches the resourceful Arlette.

ONE DAMN THING AFTER ANOTHER

Nearly ten years after his murder, Arlette is happily remarried to a phlegmatic Englishman and running a one-woman agency in Strasbourg which undertakes everything from detective investigation to the dispensing of tea and sympathy.

As she uncovers the activities of an illegal fur-trader, comforts an abandoned husband, undertakes a trip to the Argentine to retrieve a runaway delinquent, life for Arlette seems to be becoming just one damn thing after another.

And a cold voice threatening her on the telephone brings the last of Van der Valk's pigeons home to roost . . .

Also published

THE DRESDEN GREEN
GADGET
THE KING OF THE RAINY COUNTRY
A LONG SILENCE
THE NIGHT LORDS